THE
THING ABOUT
love

The Thing About Love
Copyright © 2018 by Kim Karr
ISBN-13: 978–1979372251
ISBN-10: 197937225X

Cover designer:
Michele Catalano-Creative

Cover model:
Forest Harrison

Photographer:
Wander Aguiar Photography

Editing:
Nichole Strauss, Insight Editing Services

Proofreading:
Rosa Sharon, iScream Proofreading Services

Interior Design & Formatting:
Christine Borgford, Type A Formatting

THE
THING ABOUT
love

NEW YORK TIMES BESTSELLING AUTHOR
KIM KARR

the north star

The North Star—aka Polaris—is famous for holding nearly still in our sky while the entire northern sky moves around it.

That's because it's located so close to the north celestial pole, which is the point around which the entire northern sky turns.

Polaris is significant because it marks your way due north.

As you face Polaris and stretch your arms sideways, your right-hand points due east, and your left-hand points due west. About-face of Polaris steers you due south.

Polaris is *not* the brightest star in the nighttime sky, but you can find it easily. And once you do, you'll see it shining in the northern sky every night . . . and you'll always be able to find your way.

chapter
1

Back to the Drawing Board

JULES EASTON

. . . YOU'RE NOT NERVOUS, just excited.

. . . . . . *You're not nervous, just excited.*

. . . . *You're not nervous, just excited.*

I had been chanting these five words for the past couple of blocks. The dose of calm my self-help book had assured me this phrase would trigger had yet to take effect.

I made a mental note to return that book. If anything, I was even more wound up than I had been before. Now my heart was beating faster, my palms were sweatier, and my entire body was trembling.

I had to calm down—and soon.

Having already tried smiling, closing my eyes, and thinking positively, I was entirely out of stress relievers.

Time to suck it up—and deal.

The mere thought of meeting with prospective clients always made me slightly anxious, but today I was full-out nervous.

Oh God, did I have everything I needed?

As I stepped off the curb to cross the street, I ran through the list I kept in my head. Menu options—check. Invitation samples—check. Venue photos—check. Favor ideas—check. Jaxson's business card—check.

Check.

Check.

Check.

Yes, all the checks were tucked safely in my bag.

All of a sudden it seemed to weigh a ton. Feeling like I was carrying the weight of the world on one shoulder, I attempted to switch the heavy leather tote to the other side. While doing so, the strap slipped from my sweaty grip, and my bag dropped to the ground. With a shriek, I watched in horror as all the contents tumbled out.

In the middle of the busy street, I found myself on my bare knees trying to gather my things before the light changed to green and all of my hard work turned into road kill, not to mention myself.

As I shoved the blue fabric swatch into the vast, leather rectangle, I thought about the young woman I had an appointment with in less than an hour. She was engaged to the Governor's son, and she wanted her wedding to be the most significant affair the State of Georgia had ever seen.

Beep. Beep.

Beep. Beep.

Scrambling back on my feet, I rushed to the corner with my mind still on the client I was desperate to sign. Landing this event was exactly what Easton Design & Weddings needed to prove to the community that the new management was just as capable as the previous.

The problem was I wasn't one hundred percent sure it was. But I'd keep that to myself.

There was no doubt in my mind the press received from nuptials of this magnitude would be of tremendous value.

The timing couldn't be more perfect.

I had to land this job.

Even if only to prove to myself I was more than competent enough for this position.

With the afternoon sun beating down on me, the air felt unusually thick in my lungs. I took three deep breaths while making my way along Peachtree Road. Blowing them out slowly, I glanced down at my outfit.

In a navy shift dress embroidered with white birds that I happened to catch sight of in the thrift store window only ten minutes ago, I knew I should feel confident about my upcoming appointment.

This dress was undoubtedly a sign.

Although I had gotten more than a few strange looks from passersby on the sidewalk, I didn't care because what I was wearing was more than appropriate.

Trust me.

When I heard someone shout, "Pierre, come back here," I quickly lifted my gaze just in time to see a dog trotting in my direction. Before his owner could retrieve the leash, the toy poodle was at my feet. I bent down to pet the little ten-pound cutie, and when I did, he barked so fiercely it startled me, and I went flying backward into a trashcan.

"I'm so sorry," the older man said. "Pierre tends to get excited around pretty girls."

Straightening up, I smiled. "It's fine."

Hey, at least someone got excited when he saw me.

After wiping any debris from my rear, I reached for the sanitizer in my bag and squeezed some on my hands, and then I decided it was time to hasten my pace.

This walk seemed endless today.

I probably should have driven, *but* parking was always impossible on this side of town.

When I saw someone get out of the back of a car and then watched it drive off, I considered the fact that I probably should have taken an Uber, *but* then again, that was money I didn't need to spend.

Blowing a piece of stray hair from my face, I sighed. I probably should have skipped lunch with my uncle, *but* I couldn't do that.

Sighing again, I thought about all the *'probably should haves'* and *'buts'* in my life and sped up. No time to contemplate the decisions I'd already made. They were mine, and I owned them. The thing was . . . I wanted everything to be perfect . . . I just didn't know how to make it that way.

With long strides, I glanced into the window of designer store after designer store until, at long last, I turned onto the small street that would bring me to the older and ever-so-charming area of Buckhead known as Wedding Lane.

As soon as I felt the cobblestone beneath my feet, my heartbeat finally began to slow.

I loved this part of town.

Small.

Quaint.

Quiet.

Amidst the old sidewalks and the flowering magnolias, one could find floral shops, bridal boutiques, travel agencies, fine china stores, stationary lofts, and of course the offices of almost every principal event planner in Atlanta, including my own.

It was three solid blocks of heaven.

One more turn, another lane, and then I spotted it—the battered red brick of the building I was headed toward. With all those industrial-sized windows, it made it hard to believe the place was one of the best bakeries in the southeast.

The Bride Box was a gem tucked away for those of us in the wedding business seeking out the very best of the best.

A bead of sweat dripped down my back as I once again hastened my pace, and then I was finally here. Like a kid in a candy shop, I peeked through the clear glass and there it was. A burst of delight shot through me. Even from the sidewalk, the sight made my knees go weak.

Its size.

The colors.

Its design.

The birds.

This cake was going to make a magnificent first impression, and it was going to knock my pitch right out of the park.

Even in the oppressive heat of this typical Atlanta summer day, I couldn't help but stare at it for a few long moments.

Don't be mistaken. I wasn't bragging. This place wasn't my business. I wasn't the baker. I was a wedding planner, and this was the place I had selected to meet Rory Kissinger for the very first time.

More than a dozen wedding planners had pitched the Governor's son's soon-to-be bride, but none had met her expectations. In her correspondence to me, she not only provided more than one list of wedding musts, but she also told me she expected me to *wow* her.

I would certainly say this cake should do the trick.

Finally feeling like the meeting was going to go even better than I planned, I hurried around the corner. Once at the entrance, I took a single deep breath hoping to expel any remaining jitters before I opened the front door.

I so had this.

As soon as I walked through the lobby and into the showroom, all of my senses engaged, and just like that my worries disappeared. Not only was there a delicious scent of chocolate wafting through the air, but also the sight of the bowl of icing sitting beside the cake made me drool. And don't get me started on the massive lovebirds perched so perfectly upon the top tier. Although I knew they were made from pure sugar and more than edible, they looked so real they gave me goose bumps.

There was no doubt about it—this wedding cake was not only a work of art, it was also a masterpiece.

From the doorway, I cleared my throat to alert Montgomery I had arrived. "Hi," I greeted.

"You're early," Montgomery tossed over his shoulder with his thick southern drawl as he finished transforming a panel of fondant into a swatch of elegant, edible, tree branches.

Rushing over to him, I took my sunglasses off to better admire his work and made a hush noise. "Pretend I'm not here. I just thought I'd watch you work for a bit."

With a confidence that never failed to amaze me, he placed the completed tree branch on the bottom tier, and then he glanced over at me. "Darling, I hate to say this, but I don't believe that for one minute. I know you. You came for a sample before your new clients arrive."

I shook my head. "Nope, not today."

Reaching over, he pretended to feel my forehead. "My Juliette, are you ill?"

Montgomery was the only person I allowed to call me by my proper name. After moving from New York to Atlanta to live with my uncle, I was teased in school relentlessly about all kinds of things—being the new girl, a Northerner, my New York accent, my height, my lack of southern grace. You name it, the mean girls used it. They wanted to make sure I stayed away from the boys they liked, and when they came up with the Romeo and Juliette clichés, they taunted me with them for almost a year. Ever since then Jules was the only name I ever went by.

Pushing Montgomery's hand away, I fluttered my lips in mock

protest. "Don't be ridiculous, I couldn't possibly indulge in chocolate this early in the day. That would be crazy. You know it makes me hyper. Besides, I just ate lunch and I'm way too full."

He continued to eye me with speculation. In his own way, he was a very handsome older man. Today, his salt and pepper shoulder-length hair was pulled back in a low ponytail. And beneath his slightly wrinkled, double-breasted chef's jacket that showed a gut that screamed of the sweets he ate, he wore a Tiffany-blue tie. *Nice touch.*

His houndstooth–patterned, black and white pants were, of course, to die for, but when he put on that torque blanche hat of his, which was always stuffed in his pocket, he drove the women mad, especially the mothers of the brides.

Too bad he was taken, and his husband didn't like to share. That didn't stop Montgomery from exerting his deep southern charm every chance he could.

He made a burly sigh of disappointment as he picked up the metal spatula from a cup of water on the counter. "Did I tell you this cake has four moist layers of chocolate? Four! And that each layer is not only held together by ganache filling but also filled with a tremendous amount of it as well?"

Even though he couldn't see me, I pretended to cover my ears. "Stop taunting me. It isn't nice."

Smoothing a few spots of icing with only the very tip of his tool, he ignored me. "Oh, and in case I didn't mention this either, I made an extra tier just for you. It's in the refrigerator chilling, just the way you like it."

The way he was describing the cake made it sound like a bottle of the most expensive champagne. "Montgomery," I warned. "I can't."

He shrugged. "I know, I know, you never do anything *crazy* like eat—"

Lost in the moment, I stared at the cake and licked my lips. It had been a long day, and it wasn't even dinnertime yet. One piece wouldn't hurt. In fact, it might just help by giving me that little extra spunk every girl needed once in a while.

Setting the spatula down, he got back to working on the branches. He pulled some kind of white, straw-like thingy from a drawer and then using it, he molded them into place. While he worked, he continued to describe the details of the cake until it became the only thing I could think about. Eventually, I subconsciously tuned him out as my mind wandered.

Four filled layers.

Chocolate.

Ganache.

Chilled.

With only the thought of the taste of that cake on my tongue, I practically orgasmed on the spot.

Hey, thinking dreamily of that cake was the most exciting thing to happen to me in . . . too long.

I blinked back the sad reminder of how imperfect my life was. "Well, if you insist," I told Montgomery, "but not until you're finished. We don't have much time before my clients are due to arrive."

Swapping out his tools, he ran the spatula under the tree branch and around the tier. Smoothing the icing into place with such concentration, I had no idea how he remained so steady. When he finished, he placed the metal tool back in the water along with the straw-like thingy and pushed the vessel against the backsplash. "There, now it's finished," he declared, a happy gleam in his eyes.

I clapped my hands together. "This cake is so great!"

He nodded in agreement. "Now I'll get you that piece of cake and then clean up."

"Oh, no," I declared, "I'm not eating alone. You have to share it with me."

A girl never likes to eat cake by herself unless she's in her bed drowning boy troubles in cake and ice cream.

It's a fact.

The coy look on his face made me grin. "Oh, my darling," he laughed. "I would be more than happy to." He lowered his voice. "But you have to keep it between us."

"You mean like a secret?"

He nodded.

With a curious look, I asked, "And why is that?"

Montgomery sighed deeply. "Archer thinks I need to watch my waistline."

"No!" I whispered in a gasp. Montgomery loved his sweets.

"Yes, it's true. But how can I turn you down when you so clearly need help easing whatever absurd guilt you're feeling about eating chocolate cake in the afternoon?"

"It's not guilt. It's just too much chocolate makes me hyper."

"Everything makes you hyper," he declared.

It was true.

There was no point in denying it any further, so instead, I shrugged. "It's just a thing."

He shook his head. "No, it's not *just a thing*, it's a *Jules* thing," he joked, and his southern drawl was especially thick.

Once again I found myself lifting my shoulders in an undeniable shrug. He knew me, and he knew I had quirks.

A lot of them.

Montgomery set his gaze back on the cake, and when he did, a line creased his brow.

"What is it?" I asked in alarm, worried something was wrong with the cake that I hadn't noticed.

Taking a step back, he eyed his work. Circling it, he searched for flaws, of which I was sure there would be none because Montgomery was nothing if he wasn't a perfectionist. Not a single thing was ever overlooked.

My gaze followed his. Each tier looked like driftwood, only instead of being made out of bark, the frosting, or fondant to be politically correct, was created from the most decadent white and dark chocolates.

There was also a heart piped on the middle tier as if it were carved in the tree, and inside were the couple's initials, written in Tiffany blue.

Such a perfect touch.

The branches that had been placed here and there in such a geometrically pleasing fashion were also spot on. And needless to say, the topper was exactly what the bride had ordered.

Or I hoped it was.

Birds.

Lovebirds.

I bit my lip in contemplation.

They were conventional, and from what I could tell, my prospective client was not. I had wondered about this enough that I emailed her twice to be assured I had gotten it right.

The responses she provided to me had been all over the place. In one email she stated she wanted an outdoor barn wedding, but without the cowboy boots, horses, and hay. Then she added that rustic would be okay, but she preferred modern. In another, she stated she wouldn't be able to live without those lovebirds as her wedding theme. And finally, she wrote that chocolate was her must-have flavor. Oh, I almost forgot—her PS informed me Tiffany blue was her favorite color.

I took what I could from the mix of chaos and spoke to Montgomery. Once he designed the ideal cake, I invited her and her groom-to-be to The Bride Box so I could *wow* her before taking her to my office to discuss the details of my plan for her wedding.

After spinning the cake around, Montgomery glanced over at me.

My heart was in my mouth, and my pulse was racing up my

throat to meet it. I couldn't find the air to breathe and was barely able to repeat myself. "Montgomery, what's the matter?"

"It's nothing." He waved a hand in the air.

I continued to stare at him with my heart in my throat. "Are you sure?"

"Yes," he stressed. "I'm just giving it one final look-over," he added.

Okay, he did always do that.

Didn't he?

With a grin on his face, he picked up the base. He carried the giant cake to the crystal platform on the large, distressed, wooden table behind us. And then his masterpiece was on display.

Finally, I felt like I could breathe again.

For a few seconds we both stood there and admired the cake, but then I broke free and gave in to the temptation sitting beside me. I couldn't help myself. I dipped my finger in the leftover bowl of chocolate icing and brought it to my mouth. The moan I made wasn't on purpose. "Montgomery, you outdid yourself this time."

Remaining straight-faced, he said, "You say that every time."

"This time I really do mean it," I said around a lick.

"You know I'd do anything for you."

"I know you would." I smiled at him. "But I mean it. This time, you really, really, *really*, did outdo yourself."

The corners of his lips lifted. "I'm glad you like it."

"I don't just like it," I moaned again, swiping my finger across the bowl's edge one more time. "I love it."

Never one for praise, he placed a kiss on my forehead. "Remember, Juliette, you are the one who did this."

I shook my head.

It was all him.

"Yes, you did," he insisted. "I might have made the cake, but it was your idea to present the bride with it first, to give her what she wants when she doesn't even know herself. That's the sign of a true artist."

"Maybe you're right," I admitted.

He nodded. "I'm more than right. You can do this. And I mean more than just the upcoming meeting."

"I hope so, Montgomery. I really do," I whispered.

His gaze narrowed on me. "Stop doubting yourself. Do you hear me?"

With a bright grin, I said, "Yes."

He brought his hands together. "Good, because now it's time to eat, and then clean up," he replied.

Now that was a good idea.

Grabbing the bowl of chocolate icing, he strode through the swinging door that led to the back kitchen. As it closed behind him, I was not only left with the lingering taste of chocolate on my lips but the feeling that I really could do this job.

All I had to do was prove it.

chapter 2

Bite Off More Than You Can Chew

JULES EASTON

IT DIDN'T TAKE much to make me happy.

The simple things in life seemed to be the ones that made me smile the most. I was a lot like my mother that way.

A sunny day.

The pitter-patter of rain hitting my window at night.

A kiss.

Even chocolate icing.

I licked my lips one last time and glanced around the place that had become like my second home when I needed one the most. The place I'd worked at after school for four years, only then the business name had been The Pastry Box.

As most things do, the showroom had changed over the years. No longer a retail bakery, it had been closed to the public years ago. Montgomery and Archer had decided to concentrate on the wedding trade exclusively, and it had paid off.

Now this place was used for magazine shoots, bridal party

gatherings, and wooing, yes wooing, clients. The reason everyone loved this area was that it looked like Martha Stewart's kitchen, only super-sized, and on steroids.

Painted brick walls, old wooden floors, marble counters, stainless steel appliances, refrigerated cases, and open cupboards filled with various plates, bowls, and decorating tools collected over many years. It was southern charm and New York metro combined. With the amount of sunlight streaming in, it was also the perfect backdrop for photos.

It was also the perfect sales floor.

The walls were a soft pastel blue, except the back one. That one was finished with a white glaze to allow the words scrolled across it to stand out. Every time I read, *"LOVE IS ALL YOU NEED,"* I couldn't help but roll my eyes, and this time wasn't any different.

It wasn't that I was a cynic, but *love* really wasn't all you needed. You needed air to breathe and water to survive and your phone to keep in touch with those you love.

Don't get me wrong—I was all about love. In fact, I was so much about finding the perfect love that I made it the basis for my career.

That didn't mean I understood it. In fact, I found it somewhat confusing. Love was *not* always patient. Love was *not* always kind. And love most definitely did *not* conquer all. It could happen in a fleeting moment or not even once in your life. It wasn't shared fairly, and sometimes it meant something different to different people.

Still, love was what made my world go round at Easton Design & Weddings, and that was all I needed to understand about it.

Right?

My uncle, Edward Easton, founded Easton Design & Weddings more than thirty-five years ago because he, like Montgomery, believed love was all you needed.

Since then the company had earned almost every prestigious award in the industry, including *The Knot's* Best of Weddings top pick for the past ten consecutive years.

Sadly, it was highly unlikely we would be receiving that award this year. A little more than six months ago, I had taken over the day-to-day operations of the business so my uncle could enjoy the beginning stages of his retirement. Since then I'd worked night and day, drained my entire savings account, and lost more jobs than I'd landed.

Unfortunately, the transition had not been going as smoothly as my uncle had thought it would. I had experienced more than one setback. For the first time in the company's history, the business wasn't making a profit. And worse, it was losing money.

Other than Montgomery, up until recently, no one else had known just how bad things were. Although it had killed me to keep it to myself, I had known it wouldn't remain a secret for long.

And it hadn't.

Four weeks ago the hammer fell, and now I had until the end of summer to make a success of Easton Design & Weddings or . . . I can't even think about it without wanting to cry . . . my uncle was going to be forced to sell the business.

The mandate came after my uncle asked to see the company financials. They were actually much more dismal than they appeared, but since I had infused my own money into the business, he wasn't aware of this.

Even still, based on what he saw, he had canceled most of his upcoming travel plans to meet with me twice a week for business updates and consultations. During these meetings, I always remained optimistic, but I finally had to admit I didn't know what I was doing wrong. He frowned at this and told me I didn't understand love. Although I had voiced my disagreement, he remained steadfast in his convictions.

And then today he dropped a bomb on me.

Thinking I could use the help, and hoping to motivate his son at the same time, Uncle Edward had asked my cousin to help me out. What is it they say, *'Kill two birds with one stone'*?

The thing was, my cousin wasn't anymore ready to help run a business based on love than I was. In fact, if you asked me, he was going to be completely unable to do so.

Love was the last thing on his mind.

Still, my uncle had hope.

I got it.

If I couldn't do it, maybe his son could.

More than twenty years ago, my uncle had lost his wife and son in a tragic car accident. After that devastating loss, all he did was work. And when I came to live with him, it was an adjustment on both of our parts.

It seemed like we'd just got in the swing of things when one day he came back from a wedding expo in Nevada with a foster kid who'd tried to pickpocket him. Soon he adopted that kid, and Finn became part of our small family.

I think even today he was still reeling from the effort it took to raise us both.

Boys were said to be easier to raise than girls, but Finn had been much more difficult to handle than me, and even now, he still was.

He was a wild card.

Even though Finn had been out of the toxic environment he had grown up in for a long time, he still had a dark fire in him he had yet to extinguish.

Now twenty-two years old, Finn had graduated college more than three months ago and had yet to begin to job hunt. To this end, my uncle knew very well that Finn didn't want to be in the family business. This he had made clear over and over throughout the years. However, without a plan for the future, Uncle Edward decided Finn needed to give it a try.

Finn didn't have a choice.

What my uncle didn't know was that Finn did have an interest in another field, *if you could call it that*. What he was doing with his nights was a secret between us, though, and if Finn had his way, my uncle would never find out about it.

The idea of Finn working with me still hadn't sunk in. Yet, I knew I either accepted the help or Uncle Edward was going to cancel all his vacation plans and come back to work himself. If that happened, I would never be able to prove I could make it on my own. Even if his doubts seemed less like doubts and more like reality with each passing day, I still wanted this chance.

For me.

And for him.

In my late twenties, Uncle Edward knew I was more than mature enough to run a business of this magnitude, and he also knew I wanted to be in the wedding business. Which was why he turned it over to me, to begin with.

However, today during our rather heated discussion about Finn, he told me that my quest for perfection, coupled with my impulsive nature, could be the downfall of Easton Design & Weddings. And that he wasn't sure giving me until the end of the summer to turn things around was the right thing to do.

Those words broke my heart, but they also made me more determined than ever to prove him wrong. After a very long conversation, by some miracle, he had decided to honor his promise and not rescind it before selling the business.

Proving myself wasn't going to be easy.

Of course, there was the indisputable fact that I had to turn the business around. However, there was also the fact that my failed engagement still weighed heavily on my uncle's mind. In his eyes, I had made a wrong decision, and I think he saw that as a testament to my poor decision-making abilities.

That was nearly nine months ago, and yet he continued to

refer to the less-than-logical reasons I had called the wedding off. It was safe to say he talked about it more than I did. In his opinion, Jaxson Cassidy was about as close to being the perfect one for me as anyone ever would be.

He might not have been wrong about that.

But I'd let Jaxson go.

Jaxson Cassidy.

Just his name brought a smile to my lips.

Everyone called him Sundance because he was the polar opposite of Butch Cassidy in the famous movie. Laid back and fun loving, he was more like the Sundance Kid. Jaxson, which I preferred to call him, was the Ying to my Yang.

The whole opposites attract thing described us perfectly. Where I was a bit overzealous, to put it nicely, he was laid back and easy going.

Perhaps a little too much.

I had been the one to suggest we get engaged, and so we did. I had been the one to suggest a wedding date, and Jaxson had agreed. I had been the one to pick out everything, and that worked for him.

Do you see the *I* pattern here?

In the weeks leading up to the wedding, I noticed his light seemed a little dimmer. That he wasn't shining as brightly as he normally did.

Just in case you hadn't guessed, I'm an overachiever and a bit of a perfectionist myself. Even though Jaxson swore nothing was wrong, I knew something was. And I couldn't get it out of my head. I began to wonder why he wasn't happy, and then I figured it out.

It was me.

I didn't make him happy anymore.

I wasn't the Yang to his Ying.

Being the perfectionist that I was, I wanted to be that. I wanted perfect. I wanted to be his everything, but I knew I wasn't.

This only made me question if he was *my everything*, and that was when I realized maybe he wasn't.

Ending our engagement was the best thing for both of us.

We weren't meant to be.

I felt it in my bones, and at least we remained friends, which was both good and bad. On the one hand, I loved talking to him and working with him. But, I also hated the idea that the day was going to come when he'd fall for someone else, and being close with him still, I'd not only know about it, but I'd also have to see it.

Me, on the other hand, I was beginning to think my uncle was right, and that I had made a mistake.

After nine long months, I had yet to even go on a date.

Perhaps finding Mr. Right was impossible.

Maybe finding *Mr. Almost Right* was as close as I could ever hope to get, which meant Jaxson had been my shot at love, and I had blown it because it wasn't perfect.

We weren't perfect.

Perfect.

I was beginning to hate that word.

Imperfect wasn't looking so bad.

Then again finding my North Star wasn't exactly something I had time for right now. And dating, that not only took time but energy, both of which were running low right now.

The creak of the steel door swinging open jarred me out of my more than unfortunate reality.

When I looked up, though, I smiled wide. In each hand, Montgomery held a small porcelain plate. I was certain they would be his favorite silver-lined ones if I could see the rims, which I couldn't because the pieces of cake were the size of Mount Rushmore.

Raising an eyebrow, I scolded him. "Montgomery! I thought you said we were going to share a piece, not eat the entire tier. That is way too much cake. I can't be in a chocolate coma when I meet with my prospective clients."

Before I could comment further, a pair of thick, muscled arms gripped my waist from behind, and a tight belly pressed along my back. "Not prospective client, your *new* client. Think positively, my dear," a strong English voice whispered directly into my ear. "And don't worry love, I'm not going to allow Montgomery to eat that bloody piece of cake, and you don't have to, either."

I twisted, giving into laughter at the tickling touch of a beard on my earlobe. "Archer, when did you get here? I didn't even hear you come in."

Archer was as English as Montgomery was Southern, and he was not only Montgomery's husband but also the manager of The Bride Box. With his incredibly fit physique, methodically shaved hair close to his scalp, and that single diamond stud in his ear, he was incredibly handsome.

With his deep-rooted English manners, Archer took my palm and kissed my hand. "Why my love, I've been here all day, but I was in the back office, which as you know is like being in Siberia. And since Montgomery turned off the security system yesterday when Jaxson was here doing a photo shoot for his portfolio, I didn't hear you come in, or of course, I would have greeted you properly when you arrived."

Montgomery was shaking his head at Archer.

"Jaxson was here doing a shoot, for his portfolio?" I asked, and I wondered why he hadn't told me.

Montgomery ignored my question and extended his arm to hand me the cake. "Yes, I, once again forgot to turn the alarm back on," he admitted, not looking at all sheepish about it.

Before taking the plate he was offering, I shook a finger at him. "You know it drives Archer crazy when you leave the building unsecured."

"It wasn't my fault," Montgomery sighed. "That system is much too complicated." He looked at Archer. "Even you said so."

Archer nodded. "Yes, the system has its quirks, especially when it's turned off. No matter." He waved a hand. "Tell me, how are you, love?"

"It really was nearly impossible to concentrate with that constant ding, ding, ding," Montgomery muttered under his breath.

With my gaze glued to the decadence in my hand, I ignored Montgomery's complaining, and answered Archer with a light, "How could I be anything but great when I'm about to taste this piece of heaven."

"I know, it's practically orgasm inducing." He winked, and then turned to Montgomery. "Speaking of cake, you know you can't eat that," he scolded, and then he tried to take the plate Montgomery was holding from his hand just as Montgomery was lifting his fork.

While the couple battled over the cake, I was unable to stop myself from taking a bite. I sliced the fork through the seven layers and watched as the ganache oozed along the metal of the prongs. And then I lifted the heaping size portion to my mouth, and yes, Archer was right, it was orgasm inducing.

Not that I came or anything.

But seriously, as soon as the delicious taste hit my tongue and slid down my throat, I began to wonder if it might not be better than sex, or the sex I was having with myself, ever since Jaxson and I broke up, anyway.

And if that wasn't just pathetic.

Scowling at Archer very loudly, Montgomery drew my attention, and I brought myself back to their conversation.

"—I meant the bloody cake, not the orgasms, Monty," Archer scolded. "Now give me that plate. You know you can't eat it."

Monty was his pet name for Montgomery, and although it didn't seem fitting, whenever he said it, it seemed right.

"It's my fault," I piped up. "Montgomery told me you wanted him to watch his waistline, but I insisted he have a piece with me."

"Is that what he told you?" Archer asked. So unmistakably horrified at the thought, he relinquished the plate back to Montgomery immediately, as if it were burning his fingertips.

Montgomery was making a slicing gesture across his throat, but it was too late, I'd already spoken. I had no idea where to go from there.

"That simply isn't true," Archer divulged, straightening his pink bow tie.

"Archer, please don't say another word," Montgomery begged.

Archer shook his head. "I'm sorry, Monty, but Jules needs to know. I should have told her last week."

"Told me what?" I asked, placing my fork into the cake since there was nowhere else to put it.

He turned toward me. "Last week, Monty thought he had a severe case of indigestion, but when it didn't go away, I practically had to handcuff him and force him to allow me take him to the Emergency Room. The ER doctor determined almost immediately it was not indigestion, but rather diagnosed he was having a heart attack. In a matter of minutes, my Monty had been whisked to the cardiac floor where they discovered a blockage in one of his arteries. Luckily, the cardiologist was able to open it, but our Monty needs to work on keeping it that way by eating the right foods."

Shocked, I set my plate down on the counter beside me. "Oh, my God. I had no idea. Montgomery, why didn't you tell me?"

Archer answered for him. "Because he knew how important this client was to you, and didn't want you to cancel."

Tears shimmered in my eyes. "Are you sure you're okay?"

Montgomery was nodding his head. "I'm fine, my darling. Don't listen to Archer. You know he overreacts to almost everything. It wasn't that big of a deal. And look at me—I'm fine. The doctor said to watch what I eat, and I have been. Once in a while, if I want to indulge, I should be able to. Don't you think, Juliette?"

Just then there was a pounding on the back door. It saved me from having to answer, and I was thankful for that.

At the sound, Archer slung an arm around Montgomery and took the plate from his hand at the same time. "Come with me in the back, my Monty, that must be the security company."

Montgomery looked at him in confusion.

"They are going to install a new feature that will allow you to turn the door buzzer off all by itself. You can use it whenever you need silence while leaving the alarm system intact."

Jerking his head toward me, Montgomery said, "What would I do without him? He's always trying to make my life easier. Finish your cake, Juliette. I'll be right back."

I smiled at him. "I'm not going anywhere."

And then I watched the couple as they strode into the back kitchen arm-in-arm, and sighed.

Now that was a perfect kind of love.

chapter
3

Actions Speak Louder than Words

JULES

I WASN'T A romantic, but some gestures always made my heart swell because they reminded me of my parents.

The ways in which my father used to show my mother how much he loved her were so sweet.

Their love for each other was deep, profound and full of the little things that mattered.

It was so perfect.

All I had to do was close my eyes, and I could easily remember the times my father had serenaded my mother at six in the morning because she'd gotten upset with him the night before. Or the holidays he'd had flowers sprayed in glitter before having them delivered because my mother adored sparkly things. And how sometimes he'd bring home a picnic dinner in the middle of winter to help satisfy her spring fever.

I wanted that—someone who knew me better than I knew myself. Someone to laugh with. Cry with. Be with. Someone who made my leg kick up and my toe point when he kissed me. Made my world stop. Someone to love who loved me the same way.

But my prince charming hadn't arrived yet, and he might never arrive. I had to accept that. Still, I was lucky. I got to see love all around me, and that would have to be enough—for now.

I swallowed the lump in my throat and set my teary-eyed gaze on the cake.

Feeling like this appointment was going to go off without a hitch, I quickly swiped my tears away. Pulling my portfolio of items from my bag, I began neatly arranging them around the cake.

The Tiffany blue looked terrific against the white and brown. And the rustic look really made the color pop.

Jaxson's business card had gotten intertwined with the photos of the old barns I'd found online for potential venues.

"Sundance." His nickname used as his professional name was embossed in silver upon white card stock. The S was in a scripted font, and the remaining letters were plain. There was a camera watermarked behind it. His business moniker was not so much elegant as it was practical. Easy on the eyes. A lot like he was.

I stared at it for a long while. He had always aspired to do more than weddings. He wanted to work for a prominent magazine and shoot fashion models. He wanted to work for National Geographic and photograph wild animals. He wanted to photograph anything but weddings.

Had I been the one who had held him back?

Was he finally moving on?

I shoved the card back in my bag. I'd show Rory his work back at my office. Seeing was believing, after all.

When my gaze swung back to the cake, I frowned as I focused on the heart etched into the middle tier.

A wave of alarm washed through me.

Oh, no!

No.

No.

It couldn't be.

It just couldn't be wrong.

I bent to get a closer look. With my lips twisted in contemplation, I stared at it for three long seconds.

The initials carved in the cake were RK + RH, but I was fairly confident the groom-to-be's name was Kyle Harrison, and that would mean the second set of letters should start with a K, not an R.

All of a sudden, I was so hot, and my ears felt like they were on fire. I was about to have a full-fledged panic attack, and I knew it.

This was so not the time for that.

I tried to shake it off. The cake was astonishing, so what if we had one tiny detail wrong? Everything would still be fine. Even as I tried to convince myself otherwise, I knew it wouldn't be. Not with a mistake of this magnitude.

As fast as I could, I snatched the sketchpad Montgomery always kept under the counter to double check the initials we'd agreed upon. Flipping it open, I found the rendering right away, but the heart hadn't been filled in, which meant he hadn't planned on filling it, or he was uncertain about what to fill it with.

"Montgomery," I called, but there was no answer.

Pulling my phone from my bag, I quickly thumbed through the emails from Rory Kissinger. Even after scanning them, it didn't bring me any closer to finding out her fiancé's name. All her references to him were *my fiancé* this or my *fiancé* that or *we* this and *we* that.

Tapping Google, I hurriedly searched *the Governor of Georgia's son*. Of course, he had to have two sons, whose names, of course, were Kyle and Robert.

Just my luck.

I tried adding the words *recently engaged* to my search, but I got nothing. Then again, the happy couple hadn't made any announcement yet. That would be one of my tasks if I got the job.

"Montgomery," I called again. When I got no answer, I rushed to the kitchen door and pushed it open. The room was empty. They had gone somewhere.

This couldn't be happening.

I glanced at the clock. Less than ten minutes until my clients were scheduled to arrive, and there was no time to waste. Since the name Kyle was my first instinct, I was going with it.

How hard could it be to fix?

With my stomach a queasy mess and my breathing out of control, I acted without thinking.

Hurrying back to the counter, I yanked that straw-like thingy from the cup against the backsplash and whirled back around. I just had to turn that R into a K before my clients arrived. If I didn't, I was sure I'd lose the job because the happy couple would think I was totally incompetent.

Or worse, they would think I had paired the bride with the wrong groom!

Just as the blunt tip of the tool hit the icing, someone's voice echoed from the lobby, "Are you open?"

I jumped at the deep tremble of the male voice reverberated through me. That huskiness made him sound sleepy, and dare I say sexy. Having been startled, I was a bit unsteady. Forced to stop what I was doing, I jumped into work mode.

My clients.

This had to be my clients.

Of course, the happy couple was early.

The footfalls were getting closer. With only seconds to spare, my mind started to race.

The letter repair was out of the question, and the alternatives at my disposal were limited. I could turn the cake around, step in front of it, stick my finger over the R and erase part of it, or rush the couple out of here and ignore the cake altogether.

No, forget the last one, I couldn't do that.

It was my selling point.

Pausing for a moment to catch my breath, I inhaled deeply before setting the tool down, and then I discretely just did it. I wiped away part of the top of the R and then quickly licked the frosting from my finger.

Once the evidence was gone, I stood directly in front of the cake and slowly pivoted around on my toes. Ready or not, it was time to meet Rory Kissinger and her fiancé. I didn't have a plan on how to address the smudge mark on the cake, but I hoped they wouldn't notice.

"I didn't mean to scare you."

Wide-eyed, I found myself looking at only one person, not two. A current ran up my spine, and for a moment I wondered if I knew him, but when I couldn't place him, I shook it off. "Oh, you didn't," I finally managed, the mistruth forcing me to avert my gaze.

Still walking across the lobby, he hadn't quite made it to the showroom entrance. "Well, even so, I apologize if I disturbed your work," he said.

Busted. I was busted. I had lied, and worse, he knew it.

Could he see the smudge all the way from there?

Oh, God.

Feeling my body flushing, I forced a smile on my face. "Apology accepted even though it isn't needed," I responded, feeling foolish the minute those silly words left my mouth.

"May I come in?" This stranger didn't have a southern accent, but he definitely had the southern charm.

When I swung my gaze back to answer, he was closing the distance between us. Our eyes met, and for some utterly bizarre reason, the connection felt physical.

All of a sudden, his brow creased, and he stopped in his tracks.

Had he felt it too? Perhaps just as confused as I was, he flicked his gaze away from mine and then pouted his bottom lip. It was as if he didn't like the static between us.

The flirtatious hot guy in front of me wasn't my client, but despite the fact that this should have calmed me down, my heart began to pound, and I felt that flush rush all the way up my neck. Not that it mattered what color I was because the hunk wasn't looking at me. He was doing his best to put the cake back in his line of vision.

There was still a fair distance between us, and I think the magnificence of the cake had captured his attention. That was fine because it gave me time to stare at him a bit longer than would ordinarily be socially acceptable.

Tall. Dark. Handsome. Very handsome.

Actually, he was drop-dead gorgeous. And that mouth. His lips. They looked absolutely kissable.

With his partially wet hair the color of milk chocolate spiked forward, and only somewhat combed, it appeared unruly, like he didn't give a you know what. Maybe he'd recently taken a shower and hadn't had time to finish styling it, nor had he had time to shave for that matter. He had quite the five o'clock shadow for two in the afternoon.

The fact he appeared 'undone' somehow gave him a sexier edge, if that was even possible.

His rebel good looks, along with his dark sunglasses, made him look like the kind of guy your mother warned you about.

Trouble.

Give him a leather jacket and a cigarette, and he could have been James Dean.

There was a blue T located in the upper right of his shirt with a lighter blue wave rushing over the top. Not that I would know, but my best guess was that was the logo for his employer.

The *had-to-be* security company employee must have come around the front when no one answered in the back. Montgomery and Archer were probably out back arguing over the slice of cake and waiting for him to return. They'd figure it out soon enough.

Not that it mattered. I could keep him occupied for a few minutes. It wouldn't be that great of a hardship.

The hot technician had stopped in the doorway and was standing there with one hand on the doorjamb at a point high enough to stretch his long, lean body.

I felt like I should pose in some way. Cock a hip, hold my chin up, anything to get his attention. However, before I could come up with something that wouldn't make me look like a hooker without heels, his gaze shifted my way, and he caught me staring.

Living in the moment, I pushed my small chest forward and placed a hand on my hip. Okay, I probably looked like a girl getting ready to hitchhike. All I had to do was stick my thumb out.

Great.

"May I?" he asked.

Oh, right, he had asked a question. "Yes, of course, come in," I answered.

Either not noticing or not paying any attention to my ridiculous pose, he pointed to the cake. "That's quite a showpiece."

Stepping aside to show it off, I felt very proud that I had helped with the creation, no matter how small my part had been. That was until I noticed the way he had stuck his bottom lip out in a pout once again.

Keeping my gaze fixed on him, I watched him bite that same lip, as if in contemplation. Then with a slight cock of his head, he finally said, "Birds, huh."

It wasn't a question. It wasn't said with excitement, either. I wasn't sure what to think about that. After a moment, I decided he must be overwhelmed. "Lovebirds," I clarified, not sure why that mattered. It was just my body was buzzing, and I had to say something.

As if he were done admiring the cake from afar, he eased slightly forward. One foot balanced his entire weight while his other leg bent to take a step inside the showroom, and then slowly he strode toward me.

Entirely unlike me, I found myself watching each step he took. With a body like that the man must work out, like all day, every day. There was no other explanation for how a guy could look that damned good. I had dibs on the fact the security job was part-time.

His sunglasses were still on, and although the sunlight might not have been blinding, he was. I couldn't help but take him all in. Those sexy low-slung jeans, and the way they sat on his hips. The gray T-shirt that molded to his muscled chest and was snug around his bulging upper arms.

When he rounded the large wooden table, he stroked over his sexy stubble. "They look real," he said, his tone skeptical at best.

Trying not to laugh, I slanted him a sideways glance as he moved a little closer to the table. "They're not stuffed, if that's what you are thinking. The master baker is an excellent artist, and he sculpted them out of fondant."

While looking at the cake, he took another step around the table, and this time he removed his sunglasses as if he needed to get a better look. "So you didn't make this?"

Nervous for no reason at all, I tucked a piece of hair behind my ear. "No, definitely not. I'm not even sure when the last time I baked a cake was. It might have been in my Easy Bake oven."

That earned me a sexy smirk, but then his lip pouted again as his gaze swung my way. That mouth was something to look at, but those eyes. He was close enough now that I could see them. They were blue. Really, really blue, but they were also a little red around the rims. "Sorry, you were, well . . . I saw you . . . I just thought—" he trailed off, looking sheepish, and then he shook his head. "Never mind."

Biting my lip to control my giggling, I clarified the situation to help him out. "Montgomery Laurent is the master baker, and he owns The Bride Box. I'm a wedding planner."

Almost business-like, he slipped his sunglasses into the collar of his shirt and straightened up. "Good," he said, "then you won't be upset if I tell you those birds look a little too real to be on top of something people are going to be eating."

Uncertain how to take his comment, I responded with, "Don't you like birds?"

He shrugged.

Shrugged!

And then he was standing almost at my side. "Sure, I like birds. Just not on top of a cake. Don't get me wrong, I'm certain they are appealing . . . to the right person."

Trying not to be offended, because really, what did he know about this bride, and her likes and dislikes, anyway, I decided it was time to move him along. "Are you looking for Archer?" I asked, hoping my point would come across.

Beat it, buddy.

"Archer?" he questioned, clearly distracted.

And not by the cake this time. He had fully rounded the table and was now standing less than a foot away from me.

This had to be the flirtiest technician on the planet, and I began to feel the oddest blush coat my cheeks from the manner in which he was now staring at *me*.

Those blue eyes of his darted across my face, once, twice, three times. I would have sworn they were laughing at me if I didn't feel the heat in them right between my thighs.

"Yes, Archer," I tried to say in a huff, but it came out more like a dreamy sigh.

Oh, boy.

He stepped even closer to me.

For some insane reason, my pulse started to race, and things that felt like butterflies in my belly seized me. These had to be *new client* butterflies, but I'd never gotten them like this before.

"I'm sorry if I'm staring," he said, lifting his arm, "but I think you have a little—" As the words tumbled from his mouth, his finger slowly swiped across my bottom lip.

I closed my eyes.

"Frosting, right here," he finished.

Oh my God!

My lids popped open. That was what he was looking at. Frosting on my lips. And here I had thought he might be into me. Flirting with me. Maybe even wanted to go out with me.

How embarrassing!

As if he sensed my disappointment, his eyes lowered beneath their lashes. I inhaled at the shock-like feeling that jolted through me as his gaze traveled down my entire body and then back up again.

My brain was a little flustered, and I was having trouble concentrating on any one thing. But when he held up the chocolate he'd wiped from my lip, and then slowly licked it from his finger, I was able to focus just fine. Now it was my racing heart I couldn't keep track of.

"Not bad," he breathed.

Not bad!

Furious, I blinked out of my lustful haze.

I was really ready to tell him to beat it, that was until his eyes came back to my face, and he offered me such a searing look, I let the comment go.

After all, to him, it was just a cake. He didn't know any better. It wasn't his fault.

And . . . he *was* into me.

I had been right.

In fact, by the way he was now looking at me, I thought he might just be the one to love me forever.

In that one single moment though, it wasn't love on my mind. I'd started to question what the hell I had been thinking only moments ago. Had I actually thought chocolate cake was better than sex?

If I had, I was so taking that back.

Why on earth was this security technician making me think about sex? The answer struck me so quickly, it made me weak in the knees—it was because I wanted to have it with him. And by the way his chest had started to rise and fall at a rapid pace, I knew if I asked him to meet me later, he wasn't going to refuse.

Here Montgomery thought I never did anything crazy.

The words just slipped off my tongue. "What are you doing later?"

Intrigue gleamed in his eyes as he raised a single brow. "I believe I'm meeting with you to plan the wedding, and afterward I have to go to work, but—"

Meeting with me?

A cold shiver ran down my spine at the exact moment a beep-beep alerted me that someone had come through the front door. This confused me. How could the security system have been updated already if the technician was standing in front of me?

It became painfully clear the man in front of me wasn't from the security company when a very excited young woman came rushing toward him.

This was my client.

This was Rory Kissinger.

That I knew without a doubt.

"I can't believe you got here before me," she squealed. And throwing her arms around him, she then added, "You really must love me after all."

Are you kidding me?

This guy really *was* Rory Kissinger's fiancé! They must have had a lover's quarrel, and that was why he'd practically fucked me with his eyes.

In my book that was about as close to cheating as any man could ever come. I shot him a look of disgust, but that wasn't enough. It didn't stop the anger I was feeling from building. His fiancé deserved to know just how despicable he really was.

There was no way in hell I was ever going to allow this cheat to be my client. In fact, this guy really needed to be taught a lesson.

"I can't believe you," I hissed.

That bottom lip pouted again. "Believe what?" he somehow managed to ask around the body that was wrapped around him.

His fiancé's body, that was.

All the tension and anxiety I had been feeling for weeks unfurled within me, and before I could stop myself, I had the cute little silver-rimmed plate in my hand with the giant piece of chocolate cake still sitting upon it. And then as if I'd snapped, I was lifting the plate in an arcing motion. "This!" I said with deep satisfaction.

The kitchen door pushed open while I was midway in swing, and I heard Montgomery's thick accent. "Dr. Kiss, what are you doing here?"

Dr. Kiss.

Who in the ever-loving world was Dr. Kiss?

Could it be this man wasn't Rory's fiancé, but rather someone Rory loved, and an acquaintance of Montgomery's, as well?

Dr. Kiss.

Oh my God!

Kiss, as in Kissinger.

A relative.

No!

No!

No!

Suddenly, my uncle's voice echoed in my ear. *"Always do your research so you can anticipate your client's needs."*

And I had. Or I thought I had. But what I hadn't done was Google any images of my clients, and that would have been so easy. For goodness' sake, I had just searched Rory's fiancé on my phone. All I had to do was click on images.

Oh no!

Another wave of panic struck me. The groom-to-be was the governor's son.

The governor's son.

Oh my God, the press.

The bad press.

The fall out.

I would never land another job as long as I lived.

This could mean the end of my career if I didn't turn this situation around.

Unfortunately, the perilous act I had planned on committing was already in motion. Much to my horror, I was smashing that substantial-sized piece of chocolate cake in this handsome stranger's face before I could stop myself.

Rory jumped out of the way and started screaming at once. Montgomery shouted, "What are you doing, Juliette!" And then as if that wasn't enough, the door was beeping again. A younger guy came inside with a t-shirt on, which apparently read TULANE UNIVERSITY across it.

Going to stand beside Rory, the younger man stared at me in shock like I was a lunatic, and then he turned to Rory and said, "What did he do now, honey?"

This guy had to be her fiancé.

Pulling the plate away as fast as I could, I felt dumbstruck as the cake slowly fell in pieces all over Dr. Kiss's shirt. Some of the morsels landed on the T, which I figured out was meant to represent Tulane University, not the security company.

That part was at least an understandable misunderstanding.

I might not have comprehended who everyone was, but I knew they had a connection to each other. Then again, did the specifics truly matter anymore? "I'm so sorry," I apologized, setting the plate down.

In the way those icy blue eyes were glaring at me, I wasn't sure what I should do. Taking both hands, he swiped across his nose and then shook the frosting from his fingertips. "What the hell was that for?"

Quickly dropping down to my knees, I began to pick up the morsels from the ground. When I looked up, more cake fell and landed on my own face. I ignored it and tried to answer him. "I . . . I . . . I have no idea what came over me. I thought . . . well . . . I thought . . . you were the groom-to-be and that you were coming on to me," I confessed.

He used his fingers to wipe the cake from his own lips this time. "And what? You were going to put me in my place with a piece of chocolate cake? How old are you? Twelve?"

There was no way to explain that the butterflies he had given me were something I hadn't felt in a long time, if ever, and then when I thought he was only screwing with me, well, I overreacted.

He was right. I had not only responded impulsively, but immaturely. Feeling like there was nothing further I could say that would make any sense, I stood up and glanced around for something to clean him up with. "I'll get some towels."

Rory had stopped screeching at least, but now she started laughing. I tried to catch her attention, and when I did, I silently begged her to stop. Instead, though, she strode around the table to get a little closer and then crooked a finger to swipe up some of the cake. *That was on his face.* Her laughter was out of control. I was at a loss for what to do. Dr. Kiss then glared at her too, but she didn't seem to care one bit, which was evident when she licked the frosting from her finger and made a *Mmmm that's delicious* noise.

Her fiancé, on the other hand, was still looking at Dr. Kiss with his mouth hanging open. "Remy," she said to him as she took her place beside him once again. "Come on, you can laugh. It's way too funny not to."

Remy?

Not Kyle?

Or Robert?

Was there a third son I hadn't found?

How had Google failed me?

With no time to worry about the fact that there was a messed up K on the cake where there had once been a glistening R, I started grabbing all the decorative dishtowels that were scattered around the counters. I thought about crying while I did.

I should never have doubted Montgomery.

The cake.

My client.

My life.

Once I had all the towels I could find, I rushed back to the center of the room and attempted to pat the remaining cake from Dr. Kiss's face. Montgomery was there as well and trying to ease the situation.

As to be expected, Dr. Kiss shrugged away from me. "I'll do it myself," he gritted through his teeth.

It wasn't a peace offering, but I held out one of the towels, and much to my surprise, he took it.

On my heels, Archer had come into the room and grabbed another towel from my hand to assist in removing the chocolate from his face.

When it became evident removing the cake wasn't going to be an easy job, Montgomery said, "Come on, Doc, let's go in the kitchen and get this mess cleaned up."

The glare Montgomery shot me while speaking made me feel like a child who was about to get scolded.

Even though there was absolutely no way I would be getting this job after what I'd done, I had to atone for my actions in some way. Somehow. And to do so I needed to do more than offer a simple 'I'm Sorry'.

I had acted impulsively.

Just as I was about to try to give a better explanation for my actions, not that I could just out and say I was attracted to him, Rory chased after Dr. Kiss, and somehow managed to speak around her laughter. "Looks like I'm not the only one you pissed off today, brother."

Her brother.

Of course, Dr. Kiss was her brother.

I sighed. I wished she'd told me about him. Instead, her emails had stated the appointment would be with the groom-to-be, her, and myself, only. When I asked if she was sure she didn't want to invite a family member along, she had been rather adamant she would be doing this alone.

Unmistakably, she'd changed her mind, which of course, was her prerogative. If there was any doubt that I hadn't lost the job, it vanished right then.

Her brother was apparently here for a reason—to help her make a decision. And I'd just lost his vote.

Stopping just before the kitchen door, Dr. Kiss jerked his head toward her. "This isn't funny, Rory. As soon as I get cleaned up, I'm out of here."

"Come on, Jake," she whined, "you can't go. We haven't even listened to the wedding planner's proposal."

More chocolate fell from his lips as he spoke. "Trust me, I've heard and seen enough."

"But the cake, didn't you see the cake?" she pointed. "It's perfect." Clearly, she was impressed. And clearly she loved what he had not.

Perhaps there was hope after all.

After rubbing his chin and leaving a stain of chocolate behind, her brother narrowed his gaze at her. "Not even an hour ago you told me you wanted a vintage wedding with antique Louis Vuitton suitcases and a classic Rolls Royce. How the hell do birds fit in that picture?"

"They don't," she answered almost contritely.

Wait! No birds?

I glanced from the cake to my dress, and my frown turned even deeper.

When was this day going to be over?

Those eyebrows of his rose as if to say *I told you so*. At least there wasn't any cake stuck on them.

Rory bounced on her toes over to the cake. "But that's only because I changed my mind. If I hadn't, this is exactly what I would have wanted. And besides, if you'd been listening to me the past few weeks, which you clearly were not, you would have known that lovebirds were my first choice. I might not want them for my wedding theme any longer, but that doesn't mean the cake didn't still wow me."

I had wowed her.

At least there was that.

"Rory." His tone was authoritative, and by the way his sister practically stamped her feet, it was painfully obvious he was the decision maker.

I was so screwed.

And not in the way I had thought I might be only minutes ago.

Speak of the Devil

JAKE KISSINGER

IT WASN'T LIKE vanilla was my thing, but right now I would have fucking given anything for it.

The water ran cold as I cupped my hands and splashed my face one last time. I'd been bitch-slapped, sucker-punched, even head-butted, but I'd never had anyone smash cake in my face.

It was a first.

And I hoped, a last.

I turned the faucet off and licked my lips. At last, the taste of chocolate had faded. And although it wasn't fully gone, there was the comforting fact that it wasn't in my nostrils any longer.

Monty handed me a dry towel. "Juliette can be a bit impulsive."

Taking the terrycloth from him, I patted my skin dry. "Juliette," I said, liking the way her name rolled over my tongue, and hating that I did, "is much more than impulsive."

Grabbing for my shirt, he took my vacated place at the sink and started scrubbing at the chocolate stains. "Yes, I'll admit she can also be a bit feisty, but she means well."

"You don't have to worry about that," I told him, pointing to my shirt.

He paused to glance over at me. "Maybe you could give her a second chance and listen to her proposal?"

I slid the towel down my neck and wiped away the excess water that dripped down onto my bare chest. I didn't know Monty at all. He'd been my patient last week, and I was sure he was a decent guy, but I had to call a spade a spade. "Look, I'm sure your daughter has the heart of an angel, but right now I just want to clean myself up and get the hell out of here."

The shirt was as spotless as it was going to get, and he handed it to me. "Juliette isn't my daughter, but I've known her since she was fourteen, and I can attest to the fact that she is more than competent when it comes to her job. She's also very passionate about her work, and from what I can tell about your sister, I think she would love working with Juliette."

Shrugging the damp shirt over my head, I tucked it into my jeans and then looked directly at him. "You don't seriously think I'm going to allow that woman to pitch her services to my sister after the fiasco that just took place?"

Monty eased back against the counter and crossed his arms over his chest. "Dr. Kiss, haven't you ever made a mistake?"

I mirrored his pose, kicking my Adidas out and leaning beside him to link my arms. "More times than I care to admit."

The shift in his gaze from myself to the door was anything but inconspicuous. "If you could take back the things you did that caused them to be mistakes, would you?"

Running a hand through my hair, I spoke honestly. "Sure, some of them. Heck, most of them."

After I responded, Monty fell silent a few long moments, but then he asked, "Do you go to church?"

Everyone from the south went to church. Even if you spent the majority of your youth in the north, if you had ties to Georgia, you went to church. Not at all liking the direction this conversation was going in, I paused for a moment, cocked my head to the side, and then answered with a, "I did when I was a kid."

"So you're familiar with the Bible?"

"Look," I said, "I know what you're getting at."

"Good, then you won't have a problem hearing her out."

I straightened. "I've had a long week, and I have to be back in the ER for another twelve-hour shift at five."

He glanced at his watch. "You still have plenty of time to hear at least a few of Juliette's ideas for your sister's upcoming wedding. I know she feels terrible about what she's done, and will want to make it up to you."

Make it up to me. How the hell was she going to do that? Get on her knees again. Maybe that would work. As the thought ran through my mind, it was one that most definitely did not include an audience.

"Well?" he said.

I blinked my dirty vision away.

Strictly speaking, I took care of sick people. Tending to well people who needed to feel better about themselves was a shrink's job. "I'm sorry, but no."

Monty stared at me in disappointment. "I thought you went to church?"

I felt like a douchebag.

"Look," I said. "Just because when I was a kid I was forced to listen to the whole *forgive-those-who-trespass-against-you* sermon, doesn't mean I believe in it, and it certainly doesn't apply in all situations."

Monty's face was pinched tight. "No, you're correct about that. It doesn't. But in some circumstances, it's just the right thing to do."

Guilting me.

I didn't even know this guy, and he was guilting me, and it was fucking working. I was beginning to feel my resolve flicker.

Just as I was about to answer with a *'Sure, why the hell not'* the door squeaked open and Monty's husband stuck his head in. "Everything okay in here?"

I looked past him and found Juliette staring at me. Her lips had rounded to an *O*, and her eyes were wide and filled with bewilderment. She looked flustered. Panicked even.

Archer opened the door wider, and when he did, the empty plate came into view. As soon as my gaze landed on it, I was reminded of what she'd done. Forgiveness could only go so far, but that wasn't really what was holding me back.

There was more.

Aside from experiencing the oddest sense of déjà vu in her presence that made me feel uneasy, I knew firsthand what a wildcard she was. Someone who acted before thinking wasn't anyone I could work with.

What was it they said about two peas in a pod?

Forcing myself, I averted my gaze from hers and nodded at Monty's husband. "Yeah, everything's cool. I was just getting ready to leave."

Monty's brows drew together as he looked at me.

I stuck my palm out to him. "It was nice to see you again."

The wariness in his eyes didn't stop him from shaking what was offered. "I hope once you've had time to think about things, you'll change your mind."

Not wanting to look like the asshole I couldn't stop from being, I gave him a nod and then strode toward the door.

In the other room, the chatter was loud and animated. Rory and Remy were sitting at the large wooden table, and the wedding planner had joined them.

As soon as everyone noticed I had entered, the room fell silent.

Now I really looked like a real asshole.

Fucking fantastic.

Juliette stopped talking mid-sentence. Archer, who was looking through my sister's idea book, sat frozen in place. And my sister and Remy, who were sharing a piece of *that* cake, set their forks down.

I swore even the birds perched upon the cake seemed to be staring down at me, and I found it fucking eerie.

"There you are," Rory said in delight, "You just have to taste this cake." She picked up her fork and held it out toward me. "It's so delicious."

Keeping the sarcasm to myself, I strode past Juliette and didn't stop until I reached my sister. "I'm good," I said tightly.

She pulled out the vacant chair beside her. "Well, at least sit down with us."

Looking down at her, I kept my eyes right where they were. "I already told you I was leaving."

Pouting her lips, she practically whined. "Jake, please don't leave over a silly mistake. Jules has the best ideas, and I really want you to hear them."

Huh . . .

Jules, short for Juliette.

Jules, the woman who was across from me looking like a deer in headlights.

Jules, the wedding planner who smashed cake in my face, who also happened to be the person my sister had ironically decided, after meeting with countless other planners, was the one for her.

Was Rory even for real?

Seriously, I thought I might lose it.

I didn't.

I wouldn't.

The bottom line was my baby sister was my responsibility, at least until she wed. And even though she was a fucking pain in my ass, I loved her and hated to disappoint her. With that being said, it didn't mean that sometimes she didn't push me to the limit.

Only after drawing in a deep breath could I answer her calmly. "Rory, I have to be at work in less than two hours, and now I need to get home and shower before I can grab something to eat." I bent to kiss her. "I'll call you tomorrow."

Her eyebrows bunched together. "But I'm leaving to go back to Tulane tomorrow, and we haven't made any decisions."

Standing straight, I cursed. "Shit, that's right. How about I come by after my shift and we have breakfast together?"

She popped to her feet. "Great. And we can talk about the wedding then?"

I barely suppressed a sigh. "Yes, we can talk about it then."

Throwing her arms around my neck, she said, "You really are the best."

With a shake of my head, I hugged her back. Less than twelve hours ago she was yelling at me over the phone, telling me that if I didn't show up today to meet wedding planner number fifteen, I didn't love her. "Remember that," I muttered.

"Always." She kissed me on the cheek and hurried around the table toward Juliette.

Juliette had a forced smile on her face.

"Tell me more about the wedding you did last summer," Rory demanded.

Juliette seemed lost.

Rory went on. "The one with the antique furniture set in groupings outside carpets on the grass with crystal chandeliers hanging from tents."

There was no way we were using this wedding planner, no matter how spectacular her weddings turned out to be. However, I wasn't stupid. I'd break that news to my baby sister in the morning.

After shaking Remy and Archer's hand, I strode back in the

direction I'd come in but found myself stopping mid-step when I heard my sister's burst of laughter.

Looking over my shoulder, I let my gaze settle on the quirky girl in the bird dress and took her in. Busy talking, her hands were moving with excitement, and all the tension that lined her face moments ago appeared to be gone.

Her dirty blond hair was tucked behind her ears, revealing a startling beautiful face with striking green eyes. The sun caught on the sparkle of her small diamond star-like earrings, and when it did, that feeling like I'd seen her before was stronger than ever.

Maybe she came into the ER with Archer when Monty was there or some other time. That had to be it.

I didn't know how long I stood watching her, but it must have been only a matter of seconds. Still, as if sensing my gaze, hers lifted to meet mine. Although she continued to speak, her eyes widened, and something like panic entered her expression once again.

Having no idea why I wanted to ease that panic, I lifted my hand in a goodbye gesture.

What the hell?

Once I turned, I made certain I didn't look back again.

As I made my way down the sidewalk in the blazing heat, the strangest emotion washed over me. For some reason, I was feeling like I'd been the one who had done something wrong.

As if that wasn't the most screwed up thing ever.

I mean come on . . . I could still taste her, no not her, the chocolate she threw at me . . . on my lips.

And it pissed me off.

It really did.

chapter 5

A Penny For Your Thoughts

JULES

AT FIVE A.M. it was hard to be perky, even if you were a morning person, but it was even harder when you felt like the four walls that surrounded you were closing in.

My life was such a mess.

I stretched and looked around. The ordinarily comforting feeling that being in this house had once given me had faded months ago.

Hopping out of bed, I went into the small bathroom I shared with my cousin and sighed at the mess on the counter. Bandages, tape, scissors. Sighing, I brushed my teeth and then put everything away.

After Jaxson and I broke up, I let him keep our apartment and everything in it. In order to save enough money to buy all new household necessities, I moved back home for what was supposed to be a few short months. That was nine months ago, and now with my savings entirely depleted and little money to spare, securing a place of my own had been pushed to the back burner.

Whenever I thought about it, I couldn't believe I was in my late twenties and living with my uncle and cousin.

As I climbed out of the shower, I drew on my robe and then closed my eyes and pinched the bridge of my nose.

What happened yesterday was bad.

So, so bad.

And the worst part was, Rory loved me and wanted to hire me. It was just she couldn't because she really wanted her brother's approval, and she doubted that was going to happen.

So did I.

Thank God my uncle had left Atlanta to go to his farm immediately following our lunch meeting. Having to tell him about what I'd done wasn't anything I was ready for. At least while he was gone, I didn't have to.

Heading down the back stairs to make coffee before getting ready, the dark form huddled at the kitchen table startled me. When I let out a terrified shriek, I stumbled forward. Barely keeping myself from tumbling down the stairs by grabbing the railing, I felt like I was free falling.

For a few agonizing moments, my body lurched forward into empty space and I thought, *"This is it."* I was going to fall and crack my skull or fracture my spine, or worse, be burdened with some long debilitating injury that would force me to have to kiss my job goodbye without a fight.

But then I managed to somehow keep both feet on the step. I might have saved myself, but the stack of empty dishes I had been carrying in my hands from my food binge last night wasn't so lucky. With first a roll and then a crash, the plates and bowls broke into tiny pieces all over the wooden floor.

Could my life get any worse?

"Nice," said the voice I knew, even if darkness obscured the mouth it was coming out of, I knew who it was.

"Darn you, Finn! You scared me!" I put a hand on my heart, the other still on the railing. I really thought I might just faint before I forced myself to breathe.

"Sorry," he said quietly as he got up and strode toward the broom closet.

Shakily, I sidestepped the glass and flicked the light on. Then I carefully tiptoed to the sink to pour a glass of water. With the drink in my hand, I watched as Finn grabbed the broom. Although I knew I should, I didn't want to ask him why he had been sitting in the dark.

Like a coward, I didn't want to talk with him about where he'd been all night or his new job, and that wasn't fair.

Finn was always there for me. He had been a shoulder to cry on when I needed someone. Not only had he helped me move out of my apartment after my breakup, but he had also been there for me when I started to second-guess my decision, about everything. Finn was like the brother I never had.

After gulping the water, I refilled it and turned around. "I'll do that," I told him.

"I got it," he said, sweeping the pieces into the dustpan.

It was hard not to notice the bruises on his knuckles, but I knew better than to ask if he needed anything. We'd gone round and round over his nighttime activities one too many times, and each time we argued, he only pulled away from me more and more.

Resigned to keeping my mouth shut, I leaned against the counter and took in his clothing. Jeans, T-shirt, hoodie. "You're up early or is it late?"

I already knew the answer.

Dumping the broken glass into the garbage can, he glanced over at me. "I got home a few hours ago, but I couldn't sleep. I've been sitting here thinking about today."

"Ah." There wasn't much more to say than that, so I went with,

"How about a cup of coffee?"

That got a laugh from him. "Um, no. I need to grab a few hours of sleep before I have to go to work."

Setting my glass in the sink, I walked to the other end of the counter and switched on the coffeemaker. My uncle had one of the fancy kinds that ground the beans and heated the water to just the right temperature.

After Finn put the broom away, he headed for the stairs. "What time do you want me to start, anyway?"

Opening the cupboard, I grabbed a mug and answered him. "I have to go in early, but you don't have to be there until at least ten."

He stretched and yawned. "You sure? I can come in earlier."

I pressed the brew button, and the machine spat and hissed, burping out black liquid. "I'm sure. That will give me time to figure out what you can do since at the moment we have no clients."

He cocked one eyebrow upward. "Things are that bad?"

Lifting my cup, I considered adding some whiskey, that's how bad things were. "They've been better," was all I said.

He strode over to the counter. "Jules, how bad?"

Surprise gripped me at the earnestness in his tone. "I have no more money to float the business next month," I said shakily. "I'm broke and so is it."

"What the hell are you talking about?" he demanded.

I shook my head. "Nothing. Never mind."

He leaned forward, his gaze narrowing on me. "Don't shut down, Jules. Tell me what's going on."

And so I did.

Tears filled my eyes as I told him everything. How I thought I could run this business, but couldn't. How I didn't want to disappoint Uncle Edward, but how I might have already ruined everything he had worked for his entire life. How I didn't have the money to pay next month's business expenses.

How I had failed.

How I wanted out.

Finn reached across the counter and curled his hand around mine, squeezing it reassuringly. "I'm going to get you out of this mess."

"I don't think you can," I whispered.

He squeezed my hand again. "I can try."

I smiled indulgently at him and then hugged him. "Go get some sleep. I'll see you at work in a few hours. We can talk then."

With that, he gave me a nod and turned around.

I took a sip of my coffee as his heavy black boots pounded up the steps. I appreciated the sentiment, but there wasn't anything he could do to help me. I needed ten thousand dollars to cover next month's expenses, and without any clients, that was never going to happen.

The coffee was strong and good, and I hoped it was the jolt I needed to get this day started because all I really wanted to do was climb back into bed and sleep.

I sat in the chair Finn had vacated and started to think about what to do next to turn things around. All I had was until the end of the summer, and I already knew that wasn't nearly long enough.

Then there was the accounting issue. How could I make my funds stretch far enough to pay the bills? The answer was simple—I couldn't.

Worry was high on my mind.

I needed to tell Uncle Edward he should list the business now, before it was bankrupt and impossible to sell, and I would. Soon.

The square of stained glass over the sink lightened before I realized I'd been sitting there way too long. Daylight was dawning. I had to stop moping around and get ready to go to the office.

Just as I finished loading my cup in the dishwasher, I heard my cell ringing from upstairs. Heart racing, I rushed up the steps and didn't even care when I tripped and landed hard on my knees. I just got up and kept going.

This had to be my uncle. No one else called me this early. Biting out a curse, I scrambled up the hardwood as fast as I could. The last thing I needed was for him to have any reason at all to come home, and not being able to get ahold of me would definitely be reason enough.

Almost smacking my head into the door, I pushed it open and threw myself across the bed to snatch my buzzing phone from the nightstand. I frowned at the number on the screen.

I didn't recognize it.

The cold caller was going to get a word or two from me for calling this early. That was for sure. Deflated, I answered with a very snarky, "This better be important."

"Hello, this is Rory Kissinger. Am I speaking to Jules Easton?"

I jumped to my feet. "Yes, Rory, it's me," I said sweetly. "Sorry about that. I thought—never mind. How are you?"

"I'm good. Listen, I was hoping I could see you this morning."

My pulse started going wild. "Of course. What time did you have in mind?"

"Now would be good." I glanced at the clock. "And if you could come to me, that would be terrific."

I looked at my reflection in the mirror. I was still in my robe, and my damp hair was a mess. "Sure," I said. "I can leave within the next thirty minutes."

"Super great," she said in excitement.

"Did your brother change his mind about hiring me to plan your wedding?" I asked, surprised he'd had a change of heart at all, let alone so quickly.

She hesitated before speaking. "Well, not exactly . . . but we can talk about that when you get here. I'll text you the address."

At this point, did it truly matter? "Okay, can't wait to hear what you have to say. See you soon."

"Jules, wait," she said.

"Yes," I answered.

"Do you think you could hurry?"

"Yes, of course, I can," I said, and then I hung up, wondering if there was a fire sale or something, before rushing around like a crazy woman to get ready.

It wasn't like I had anything to lose.

Little did I know just how untrue that statement would turn out to be.

chapter
6

From the Fire into the Frying Pan

JAKE

THE SWELTERING HEAT was really starting to piss me off. Then again, just about everything was doing that lately.

Warm days had every Tom, Dick, and Harry out on the street. Mix the extremely high temperatures with alcohol, drugs, and handguns and the results weren't anything pretty.

As I headed across the large room, the green linoleum felt especially hard under my feet. After fifteen hours on them, anything would.

The twenty-six beds lining the three U-shaped walls were cluttered with wires, monitors, and charts, but for now, everything in this unit was quiet. Exhaling a deep breath, I unwrapped my stethoscope from my neck and shoved it into my pocket.

Walking out to the reception area to dictate some notes, I was pleasantly surprised when the main ER doors opened, and the sunlight practically blinded me. Thank fuck this night was over.

In came a man with his hand wrapped in a bag of ice. He wasn't running or screaming, so it was safe to assume all his appendages were still attached. As he waited in line at the window to give Gladys, the night receptionist, his information, the night nurse looked over at me. "What do you say, you and me one last time?"

It didn't go over my head that she was talking about more than the patient. I shook my head. "Not a chance."

Those long lashes of hers blinked. "Come on, Dr. Kiss, just one more," she purred.

That whole *don't dip your pen in the company ink* thing, yeah, well, I think I'd finally learned my lesson. "About that. Could you stop calling me Dr. Kiss? Now I have patients calling me that in public."

She threw her head back in laughter, and her brunette hair swung back and forth. "Oh, what I wouldn't give to see your face when they do that."

I eased back against the counter. Carly was, for the most part, cool about our past one-night stand. I think she just liked to press my buttons to see my uncomfortable reaction when she brought it up, more than anything else. We both knew it wasn't the right thing to do since we worked together, but at the time, it didn't seem to matter.

The hookup took place right after I'd learned my grandmother didn't have long to live, and the gravity of that had sent me spiraling. She was the one constant in my life, and in my sister's as well. Losing her was going to be devastating for us both. Carly was here that night my grandmother was brought in, and that morning when I learned the news. All I had wanted to do was forget, even if just for a little while. And she helped me do that.

The man with the bandaged hand rapped on the counter, and when his bag of ice clanked, I flicked my gaze his way. Who knew what he had done. Punched the wall? Slammed his hand in the car door? After the night I'd had, something that simple would be like a wet dream.

He had just finished up at reception and was walking toward the waiting room when Gladys handed Carly the chart and then turned to me. She was just about to update me on the specifics when I stopped her with my hands in the air. "No. No. No. No way."

"But, Dr. Kissinger—"

I cut her off. "You're going to have to call Dr. Hall. I'm sorry, but I'm out of here."

Gladys was in her early sixties and had been working at this hospital for over thirty years. No matter who said they were in charge, we all knew she was the reason things ran smoothly.

So when that stare of hers narrowed on me, and she pursed her lips and raised her brow at the same time, I might have second thought my decision, for about a half a second. "You can't intimidate me," I smirked. "Don't forget, I know what a kitten you really are, even when your claws are out."

With a huff, she turned around and picked up the phone. Overhead, her voice bellowed. "Dr. Hall, you're needed in the ER."

"Not even a stat," I muttered under my breath.

I knew she heard me by the shake of her shoulders, but she didn't turn around. That was okay. I'd make it up to her by bringing her one of those milkshake-like drinks from Starbucks she liked so much on my next shift.

Carly was giggling under her breath, and I looked back over at her. "Don't you dare let her hear you," I mumbled.

She put a finger up to her lips. "I wouldn't think of it."

Good thing Gladys was busy with another patient.

"You know," Carly said low, "why don't you stick around? I'm off in thirty minutes. We could grab a coffee or something."

Something.

I started to log into the computer. "Sorry, I can't. I have to meet my sister for breakfast."

So much for the whole *she was fine with the way things* were.

Guess I had that wrong.

"Maybe next time," she said breezily.

Not that this was the place, but I thought maybe I should just tell her there wasn't going to be a next time. That it was best if we remained colleagues and keep it at that. I wasn't really into her, or maybe I just wasn't in the right headspace.

Learning the person I had relied on wasn't going to be around much longer changed me, made me look at things differently, set me straight.

Gone were the nights of drinking and partying, and meaningless sex. They just weren't as appealing as they once had been. I had very little time left with my grandmother, and I wanted to spend what there was wisely.

Just as I was about to open my mouth to let Carly down as tactfully as I could, someone frantically yelled, "Dr. Kissinger!"

I wielded around to find a very frazzled first-year resident shoving a chart in my face. "Dr. Kissinger, I need your help."

"Where's your attending?" I asked pointedly.

Her distress was more than evident. "I don't know. I can't find him, and I'm next up to take the lead."

"First of all, you need to relax."

She took a deep breath.

"Okay, that's better. Now, what's going on?" I asked, wanting so much to tell her to find someone else to seek advice from, but at the same time not being able to.

"There's a knife wound victim on his way in. The paramedics will be here in less than two minutes, and I'm not sure where to start."

A siren screamed in the distance. Hearing it, I took the chart from her and quickly looked it over.

Fifty-year-old male.

Multiple ER visits.

History of alcohol abuse.

The poster child for this ER.

I so had this.

Grady Memorial Hospital was the largest healthcare facility in the state of Georgia and also the fifth-largest public hospital in the United States. It was not only one of the busiest ERs in the southeast, but also one of the busiest Level I trauma centers in the country.

We saw just about everything, and nothing was a surprise.

Not even sixty seconds into my chart review, the doors flew open, and three paramedics came rushing through. As soon as they reached the holding room, they moved the bloody body from their transport table and onto the trauma gurney.

The paramedic gave a rundown of the patient's current condition and the first-year nodded in acknowledgment. Well, that was a good sign that she wasn't completely lost, but really, where was her attending?

Rushing over to the patient, I pulled out my stethoscope and immediately began to assess him. The moment I looked into his bloodshot eyes, he spasmed and jerked in agitation. The signs were pretty clear, and his history had already spelled it out. "He's drunk. Very drunk," I told the intern. "The first thing you need to do is sedate him with a milligram of diazepam to help calm him down."

"Okay," she responded, and for a moment I seriously thought she was going to write it down. Thank fuck she didn't.

Not knowing if she'd taken the time to read the chart before handing it off to me, I went ahead and gave her the rundown of what I'd picked up in the few seconds I'd scanned it. "He's an alcoholic, which means his blood is thin, and he won't clot. Once you get back in the trauma unit, you need to run an Autoplex solution in his IV before you do any cutting or he might bleed out."

When there was no response, I glanced over and caught her blank stare.

"Autoplex," I repeated. "Got it?"

Still with the blank stare.

"It's a plasma-based coagulant."

"Yes, yes," she said as if it finally clicked. "Where do I get that?"

"You'll have to order it from the blood bank as soon as you cross through the doors."

She nodded. "Okay, I got it."

Assessing the wound site, I took her hands and showed her how to apply the right amount of pressure.

She knew what she was doing because she took over without me having to prompt her. It was clear, she was just nervous to be on her own.

I wasn't judging.

All of us in here had gone through it.

Lucky for her, two more first-year residents came rushing through the trauma unit doors and got right to work.

"Thank you, Dr. Kissinger," they all said in unison.

I nodded and watched as they tore through the set of doors, and I hoped in the future they all could respond a whole hell of a lot faster than they had.

When I turned around, I came face-to-face with the chief attending. I shook my head. "There you are."

Dr. Peter Wright was standing behind me with his arms crossed and looking just as exhausted as I felt. "I thought this time she was going to get it on her own. I really did."

"Yeah, well, she's just started her first year," I told him.

He sighed. "I know. I know. But potential without experience seems to be the story of my life lately. You could change that, you know. Are you ready to come show them all how it's done and join us in the trauma unit?"

Dr. Wright had moved from New York to Atlanta the same time I started working at this hospital. He said it was for the warmer weather and to begin the early stages of retirement, but as far as I could tell, he was far from retiring. He was, however, always looking to bring me under his wing.

This time when I took my stethoscope off, I swore I wasn't putting it back on until Monday. "Not happening, Peter. You know that."

As always, his face fell. There was this haunted undertone to almost every one of our conversations. I never understood why. "You sure you won't change your mind?" He was almost pleading. "I have an open spot in the Trauma Unit, and it's yours if you want it. You don't have to wait to move to New York to do the job."

I shook my head. These days New York seemed like a pipe dream instead of reality. "If I've told you once, I've told you a thousand times, I'm not changing my mind about New York. They're holding my spot indefinitely."

He squeezed my shoulder. "You know you would have made your father proud no matter where you worked. Even here, in Atlanta."

"Peter!" I warned.

He held his hands up. "I'm done trying."

I doubted that.

All through my residency, he had steered me away from New York Presbyterian. "Good," I said, "because I'm finished talking about it, and besides, I'm out of here for the day."

Clapping his hand on my shoulder, he said, "Have a good day, Jake."

"You too, Peter."

"Hey, Jake, how about dinner next Sunday?"

I made a face. "I don't think so. Mimi isn't doing well and I want to spend as much time with her as I can."

He nodded in understanding. "I'm sorry to hear that. I'll be in touch to check on her when I get back from the City."

"You headed back to New York again?"

"Yes, for a few days, but I'll be back."

"Can't stay away," I joked.

"No, son, I can't."

With that, I headed down the hall and pushed the elevator button. I had a stop to make before going to see my sister.

And unfortunately, that stop was in the ICU.

The hospital complex took up multiple city blocks. To say it was huge was an understatement of epic proportion. After walking down three corridors and across two walkways, I was finally in the Crawford Wing. Taking the elevator up to the fifth floor, I stood outside my grandmother's room and stared at it through the glass for a few long moments.

Beatrice Beau Crawford Alexander might have once been America's most revered media mogul, and the richest person in Atlanta, but to me, she has been and always would be Mimi.

At sixty-nine, she should have had a decent number of years left. But lying in that hospital bed looking so frail and small, she looked more like ninety, and I knew her time was running out.

Famously private and ironically media shy, she still remained on the board of directors of Crawford Enterprises, but her involvement over the last couple of years had been minimal at best.

Her hope was always to live long enough to pass the torch to my sister, and Rory wasn't quite ready to assume her role in the company. Until she was, the company was being run by a half dozen suits who I hoped like fuck knew what they were doing.

Beatrice Beau Crawford was, by all accounts, a true southern belle, and the greatest lover of dogs I'd ever known.

Aside from successfully taking the helm of her father's business when his brothers tried to take it from her, she was also a canine lover and an avid gardener. So much so, she was elected the Peachtree Garden Club president every year for ten years in a row.

Damn, why didn't I think to bring her some of her beloved Cherokee Roses?

Cursing myself, I took a moment to peruse her chart. Her vitals hadn't improved, and the newest tumors weren't responding to this round of chemotherapy. By the looks of things inside, another remission was highly unlikely. I wasn't an oncologist, but I didn't need to be to know her condition was worsening, and quickly.

When I opened the door, the seal broke, and a little hiss of air was released. Inside, the medical equipment was doing its job—pumping and monitoring and keeping everyone informed of her current state.

God, she hated those machines, and I hated having to see her hooked up to them.

Her eyes were closed, but I knew she was awake when she reached to fix the scarf around her head before opening them.

Once regal and beautiful, my grandmother now looked so ill. Her eyes had sunk back into her skull, her once able body looked so frail, and her arms too thin.

"There you are," she said with a mustered smile. "I was beginning to think you'd forgotten about me."

Grabbing a chair from the corner, I kissed her cheek before sitting down. "Like you'd ever let me do that?"

"Well, that's true," she said, and then tried to sit up. I wanted to help her, but I knew how much she hated that. However, when she couldn't manage, she looked at me. Without a word, I assisted her.

Alarm bells went off in my head.

Once she was settled, I held her hand. It felt so cold, and I rubbed my thumb over the top of it to try to warm it. "How do you feel today?" I asked.

Reaching for the white Styrofoam cup on the bedside table, she took a sip from the straw before answering. "Not very well, I'm afraid. Sleeping around here is impossible. And that's why I've been waiting for you to get here."

I raised a brow.

"Don't give me that look. There are some things I need to talk to you about."

I took the cup from her and set it down. "Oh yeah, what are they?"

Her eyes became laser-sharp when she looked at me. "I'm stopping my treatments. They aren't working, but they are making me very sick. I want to go home."

Suddenly the beeps and bleeps and pumping sounds in the room seemed even louder. But somehow I managed to hold her stare. "Mimi, you can't do that. You have to fight."

"I've been fighting long enough, Jake. It's time to stop."

"I don't think that's a good idea."

She had the bluest eyes, and I swore there were times they looked like storm clouds. "Well, I do," she said sharply. "And I want to die at home in a place that isn't filled with strangers."

Sadness thundered through my body. "I'll see what I can do."

"Good," she said. "I was confident you would take care of it."

I hadn't said I would. I'd said I could try, but I wasn't about to tell Mimi that. Besides, there was something in her voice that was more pleading than demanding, and it killed me not to be able to say yes right away.

"And there's something else."

"Oh yeah, what's that?" I whispered as I stared at her more than serious face.

She squeezed my hand. "I want to see your sister get married."

The before I die, was left off, but it was more than implied. There was a lump the size of Georgia in my throat. What else could I say except, "I can make that happen."

"Good," she said again. "I'm glad that's settled. Now, what about you?"

"What about me?"

She glared at me hard enough to burn a hole in my forehead.

"You know exactly what I'm talking about."

I shook my head, nothing but blankness coming to mind.

She sighed. "You, Jake. Your own life. You need to start building one that doesn't center around Rory and I. What about Bridget?"

"Bridget?" I rolled my eyes. Bridget and I had been a thing as residents in New York, but once our training was over, so were we. We both wanted different things. She wanted love and marriage. I didn't. There was no room for compromise on either of our parts.

"Yes, Bridget. And don't roll your eyes at me."

"Sorry," I said. "But we've been over for more than a year, and as far as I can tell, your mind is still as sharp as a tack, so you already know that."

Mimi gave me a little shrug. "You could call her and see how she's doing. Take that job in New York that is waiting for you and be closer to her. See what happens."

"No, Mimi, I can't."

She frowned. "Why not? Was the sex not good?"

Both of my brows popped. "You know I am not going to discuss sex with you, and besides you know why."

The white sheets seemed to swallow her up. "Jake, it's time you stopped taking care of everyone around you and take care of yourself. If you want that job in New York, you should go now."

I shook my head. "They are holding it for me. I'll go when I'm ready."

She shook hers. "Sometimes you can be so stubborn."

"Wonder who I take after?"

She gave me a smile, it was faint and weak, but it was still a smile. "All I'm trying to tell you, Jake, is you can stop waiting around. Rory will be married soon, and you won't have to take care of her anymore. And me, well—"

I cut her off. I couldn't hear the words. "Mimi, you will still be the same hard-headed mule you've always been."

Fighting a smile, she drew in a breath. "Go to New York, Jake. Live your life."

"I am living my life."

The look she tossed at me was doubtful. "You work and spend time with me. That isn't living your life."

"I think it is."

She waved a hand "You're a bad liar. You always have been. Go to New York. Look up Bridget. Maybe things will be different when you see her again. Perhaps the chemistry will pop the second time around."

"Nothing will have changed. We want different things. That's the end of our story."

"Oh, sweetheart," she sighed. "I wish I could see you fall in love and get married."

I gave her hand another squeeze. "Mimi, don't ask me for something I can't give you. You know I'm not looking for love."

This time her sigh was resolute. "Someday, Jake, love will find you. And when it does, you won't have a choice but to accept it."

"I will always have a choice."

She shook her head. "Just wait and see," she said almost wistfully. "Just wait and see."

I let her have the last word.

She always made sure she did.

"Jake."

"Yes?"

"You didn't get one of those letters this year, did you?"

Those letters. The ones I'd gotten every year for fourteen years on off-white heavy stock paper tri-folded in the oddest way with the same six typed words,

I'm sorry. It wasn't your fault.

The letters postmarked from New York City. "No, I didn't get one last year or this year so far, anyway."

"Good," she said.

After that she closed her eyes, and when she did, I knew that I had to make my sister's wedding happen fast.

Time was running out.

It was in the sound of her voice.

The distance in her eyes.

And the sad way she looked at me.

Yet the words *fast* and *wedding* weren't synonymous, unless you hopped on a plane to Vegas. Every wedding planner my sister and I had met with was booked out for months. They had also stressed that it was going to take more than a year to plan the type of affair my sister wanted.

A thought came to mind, and I wanted to set it on fire.

The wedding planner from yesterday.

God help me, but she was the only one we'd met with who was more than accommodating to our schedules. It appeared that perhaps her schedule was wide open. She also seemed like the most likely person to help me do what I needed to do, quickly. She was eager, and spunky, and maybe even an over-achiever.

Juliette.

Jules.

Shoot. Me. Now.

chapter
7

Take Your Head Out of Your Ass

JULES

ROSEWOOD!

Rory Kissinger was at the house known as Rosewood. The McMansion on West Paces Ferry Road was located across the street from the Governor's estate. And I used the term *across the street* loosely. It was actually more like across half a mile.

Coincidence?

I highly doubted it.

Stopping at the entrance located in the affluent neighborhood of Tuxedo Park in Buckhead, I pressed the button to gain access, and while I waited, I quickly brought up Google and typed in *Beatrice Crawford*.

As the gates began to open, I scanned through her biography. The article I was reading called her a recluse. A heartless woman who only tolerated perfection. Someone who'd divorced her husband because of his sex addiction and disowned her only daughter because of her issues with alcohol. And then there it was, the estranged daughter named Monica, who had two children.

Were Jake and Rory her grandchildren?

I read on, and there it was.

Jake and Rory were her grandchildren!

I thumped my palm against my forehead as I pulled through the massive iron gates, and then I gazed up at the two-story white brick manse in awe.

Rory was a Crawford.

A Crawford.

One of the founding families and the most influential names in Atlanta.

And I hadn't had a clue.

Uncle Edward was so right. I really did have my head up my *you know what* these days. Clearly, I hadn't done enough research on my lost client. Here I thought the draw of the event would be Rory marrying the Governor's son, but it was definitely the other way around.

And the wedding was going to be so much bigger than I had initially anticipated.

A Crawford getting married would be front page, Page Six news, across the country news.

Putting my little Miata in park, I slowly climbed out and breathed in the warmth. The dense air smelled as fragrant as a bouquet of flowers, and I knew there had to be a rather large garden around back.

As soon as I took my first step, one of my heels caught in the crevices between the cobblestones of the walkway. I made a mental note to slow my ordinarily quick pace in these shoes. The nude pumps were all I had to go with my navy silk dress. I figured after the previous day's debacle, polished and professional was the way to go.

I'd even pulled my shoulder-length dirty blonde locks back into a low chignon. Then again, I hadn't much time to do much else.

The residence sat in the middle of the property, almost on top of a hill. The beautifully landscaped grounds were shaded with maple and spruce trees and birdbaths, and angel's wings could be seen in the pockets of lush green grass.

Walking painstakingly slow, I used the extra time to glance around. There were fountains on either side of the house, boxwood hedges that seemed to wind through pathways for miles, and I thought I could see the tops of some colossal stone statues through the dozens of Magnolia trees.

The grounds were absolutely breathtaking.

Ringing the bell, I stared at the large glossy red doors and waited patiently. I had no idea why I was there, but I hoped it was for a second chance. I wished I could have a do-over, but my head wasn't in the clouds. That only happened in the movies.

When I heard the purr of an engine, I glanced over my shoulder. I was surprised to see a vintage black Jaguar pulling in with the top down. It was already so hot. Still, the car was totally awesome. The sun was blinding me, and I couldn't see who was behind the wheel. Before I could catch a glimpse of who was driving it, the front door opened wide.

"You made it." Rory threw her arms around me and then practically pulled me inside.

Tripping over a tangle of leashes and landing in a mound of suitcases in the grand foyer, I really wished I'd gone for the flats. You'd think I would have known better by now not to wear heels. I was just too clumsy in them. No matter how hard I tried, I couldn't walk very well in them.

"I am so sorry. Are you okay?" Rory asked, with that slight sliver of a southern drawl she had.

I shook it off and smiled. "I'm fine."

"Oh, phew. I'd hate to have to call my brother."

Light from crystal chandeliers glinted off the gilt-framed oil paintings that hung on the walls, and I marveled at how beautiful they were. "Should we move them out of the way?"

She shook her head. "Remy will be here soon, and he'll be loading them in the SUV. He would have been here by now to meet with you, but his father's security detail hung him up. Something about our new apartment needing to be cleared."

Security detail.

Go figure.

It was such a different kind of life.

As was this place. I couldn't help but look all around me. "Oh, that's right. I overheard you yesterday when you told your brother you were headed back to college today. Isn't it early for school to start?"

With a wave of her hand, she led me past the grand staircase. "Yes, you're right. Classes don't start for two more weeks, but since it's my senior year and I'm the sorority president, I have way too much to do, and thought it would be best to get started early."

Taking small steps, I tried my best not to slide across the highly polished black and white tiled floor. "Wow, president. I bet that keeps you pretty busy."

She stopped at a set of large wooden doors and turned the ornate brass handles. "It does, and that's why I wanted to talk to you before I left."

My eyes were flickering all around. "You peaked my interest, for sure, but first, I have to ask, do you live here?"

With a push of both doors, she answered me. "Yes. It's my grandmother's house."

"I remember reading online that this house has twelve bedrooms and each is painted a different shade of blue?"

She laughed. "Yes, it's true, but that's probably about the only thing you read that is. My grandmother wasn't trying to ward off evil spirits, nor does she sleep in a different bed every night. Her mother loved the color blue and decorated each one. Mimi just never changed them. There was no need to, she said."

I nodded. "I can understand that."

She shrugged. "Well, you haven't seen them yet. They are a bit extravagant and over the top, but really beautiful at the same time."

Extravagant.

Interesting.

The room we walked into had at least a twelve-foot ornately carved wooden table in the middle of it. It had to be the formal dining room, and it too was extravagant with its silk wallpaper, sterling silver, and chinaware.

Rory spoke to an older man in his sixties who was dressed in traditional butler attire. He wore black tails, a white shirt, cufflinks, and gloves, and he was setting a bowl of fruit on the sideboard next to several large covered silver platters. "Hi, Roger. My guest has arrived."

"Miss Rory," he greeted and then bowed. His voice was deep, proper, but still very Southern. "Breakfast is ready. Would you care for tea this morning?"

"Yes, please."

"And you, madam?" he asked me.

Madam.

I wanted to giggle. "Coffee for me, please," I managed without an embarrassing sound.

"And we'll both have orange juice," Rory told him.

"Of course." He bowed once again and then disappeared through a door in the back of the room.

Rory went over to the buffet and picked up two plates.

On her heels, I took one from her, and because I was impatient, I couldn't wait any longer. "So," I said. "What did you want to talk to me about?"

I crossed my fingers.

She lifted the lid to the first serving dish to uncover pancakes. "Well, I thought that was obvious, I want to hire you."

My heart started to pound. "What about your brother?"

Lifting a pancake with the giant fork, she looked it over. They appeared to be buckwheat, and she scrunched her nose as she set it back down. "That's what I wanted to talk to you about. After meeting with you yesterday, I think you get my style more than anyone else. Actually, I think you get me."

Not picky myself, I took a pancake. "That's really sweet of you. I appreciate it."

She opened the next serving dish and grinned at the waffles. "It's true. And like I told you yesterday, Remy and I have been together since we were fourteen. He's my soulmate."

Soulmates?

Did they really exist?

"How do you know?" I asked, unfiltered and inappropriate. I wanted to slap my hand over my mouth as soon as the words left it. "Never mind, I shouldn't have asked that. I'm sure it's not only personal but complicated."

Then again when was love anything but?

"No, no, it's fine," she said with a wave of her free hand. "I don't mind answering. It's simple really. We're best friends, we challenge each other, and we can't stand to be apart. What else matters?"

I stared down at my plate in thought. She had a point. What else did matter?

"I know I've been all over the place with what I want. But that's because I want our wedding to be perfect, which is why I want you to help me convince my brother to hire you."

Jerking my head toward her, I almost dropped my plate. "Rory, I smashed cake in his face yesterday. I don't think I can come back from that. He probably hates me."

"Hate is a strong word."

"Dislike," I restated. "Either way, I really doubt there's anything I can do to sway him my way."

I had to be honest.

Scooping scrambled eggs onto the gold-rimmed china, she said matter of factly, "Oh, he'll get over it. In fact, if I know my brother, he probably already has."

"I don't know about that," I responded, and used the tongs to pick up a piece of toast. "He looked pretty angry the way his brow creased and his lips pouted."

She popped a croissant onto her dish with her fingers. "Oh, you mean that brooding look he has going on," she laughed. "It's nothing. He's been wearing it a lot lately. He has a lot on his mind, that's all. Besides, in the grand scheme of things, what you did wasn't that bad. And, if he takes the time to really think about it, it was almost commendable."

When I lifted the lid of the next silver dish, the smell of bacon wafted under my nose. It smelled so good, but my stomach was still upset, and I knew better than to overeat. "I'm not sure he'll ever see it that way," I laughed and closed the lid.

"Well," Rory said. "As a matter of fact, that is why I asked you to come over. Now hurry up and finish getting your food so we can get to work. We don't have much time."

All I could do was what she'd told me to do—hurry.

Grabbing an apple, she practically pranced over to the long table. With her shiny long brown locks pulled back in a hairband, and her bright pink pants with white halter-top, she looked like an actual modern southern bell.

Quickly placing some peach slices on my plate, I traipsed over and sat next to her. Once I put my napkin on my lap, I said, "Okay, I'm ready."

Just when she was about to speak, a text went off on her phone. "Give me one sec, that's Remy."

Roger had already served the coffee, tea, and juice. As I poured cream into my cup, I glanced down at the notebook Rory had laid on the table, and my heart started to pound.

On the page it had fallen open to, Rory had written different ways to invite the guests to her event. It wasn't the phrasing I was staring at though, but the names she had scribed. They read, "Rory Beatrice & Kyle Remington."

I couldn't believe it.

Monty must have done his research and known that Kyle went by the name Remington, or maybe he even knew her fiancé preferred to be called Remy.

Google hadn't failed me.

I had failed me.

Setting the creamer down, I felt like the pit in my stomach had morphed into a tennis ball.

All of a sudden it became crystal clear why I wasn't able to sign clients and make a go out of running my own business. I was focusing on all the wrong things. Whereas, my uncle had always focused on the couple first and the business second, I had been spending most of my time on the dynamics of running the business. It was so time-consuming. The thing was I wasn't sure I could do both and do them well, and that worried me.

I wasn't programmed that way.

"Okay," Rory said, setting her phone back down. "He'll be here in twenty minutes to pick me up. That doesn't give us much time to strategize about my brother."

With my hand already shaking on my glass, I found myself once again jerking my head in her direction. "What exactly do you mean by *strategize* about your brother?"

She took a bite of her croissant and chewed it. "Well, the term strategize might be a stretch. All we need to do is come up with a way for you to win my brother over. And the best place to start is to appeal to his bleeding heart."

I practically choked on my glass of juice. "His bleeding heart?"

"Yes, he's a bleeding heart."

I chuckled. "He seemed anything but."

Again, I had to be honest.

"No, really, he is. I promise you," she reassured me, dabbing her mouth with her napkin. "It's the whole doctor thing. He's a lot like our father was in that way. I wish I could be more patient and kind like him, but I've always been business minded. There's no changing that. Anyway, here's what I'm thinking."

As we ate breakfast, she disclosed her plan to get her brother on board. It not only included me apologizing, but appealing to his humanity. According to her, the doctor in him couldn't turn away from a person in need.

I didn't quite understand if I was supposed to feign being ill or if she thought I was so off-the-wall crazy that all I had to do was talk to him, and he'd feel sorry for me when he took the time to listen.

"Finish your coffee," she said. "I'll give you a tour of the bedrooms in the west wing, and then we'll finish talking while I wait for Remy."

Setting my cup down, I lifted my napkin and placed it beside my plate. "Okay, I'm ready."

Although I wasn't certain, I was.

The conversation had turned what I had eaten into sludge. Her brother didn't like me, and she wanted me to turn that around.

Like I could do that.

The thing was, she was convinced I could.

And I wanted to believe I could too, but really . . . talk about a long shot.

chapter
8

Picture Paints a Thousand Words

JULES

THE OLD STAIRCASE creaked under my feet as I climbed it.

At the landing, Rory and I had the option of going right or left. "This way," she declared and veered to the right.

I followed without question. I was anxious for a look. Curious, was probably a better word.

"My bedroom and my grandmother's are to the left, but they are not blue, and not nearly as fun to look at," she laughed. "Mine is pink, and Mimi's is gold."

I laughed along with her. "I guess someone had to change it up."

Rosewood's southern elegance was straight out of *Gone with the Wind*. Polished dark wooden stairs and brocade gold draperies, walls painted white, but not looking sterile in the least and regal carpets that belonged in a palace.

"Miss Rory," Roger called, from the bottom of the stairs.

We both turned to see him holding up a phone. "Yes, Roger?" she asked.

"Mr. Remy is on the phone, and he needs to speak with you. He says it's urgent."

With a shake of her head, she said, "I just hung up with him." She must have left her cell on the table in the dining room.

She started to grin. "He must miss me," she said and then looked in my direction. "Jules, do you mind having a look at the bedrooms without me? I'll meet you in the room next to the dining room in five minutes."

"That's fine," I answered. I figured I might not get to see anything like this again, and I was curious.

Rory pranced down the stairs and took the phone. "Remy, baby, what is it?"

The hallway at the top of the second flight of stairs was relatively long, and I started down it. The doors were opened, and each bedroom was decorated more beautifully than the next. And yes, each was a different shade of blue.

Just how many shades of blue actually existed?

At the end of the hall was another flight of stairs. That article I had read online about Rosewood so many years ago had spoken of a secret room. I wondered if what they had written was true. Since this wing appeared entirely unoccupied, I decided to find out and hoped that cliché about curiosity killing the cat wasn't true.

The stairs were narrow and the lighting dim. I jumped a few times when the boards beneath my feet creaked, but once I got to the landing, I breathed a sigh of relief. There was only a short hallway with two doors. No ghosts or goblins or trap doors. Both of the standard-looking doors were slightly ajar, but not entirely opened.

I should have taken that as a sign that privacy was required.

I didn't.

In my quest to see if these rooms were also blue, my fingertips nudged the door open just enough to see the wall, and yes, it too was blue, but not the same as the others.

Then again, it was the bathroom, not the bedroom, and the sound of water running should have sent me running.

It didn't because I could see the reflection of who was under the spray in the mirror.

Perfectly.

I gasped and jumped to the side. In my direct line of sight was a huge glass wall and *he* was just beyond it.

My pulse was beating so hard I could feel it pounding at all my pulse points. I needed to leave. Yet, I couldn't move. Or maybe it was more like I didn't want to.

Steam hovered in the air, but there was not nearly enough of it to obscure anything. He was naked. His eyes were closed. And his head bent as the water sluiced over him. With one hand on the wall, the other was sliding slowly down his belly, and it landed between his thighs.

Oh, God.

Now I really couldn't move. I was frozen in place. His hand was on his cock. I swallowed the noise my throat tried to make, but I was sure I didn't do a good job of it. Thank you, Jesus. He didn't seem to notice. No, he definitely didn't notice because oh, my God, he was stroking himself. Slowly. Deliciously. Up, then down, and a twist of his palm around the head of his cock.

I shouldn't have been watching, and yet I couldn't look away. This was private. For him only. Not for me. And definitely not for my viewing pleasure.

When he moved his wrist faster, I had to stifle my sudden harsh breath with my hand. My eyes were glued to his body, and although I should leave, I didn't.

Jake, doing this to himself, was the most erotic thing I'd ever seen. The only thing that prevented me from reaching between my own legs to get myself off was my perverted fascination with wanting to watch him come. Oh, and of course the terror of getting caught.

Like the cake incident wasn't unfortunate enough.

His mouth opened, water filling it and overflowing when he tipped his face into the spray.

I watched him.

Soon he was fucking into his fist with a deliberation that made me weak at the knees, and still I watched. I watched the way his muscles corded in his arms, the way his cock moved within the confines of his fist, the way his face contorted into pure pleasure.

I watched.

Looking at Jake about to come made him seem like the sexiest man I had ever seen.

His cock disappeared inside his curled fingers, and this stroke seemed somehow more determined. Up, down, a twist around his crown, and then another twist. This time his hand dipped down, and then lower still.

I pressed my thighs together to ward off the ache of arousal that was flooding me. I couldn't hear him, but I wished I could. I knew what he was feeling, though, because I could see his mouth open and his face twist with satisfaction. He was close. I could tell. And then soon enough, his taut belly strained, the muscles in his legs bunched, and then it happened—his desire jetted out.

Oh, God.

I watched.

Never in my life had I wanted to make myself come like I did at that moment. Still, it was all kinds of wrong. I shouldn't have been watching him. I knew this, of course. Chiding myself, I licked salt from my upper lip and slowly, cautiously took a step back.

Guilt washed over me.

This was so wrong of me.

When had I turned so bad?

"Miss Easton, is everything okay?"

That voice. I knew that voice. It was Roger.

Oh, God!

No. No. No.

Before I even dared shift my gaze, I took a step and then another, and another still away from the door. My heart was beating like a drum. And although my sight was a little blurry from looking through the steam of the bathroom, I forced myself not to appear petrified as my head snapped in the direction of where Roger was standing.

He had no idea Jake was in there.

Right?

No idea what I was doing.

Right?

I couldn't look guilty.

Couldn't.

On trembling legs, I made myself walk toward him. "Oh, Roger, I got lost, I was looking for another way down."

The look he gave me was sympathetic and not at all suspicious. "Madam, this way. Follow me."

My escape was slow and unsteady.

Oh, my God.

The image of Jake was still in my head, and my body wouldn't stop trembling. However, way too soon I was standing at the bottom of the staircase in the grand foyer, and I had to pull myself together.

But what I had seen changed everything.

And I knew I'd do whatever I had to in order to make things right between us.

chapter 9

Sitting on the Fence

JULES

THE HOUSE WAS an authentic mansion.

And the room I was about to enter with flushed cheeks must have once been a parlor. A place where the young women received gentleman callers and the two of them sat properly while they sipped iced-tea and spoke of polite, but boring things.

Nothing taboo was allowed.

Definitely not masturbation.

And they most definitely were not permitted to discuss the idea of watching someone masturbate.

I looked around and wondered how many women had broken that rule. Watched the man of the house like I had.

There were silk draperies and oriental carpets and more oil paintings, if only they could talk.

Forget that.

What if they told on me?

The room was soft and light. Painted and covered in ivory, cream, taupe, and yellow with blue accents. It was as bright as the sunny day outside. Antique tables and tufted velvet sofas with wingback chairs were spread across the space in various seating arrangements, but the focal point was most definitely the huge marble fireplace.

And there were also dogs in the room.

Lots of dogs.

Seven, if I counted correctly.

"So," Rory said, "What did you think?"

I think your brother is super hot and I want to jump his bones. "It's amazing," I answered. "The rooms are so big . . . I mean so grand."

Whoops.

"Aren't they," she smiled. "My grandmother used to fill them with guests every weekend. She loves this house, almost as much as her dogs, and I guess I do as well. It just has so much charm." Rory was crouching down petting one of the dogs.

"Yes, it does." I had to get off the room topic, or the image of Jake in the blue bathroom was never going to leave my mind. "Was everything okay with Remy?" I asked.

"Oh well, it wasn't quite an emergency. He just couldn't decide what to pack for Fall Ball. I told him to bring his tuxedo. We are going all out this year. I'm going to wear a gown and the highest heels I can find."

"Sounds fun."

"It will be. So, anyway," she said, "about my brother. Don't you agree?"

"About which part?" My mind was still on his cock, and she most definitely didn't mean *that* part of him.

"That you need to win him over."

No, would have been my answer before the bathroom incident, but now, I honestly didn't know. I wanted to win him over all right— right into my bed. That was so wrong, so I said nothing.

As Rory made her way around the room saying goodbye and

petting each and every dog, I realized I had to be honest. This was about my career, not my libido.

I spoke up. "I think the best way to convince your brother I'm right for the job is to be straightforward and tell him my ideas. Let the plan sell itself."

She scoffed as if she knew something I didn't, and then she pointed to the enormous sable-colored German Shepard lying on the sofa. "This is Mr. Darcy," Rory said, kissing the dog's head.

He wore a wide black leather collar with spikes on it around his neck. I stepped over to where Rory had taken a seat on the sofa. "Well hello there, Mr. Darcy."

I loved dogs.

As soon as I got close, he barked really loud.

Too bad they didn't love me.

"Mr. Darcy, be nice," Rory admonished, shaking her finger at him. "Jules is here to help us." As soon as she gave him a small pet, he calmed right down.

"How did you do that?" I asked.

"He's really a big softie. All bark and no bite. Don't let his size intimidate you."

Just as I bent to attempt to pet him once again, I heard the familiar sound of a husky throat clearing.

Rory and I both jerked our heads up to find Jake leaning against the doorjamb, holding a glass of orange juice and popping a grape into his mouth. The mouth I had seen open in ecstasy just moments ago.

I froze like a kid who'd just gotten caught with her hand in the cookie jar. I wasn't prepared with the best way to address him yet, especially after what I'd just witnessed.

If I took Rory's advice, all I had to do was pretend to faint, and he'd be sympathetic to my condition.

It was simple case of *doctor, doctor.*

Then again, I wasn't much of an actress, and besides, what if I really hurt myself as I fell to the ground? The whole wolf in sheep's clothing thing terrified me.

"You're just like your brother, aren't you, Mr. Darcy?" Rory cooed.

I wondered which part of what she'd said moments ago she was referring to. The softie, the bark, or the size. The last one had me blushing. He was big. No, he was huge. And I knew that firsthand.

My heart started fluttering as I thought back.

Shame on me.

Knowing I couldn't avoid the well-endowed man since he was right in front of me, I lifted my gaze. Jake's eyes might have been even more bloodshot than they had been yesterday, but that didn't detract from his incredibly good looks. His hair was wet, of course, and he was in jeans and a T-shirt. I hated to even think the way I was, but God, he really was so sexy both in and out of clothes.

"Hey, you finally made it," Rory said. "I was beginning to think you were going to stand me up."

Oh my God, she'd engineered this meeting and hadn't told me.

So much for the sweet girl routine.

Jake shoved his hands in his pockets and strode into the room. "You didn't tell me you'd invited Juliette."

Juliette.

I wanted to correct him, tell him my name was Jules not Juliette, but his glare was much too fierce for me to say anything but, "Hi." I gave him a slight wave and wished the seeping flush to stop creeping up my neck.

He nodded or cringed, I couldn't be certain. That was better than giving me the finger, I supposed. "I stopped to see Mimi first," he told his sister.

Who was Mimi?

Another dog?

Rory stiffened, and her voice cracked when she spoke. "Is she any better? Last night when I went to see her, her stomach was bothering her, and she couldn't eat."

Okay, Mimi wasn't a dog.

Stopping at the first dog he came to, Jake crouched down to pet him. "Nothing's changed, but she wants to come home."

Now I knew who Mimi was. She was Beatrice Crawford, their grandmother, and she was sick.

Rory rested her head on Mr. Darcy's big body and hugged him tightly. "Will she be able to?"

Jake glanced over at her. "I'm doing my best to make it happen."

Rory bolted up. "Should I stay home so she isn't here alone?"

Almost adamantly, Jake shook his head. "No, I'm moving back into my old room. You know she wants you to finish school."

The room at the top of the stairs.

Rory nodded and went back to petting the dog.

"Rory," he said.

She looked up.

"I think you should move the wedding date up."

"Why?"

The look on his face was heartbreaking. "She's stopping her treatments."

"I don't understand. Why would she do that?"

"It's making her sick, Rory, and it's not working."

"You can't let her do this."

"It's not my choice." His voice was barely audible.

"But her doctors said she had more time," Rory whispered, wiping a tear away.

A few of the other dogs had gathered around Jake and he was showing each of them some attention when he glanced up at her with such sadness in his eyes I felt like I might weep. "I don't think she does."

"How long then?"

He stood and strode toward us. "I don't know, but she wants to see you get married and I think we should give her that."

"Of course we will," Rory cried. "When should I move the date to?"

"As soon as possible. Labor Day weekend if you can."

Labor Day weekend was less than five weeks away!

"Then I should just stay home."

Jake had shoved his hands into his pockets. "Rory, she won't come home if you do that. You know how important it is to her that you finish school and start working at Crawford Enterprises."

Wondering if I should excuse myself, I went to stand up, except Rory put her hand on my knee to stop me. Staying where I was, I instead leaned over to pet the little sand-colored Yorkie that had somehow ended up at my feet. Her collar was hot pink and almost bigger than her. The jewel-encrusted nametag read, "Daisy." Daisy was adorable. She licked my hand, and I let her.

Rory slid to the Oriental rug and kissed her, too. "It's okay Daisy, Mimi will be home soon."

Apparently, her grandmother had a great love for dogs, and it was also evident it was shared by her grandchildren.

More tears slid down her cheeks, and I felt a pain in my heart for her. A few moments later, she looked up at her brother. "If I go back to school, I won't be able to plan the wedding. Will you work with Jules to plan the wedding?"

Wait!

What?

The pained look on his face was to be expected, but his single word response was anything but. In fact, it truly surprised me. "Yes."

Rory reached up and grabbed my hand. "Jules, will you do it? Will you work with Jake to create my dream wedding in time for my grandmother to be a part of it?"

Uncomfortable with the fact those two sets of blue eyes were on me—one sweet and kind, the other hard and angry—I forced a smile to spread across my lips and then took a moment to ponder my answer.

It wasn't as simple as it should have been. There were too many factors. I was supposed to work with Rory, not her brother. And this was supposed to be a hard sell. It wasn't supposed to be a slam-dunk. Besides, what if I couldn't do it?

Not only did I have to plan the wedding of the decade, but I also had less than five weeks to do it in.

My heart was pounding stupidly hard in my chest as I opened my mouth and said, "Yes."

"Yah! I'm so excited," Rory blurted out. "I can't wait to see what you come up with. Oh, and I almost forgot why I brought you in here. Look," she pointed to a large photograph sitting on the mantel.

There were many others scattered along the space, but that one stood out. "Who is it?" I asked.

"My great-grandmother in her wedding gown. And I thought I might wear it."

Surprised by this, I stood on shaky legs. I wasn't looking at the ground as I walked, and I stepped right on one of the dog toys. I caught myself this time before tripping though, and other than my hands flying in the air, I hadn't made that much of a scene.

Thank goodness it wasn't one of the dogs that I stepped on.

Jake chuckled, low and deep in his throat, and although it shouldn't have turned me on, it did.

Rory was kissing the dog with a big wide pink collar and hadn't noticed.

With my head held high, I walked past Jake. To avoid one of the dogs, I had to sidestep though. When I did, I brushed the skin of Jake's muscular arm, and those pesky butterflies took full flight in my belly.

I ignored them as best I could.

Over at the mantel, I picked up the photo and tried to calm my racing heart.

"I believe it was actually her mother's." Jake was standing next to me, and he smelled so good.

"It's beautiful," I marveled. And it was. In the photo, the elegant woman was sitting on the back of a vintage Rolls Royce, and her dress was long and flowing and made from pure silk and the most beautiful tulle. It was something right out of Great Gatsby.

"Do you think you can secure that place we talked about yesterday?" Rory asked.

Lost in thought, I blinked and looked over at her. "Where was this photo taken?" I asked.

"I'm not sure." She glanced at Jake. "Do you know?"

He took the picture from me with the hand he'd used to jerk off and stared at it. "I think it was taken here."

"Didn't that place you talked about have an outdoor ballroom?" Rory asked.

I looked out the French doors at the beautiful view and wondered if the photo was taken here almost one hundred years ago. "Yes, it does."

She had picked up one the dogs and was cradling her like a baby. "What was it called again?"

"Lanier Islands in Buford. And it has the most stunning lake views."

"It sounds perfect," Rory said dreamily, "Doesn't it, Myrtle?" she asked the dog she was holding before setting her down.

"I can certainly call and inquire about it, but unless there has been a cancellation, it is highly unlikely they'll have an opening."

The front door opened and a voice boomed, "Rory, are you ready?"

"Remy, I'll be right there," she called, and kissed her brother and hugged me. "I trust the two of you to make my day magical. I have to go." And then she was off, leaving Jake and I staring at the door she trotted out of.

He handed back the photo, and when he did, something flickered in his gaze. I held my breath as we stared into each other's eyes.

I couldn't stop my eyes from dropping to that mouth that he just loved to pout. Afraid he was going to catch sight of my desire, I averted my gaze, only to find he was looking at my lips.

They parted under his stare.

Quickly, his gaze returned to mine, and then he reached in his back pocket to pull out his wallet.

I didn't want to look inside. What if he had a condom in there, and I saw it? Yet my curiosity got the best of me, and I snuck a peek. Nothing. I saw no condom outline. Phew. That would have been embarrassing.

All business-like, he handed me a card. "Call me when you have something to discuss, and we can meet then."

I held a hand up. "Wait. It doesn't work that way. We need to discuss the budget, so I can secure a venue and pick a date."

He set his card on the mantel. "There isn't a budget. Whatever it costs is what it costs, and the rest is up to you."

"Everyone has a budget," I protested.

"There is no budget," he insisted through gritted teeth. "Make this wedding everything my sister wants and more." He pointed to the card. "And like I said, call me when you have something to discuss."

I picked up the card and stared at it. Like Jaxson's it was simple. But instead of the picture of a camera, it bore the caduceus with its two snakes and wings used to symbolize medicine, and read:

Dr. Jake Kissinger
Grady Memorial Hospital Emergency Medicine Department

404–616–1000 (main)
404–121–4321 (cell)

When I looked up, he was gone. I heard his voice in the foyer and all of a sudden the fact that I had to work closely with him became very real.

Him.

The jackass.

Him.

The guy with the big dick.

Him.

The hot doctor with the kissable lips.

Dr. Kiss.

I meant Dr. Kissinger, of course.

chapter
10

At the Drop of a Hat

JULES

THERE WAS A genuine possibility my ear was going to fall off.

And that was no joke.

For the past three days, Finn and I had done nothing but make phone call after phone call. The only place in the entire state of Georgia we were booking a wedding of this size on such short notice was the Moose Club, and that too was no joke.

Yet still, the pompous Dr. Jake Kissinger couldn't even manage to meet me on time to discuss the alternative.

I glanced at my watch. He was late. Albeit only three minutes late, but nonetheless, he was late. Maybe he wasn't coming. I wouldn't doubt it. He hadn't exactly been welcoming when I tried to correspond with him. In fact, he had been downright rude.

Looking down at my phone, I pulled up my text correspondence with him, and reread it to make sure I hadn't misunderstood our date. Well, not our date, but our scheduled appointment.

Me: Having trouble securing a location for the date you gave me. Any chance I can move it a little later into the month of September?

Him: No. Rory and Remy have a long weekend, and I've already taken the time off. Make it work.

Me: Is there any chance you can meet me tomorrow to discuss?

Him: Do you have a plan to present?

Me: Not exactly.

Him: Then no, I can't.

Me: I do have something to talk about though. Fifteen minutes is all I need. Please.

Him: Fine. Make it later in the afternoon. Where do you want to meet? The bakery?

Me: No. How about Octane at three?

Him: Fine.

Fine. Fine. Fine.

I really despised that word.

Okay, so there were no alternative dates. Labor Day weekend it was. Rory and Remy would have time off from school to get married. And, there was more to it, I knew, and I got it. However, like I said, there were no suitable locations available.

The only thing I could think to do was see if he could exert his influence to sway the manager of the Cherokee Town & Country Club to allow us to use the grounds. And that was why I was meeting with him, and the only reason. Because really I would have rather been pulling my eyelashes out one by one than sitting here.

All the ballrooms at the country club were booked, and the manager wouldn't even entertain the idea of using the grounds. Yet, it was an option. Of course doing so meant if it rained we were screwed. Still, there was no other alternative other than the Moose Club.

It was all I had.

And I needed the sexy jackass's help to get it done.

God help me.

Closing the text, I went back to pretending I was making progress by searching for the perfect invitation. While I was at it, I ordered myself to stop watching the door of the coffee shop. And then while I was at that, I pretended I was doing a great job of not watching it.

Sadly, pretending was all I could do.

I totally was.

Forcing myself, I flicked my gaze away. The colorful booths and stools were crowded with college students. The lights were too bright and the voices too loud. It was way too over-stimulating in here to truly concentrate.

In my college days, I'd hung out at this coffee shop all the time. It was strange how I'd forgotten how noisy the place could be. Forgotten how busy the place was. And not realized what a wrong choice it was for a meeting. I should have selected somewhere quieter. But I knew the brooding doctor would probably have to be to work by five, so I'd chosen Octane in Atlantic Station because it was halfway between Buckhead and Grady, and should have been convenient for him.

I was just about to text him and ask if he'd like to reschedule when I got a text from Finn.

Finn: Sunshine Farms had a cancellation.

Me: Are you serious?

Finn: Jules, get real. Why would I tell you that if I wasn't?

Me: Sorry. Can you send me pictures of the venue? I'm not familiar with it. Where is it anyway?

Finn: I'm headed out. Pull it up on Google. It's about an hour drive east. And they also told me they have a wedding tonight, so if you'd like a tour, you should be there before five.

Me: Thanks.

It was Friday, and he had been working twelve-hour days just like me, so I wasn't about to fault him for wanting to leave at three.

Searching for the venue on my phone, I couldn't believe my luck. Now I just hoped it was suited for a wedding of this stature.

With my anxiety level at an all-time high, I thumbed through the pictures. It looked decent. Not great. The hay barrels everywhere were an immediate turnoff, but I could have them removed and dress the shabby barn up. I'd have to go see it in person first before making a decision.

"Hey, sorry I'm late. It took a while to find a place to park."

I looked up as Jake slid into the seat across from me. He was in his standard jeans and Adidas, but this time he was wearing an Atlanta Hawks golf shirt instead of a T-shirt. It appeared his hair was once again wet, but it was hidden under his Atlanta Hawks baseball hat, so I couldn't be sure. I wanted to ask him if he lived in the shower, but obviously, I didn't. "Hi. It's fine."

Pulling off his cap, he ran a hand through his wet hair as he glanced around the shop. "I haven't been in here before. Cool place."

I kept an easy smile on my face, my breezy manner intact even though my excitement about the potential venue had me wanting to jump up and down. "I used to come here all the time, and I figured it was close enough to the hospital that you wouldn't be late for work."

His eyes flicked over me from my head to my chest. I had dressed to impress, and I thought I was doing just that. I had styled my hair straight and sleek in its bob-like shape. I wore a black and white printed silk tank top and black wide-leg pants with wedges. I was put together and professional, but not stuffy. His gaze came back to my face, and he heaved a heavy sigh of irritation. "I'm not working tonight. So tell me, what am I doing here?"

God, he really was an ass. "How about a coffee first?"

He looked around for the waitress, and then muttered, "Oh, shit."

"Jake, this is a surprise. I've never seen you here." The voice was sickeningly sweet.

The woman who came into view was not the waitress, but rather a very beautiful woman wearing Grady Memorial Hospital's signature black scrubs.

Jake went to his feet. "Hey Carly, yeah, this is my first time."

The nurse looked at me. "Hi," she said, and I could tell right away she was accessing me.

"Carly, this is Jules Easton, she's helping me plan my sister's wedding."

"Oh," she said and in her tinkly laughter, "that's why you're here. It makes sense now."

As if he couldn't just be meeting me for coffee?

She batted her lashes and smiled at him, and it was a smile that left no question of her intentions. "Well, I should be getting to work. I'm sure I'll see you soon," she directed to Jake.

Jake looked very uncomfortable, and I could tell they either had something going on or were about to embark on that something. "Yeah, see you around."

I wasn't a jealous person, but a surge of venom coursed through my veins. "Bye Carly, it was nice to meet you."

She gave me a little wave, and I looked over at Jake, who was frowning. "Girlfriend?" I asked.

"No," he said quickly. "I don't have a girlfriend."

Oh, that was good to know. "I was only asking for wedding planning purposes."

Liar.

He stared at me. Did he see right through me? I was fairly confident he did. "So," he said, tapping his fingers on the table, "tell me what I'm doing here."

I squirmed a little under the intensity of his stare. "Well, I asked you here because . . ." I looked down at the table. "Because . . ." I looked back up to find him now glaring at me with a raised brow.

What the ever-loving hell?

Why was I so nervous and tongue-twisted around him?

I cleared my throat. "Because I found a venue for the wedding," I finally said cheerily, although I felt a flush coat my cheeks at the mistruth.

It wasn't really why I asked him here, but still, it was true.

"Then I suggest you do whatever it is you do," he shot back.

Not a *that's great*, or *fantastic*, or even a high-five.

I pushed down my irritation, reminding myself that in this most unusual case of the unavailable client, he was the closest thing I had to one. And, since I had recently figured out my focus hadn't been entirely on the client as it should be, I had to play nice.

Although this client was all kinds of irritating, perhaps he didn't understand and needed to be schooled. "That's just it, Jake, I don't act alone. I don't make major decisions on my own. I need input from you about *your* sister's wedding."

His glare turned almost hostile.

I swallowed. Okay, perhaps I took it a bit too far, and he never did tell me to call him by his first name. I'd start with that. "Dr. Kissinger, I mean."

"Jake is fine," he said through gritted teeth.

"Okay, Jake," I said firmly, "what I do is work with the clients to make their dream day come true, and in this case, whether you like it or not, you are my client by proxy."

His response to that was to sigh and relax against the booth. He crossed his arms over his chest and hit me with, "So, let me get this straight. You want to make my dreams come true?"

"Well, yes and no."

That brought the most condescending smirk I'd ever seen to his hot lips. "You might change your mind after I tell you what they are." His tone was sly, hot, and flirtatious.

Dirty, dirty, doctor.

I wasn't insulted by his comment or agitated like I probably should have been, but rather my insides felt all warm and fuzzy.

Wait!

I had to get real here.

I had a job to do.

There was no time for crushes. Just as there was no time for resentment. He was acting difficult on purpose. That was clear.

"Look, Jake." I held up my hands in surrender. "What I did was unprofessional and—"

"And what?" he asked coyly.

"And I apologize," I hurried to finish.

"Hi."

We both jerked our heads toward the end of the booth. Enough of the interruptions already. This time at least it was the waitress and not another want-to-be-girlfriend.

Jake mustered up a smile for the girl who had finally come to take his order. Damn, I should have asked him what his dreams were while we were in the moment. Then again, watching the way he lit up for this woman, maybe I didn't want to know.

"I'm Sara. Sorry about the wait. It's crazy in here today."

"It's fine," Jake said.

Sara smiled at him. "What can I get you?"

He peered up at the menu board. "I'll have an extra tall latte macchiato with an extra shot. No, make that two extra shots."

Sara smiled wider. "That's a lot of extras. You must really want to stay awake."

The debonair charm he exuded in her presence agitated me because it was the same charm he'd shown me—before I'd smashed cake in his face. And the same charm he'd shown Carly, I reminded myself. "Just waking up, actually. I worked all night."

"Oh, then I'll be sure to make it extra strong," she said with a wink.

Jake smiled in return, and I swear she started to blush right there. Seconds later she looked at me. "Another Vanilla Latte for you?"

"Actually, no," I smiled, but mine was more than fake, "I'll have what he's having."

She scribbled the number two down. "Were you up late working, too?" she asked.

"No, but I'm going to be up late tonight."

"Ah," she remarked, like Jake and I were going to be going at it like bunnies all night long. The thought had me blushing.

"I have to . . . never mind." I decided it was best to discuss the farm with Jake before just blurting the location out to the waitress.

She winked at me. "Gotcha. Two high-octanes coming up," she said, and then walked away.

"Okay." I propped my chin on my fist. "Get whatever it is you need to off your chest."

He quirked an eyebrow at me. "You sure you can handle that?"

I ignored his sarcasm and answered directly. "Yes. I'm more than sure."

The surrounding air thickened with my challenge. "Fine. Here it goes. I only agreed to work with you because I needed someone who was available now. Every other wedding planner is booked out for months."

I threw my shoulders back in deference to his comment. "I don't really care why you agreed to hire me, or what you think of me for that matter. The only thing that matters is that your sister has entrusted me to engineer her perfect day, and contrary to what you might think, I *am* more than capable of doing that."

His already narrowed eyes shone with a spark of challenge as he said with threatening calmness, "That has yet to be seen."

I closed my eyes.

Bleeding heart my ass.

He wasn't patient, nor was he kind. What he was, however, was the prince of darkness. An arrogant ass I wanted nothing to do with. And what made matters worse was somehow he had figured out what my weaknesses were, and he was purposely exploiting them.

I could do this job.

I could do this job.

I could do this job.

So what if his opinion of me wasn't positive. I didn't care. I knew my capabilities, and I knew I could do this job.

I could do this job.

I could do this job.

I could do this job.

That damn self-help book and its silent chanting. That technique did not work, and I was proof positive of it.

I opened my eyes and stared at him stonily. "With that out of the way, now are you ready to move on to why I asked to meet with you?"

"Not quite. There's one more thing." His gaze went to the counter. "Sara."

She turned back from the counter. "I'll have a piece of that chocolate cake as well."

Surprise flared in my eyes. "You wouldn't dare?"

Jake slipped on that intimidating mask of his. "Wouldn't I?"

I gulped, suddenly wondering why I thought it was a good idea to poke the tiger. "Jake," I warned. "I don't have time to go home and get cleaned up. I have to drive out to Monroe after I leave here to meet—"

"Two high-octanes and one piece of chocolate cake." Sara set the oversized cups on the table, along with a fairly healthy serving of cake. "Enjoy!"

As soon as she was gone, Jake glared at me. "Don't stop now," Jake insisted. "To meet with who, your boyfriend for a date? Your lover for a rendezvous?"

Enough was enough. I tucked a piece of hair behind my ear and then placed both of my hands on the table to lean forward. "For your information, I do not have a boyfriend, and I have never had a lover who I've had to rendezvous with. What I am going to do with my Friday night is drive over an hour to the only place I can find that is available for *your* sister's wedding besides the Moose Club or the grounds at your country club, which is what I wanted to talk to you about. And just so we're both on the same page, you can smash that cake in my face, you can make me feel incapable, you can avoid talking to me, you can even act like a condescending, pompous ass, but I'm not quitting."

Jake's demeanor seemed to change almost instantly from anger to amusement. "A condescending, pompous ass? Wow. That's pretty harsh."

I shrugged. "It's the truth."

He forked a piece of cake and then leaned back to nibble on it as he studied me, and just like that his mirth was gone too, leaving nothing but seriousness in its wake. "Look, Juliette—"

I jutted my chin out in defiance. "I'd prefer you call me Jules."

"Fine, Jules." He set his fork down and stuck out his hand. "For the sake of my sister, I'm willing to move on from the cake incident and focus on the wedding."

My eyes dropped to his hand in suspicion. What had triggered his abrupt change of heart?

My outburst?

My tone?

My own bleeding heart?

Or was he still going to smash that cake in my face, and just biding his time until I let my guard down?

His gaze was unwavering as he waited for me to accept his gesture.

Maybe he was being sincere?

I tried not to tremble when I reached out and slid my small hand into his large one. "Fine," I said, using his very own annoying word on him.

Let's see how he liked it.

As soon as our hands came together, though, I wasn't thinking about what he liked or didn't. I wasn't really thinking at all. The friction of the rougher skin of his palm against the softer skin of mine was sending sparks shooting from the tips of my fingers all the way to my toes.

Oh, no! I was not going to allow myself to be attracted to this pompous ass.

Quite abruptly, as if he was thinking something along those very same lines, Jake ripped his hand from mine and reached for his coffee cup. "There isn't much in Monroe. What is this place you'll be looking at, a farm?"

Still shaken from the sizzle that had just passed between us, I answered hoarsely. "It is. The place is called Sunshine Farms. Have you heard of it?"

He swallowed his coffee, and then set his cup down. "No, I haven't."

"From what I can tell, it has a suitable size barn."

He pouted his lip. "I think you need to understand something about my sister."

"What's that?"

An emotion I couldn't decipher flashed across his face. "Rory has been treated like a princess her entire life. It's not her fault. It's just the way it is. So, when she says she wants to get married in a barn, I can't help but think she doesn't really mean a barn in the actual sense of the word."

I scrunched my brows together in confusion. "Okay, then, tell me, what does she mean?"

At first, he said nothing. Then the corners of his lips twitched up. It wasn't a smile, but it was close enough. "Knowing my sister, she thinks a barn is a magical place that smells like roses, not horse shit. And that it is a place where the ground sparkles with glitter, not littered with dirt and hay."

Tension eased inside me, and I found my own smile easily enough. "You see, here's the thing, I can make those things happen. That's my job!"

Again, he said nothing, but his lips had thinned and the look he gave me was filled with doubt.

"Jake . . ." I began, stuttering at the way my pulse sped up when I said his name.

The blank mask was back. He was so hard to read. "Yeah," he answered.

The table between us was so small that when I shifted to sit up straighter, my knees bumped his. I couldn't stop the hitch of my breath or the thump of my heart that resulted from the contact. "Why don't you come with me to see the farm? If you don't think it's something your sister might like, I won't pursue it. But you should know, the only other suitable alternative was Cherokee Town & Country Club, but I'll need you to talk to the manager about it."

He ran his hands down his face. "I really don't like that place, but that aside, why would I need to talk to the manager?"

I stared down at the veneer tabletop and traced one of the lines in the hatched pattern.

"Jules," he demanded. "Tell me."

Drawing in a breath, I glanced up. He could be very domineering. "Because the ballrooms are taken, but the grounds are available. I just can't get the manager to consider my suggestion."

"You mean you want to hold the wedding outdoors?"

I slowly nodded.

"With no cover and no indoor facilities?" He practically shouted the words in a way that they didn't really come out as a question and also made my idea seem ridiculous.

I attempted not to bristle at the clipped tone. "Yes."

He shook his head adamantly. "That's absolutely out of the question. My grandmother can't be out in the heat all day."

My stomach flipped. I hadn't thought about that. "You're right. I'm sorry. Then it has to be the farm."

His eyebrows drew together.

"And if we leave right now, we can get there before the event starts and have a look around."

Jake's lips twitched, and he let out a low huff that wasn't quite a laugh as he shook his head. "Do you ever give up?"

I struggled not to laugh. "No, I don't."

When he reached into his back pocket for his wallet, amusement might have been glittering in his eyes. I couldn't be sure. "Yeah, I'm starting to figure that out."

I reached in my purse. "I got this. I invited you."

Standing up, he tossed two twenties on the table. "Consider it part of the deposit you have yet to ask me for."

"About that," I said, getting to my feet.

He waved a hand through the air to usher me forward. "You mean you want to get paid for what you're doing? And here I thought you were doing it for the sheer pleasure of aggravating me."

I gave him a shove as I passed him. *And he liked it.* I could tell by the small amount of wickedness that gleamed in his eyes.

The kinetic energy that zinged between us threw me off my game, not that I had game to begin with.

In my wedges, I couldn't walk that fast, and I especially couldn't walk and talk at the same time, so I stopped and jerked my head over my shoulder. "Actually, there is a set fee I should probably go over with you."

His response was to place his hand on the small of my back and whisper in my ear. "I'm not at all serious. Just email me your requirements, and I'll get you what you need."

Had he actually been joking around?

He had.

Tingles of arousal shot through my core. I liked this side of him. Then again I was beginning to wonder if I wasn't oddly attracted to all sides of him. "Yes, sure, I'll do that, but don't you want to know how much the fee is before you just blindly agree to make payment?"

He pushed past me and opened the door for me to walk through. "I never enter into anything blindly," he said somewhat coyly, and I could feel his heat as I passed by him.

Oh, my.

Out on the sidewalk, the sun beat down on my skin, hot and humid. Quickly, I rummaged in my purse for my keys. "Did you want to catch a ride with me or drive yourself?"

When he didn't respond, I looked up at him.

He was staring at me in utter annoyance once again.

"What?" I asked.

"I don't *catch* a ride with anyone. But if you'd like, you can *catch* a ride with me."

I was trapped in his gaze. "I can't. My car is here."

That stare of his remained pinned to mine, but it shifted to something other than annoyance. I think it was more like amusement. I didn't care what it was because it was smoldering hot. "There's an easy solution to that, Jules."

"What's that?" I asked, my voice husky, shaky, and totally off key.

"I'll bring you back here after."

Dah! was what he didn't say. He didn't have to though. Okay, I wasn't thinking clearly because I'd have had to do the same thing.

Seriously though, there was no way he didn't know the effect he had on a woman when he did that whole *intense-look* thing. Like I could say no even if I wanted to. "Sure. If it isn't too much trouble."

And there he went shocking me with a dose of that charm of his. "It's no trouble at all."

A smile prodded my lips. "Okay. I just need to get my briefcase."

"Where are you parked?" he asked.

I pointed up the street. "In the garage at the corner."

He shoved his hands into his pockets. "That's where I am as well."

"Good. That means we will be able to get on the road quicker," I said.

He shook his head and started walking. "Do you always go one-hundred miles an hour?"

I shrugged. "It's just that I want to arrive at the farm before the event starts so I can see it without people everywhere."

"Oh, we'll get there on time. Trust me."

The heat practically radiated from the concrete as we walked. That's how hot it was. And it didn't help it was radiating off him as well. Neither of us said much. We just looked around at the chaos of the upcoming rush hour and walked.

At the garage, I pressed the elevator button, and when the doors opened, we both stepped inside. Surprisingly, we didn't gravitate to opposite corners like is the norm.

Standing beside Jake in the coolness of the elevator, I looked over at him and asked, "Were you really going to smash that piece of cake in my face?"

Throwing me a quelling look, he answered with, "Do you really want to know?"

The doors opened, and the blast of hot air was almost unbearable. "Yes, I do," I answered, and then I stepped out.

Walking beside me, he leveled me with that heavy dark gaze of his. "It's probably best if I don't answer that."

"So you were." I frowned and hit the button on my remote before pulling on the handle to my car door.

He gave me a slight shake of his head that was so much hotter than it should have been. "I didn't say that."

I got inside and grabbed my big leather bag. When I went to get out, he offered me his hand in assistance. I took it and hadn't realized how close he was until I was standing on my feet and only inches from his face.

Teetering on my wedges, I froze, but my pulse sped up. "But you didn't say you weren't, either."

He didn't move.

Neither did I.

He didn't speak.

Neither did I.

Surprise had transformed into a quell of nervous flutters in my belly.

This close, I could see his blue eyes. I could see the way his shirt sculpted his body and the superb strength in his shoulders and arms.

I could see his strong jaw. And I could see how pillowy soft those lips might just be. All he had to do was lean in a little more and kiss me, and I would know.

Oh God, oh God, oh God.

For a moment I forgot I didn't really know him and got lost in time. I wasn't even sure I was breathing.

His gaze seemed to go liquid with a heat I felt between my thighs. "Some things are better left unknown," he whispered.

Staring at him, I felt my palms turn clammy as my heart rate increased. "And some things are better when you know what to expect."

His beautiful eyes flickered to my lips. "That can be true, too."

We were no longer talking about the cake, and I suddenly felt overwhelmingly, deliciously surrounded by him.

"Hey, Miss, are you leaving?" a man yelled from his car.

Jake stepped back and shoved his hands in his pockets like we'd just gotten caught doing something we shouldn't be doing "No, she's not," he called, "but I am. I'm right over there if you want to wait a minute."

My head jerked to where he was pointing, and I stood open-mouthed. The vintage black jag I'd seen pulling into Rosewood days ago was his. And I was going to get to ride in it. It made me feel giddy. Or maybe it was him that made me feel the way I did.

Closing my door, we started toward the car.

All of a sudden I had a sinking feeling in my stomach.

It wasn't because I had the insurmountable task of planning the wedding of the decade in less than five weeks. Instead, it was because this man with his brooding disposition and impatient temperament did something to me no one had ever done. He penetrated a layer buried somewhere deep inside me. It felt like an arrow had been speared through my heart.

And that made me want to turn and run the other way.

As fast as I could.

Wedges or not.

chapter
11

Barking Up the Wrong Tree

JAKE

THE FARMHOUSE WAS classic Americana.

With its white wraparound porch and the pair of rocking chairs swaying in the wind, it looked like something that belonged on a Norman Rockwell Christmas card.

Rustic.

Quaint.

Quiet.

And nothing I pictured as the backdrop for my sister's wedding.

Turning the music down, I came to a stop under a giant Maple tree and glanced over at Jules. "Are you sure this is the right place because I don't see a barn anywhere?"

"You're such a city boy," she quipped.

The top was down, and a few of the leaves from the canopy overhead floated down. "What's that supposed to mean?" I asked.

"Barns aren't like garages. They don't always have to be close to the house." She twisted her head to look around. "I'm sure it's around here somewhere."

This woman really knew how to push my buttons.

Either oblivious to this fact, or indifferent, she shaded her eyes and continued on with her search. "I'm surprised there isn't a sign anywhere."

A leaf landed on my steering wheel, and I swiped it away. "Are we in the right place or not?"

She glanced down at her phone. "Just give me a second. Will you?"

Frustration was slowly burning through my veins. Impatient to get this unplanned visit over with, I grabbed through the air at the next leaf that dared drop into my car before it made a landing, and tossed it out along with the other.

Pointing her finger down the hill and to the east, she said, "According to Google maps, it's a half-mile in that direction."

As soon as I pressed down on the accelerator to turn off the country lane and onto the dirt road ahead, my wheels started to spin. I stopped immediately and put the car in park.

Shit.

With a yank of her hair tie, she freed her hair, and it seemed to be dancing along with the slight breeze. "You might want to go a little easy there, big boy."

Color had tinged her cheeks from the wind, causing her tanned skin to appear rosy. With her green eyes and the sparkle from her earrings reflecting off the sun, it looked beautiful. *She was beautiful.* Shaking the thought away, I peered over my Ray-Bans at her. "I do know how to drive."

"Yes, I'm sure you do, on city roads. But how often do you drive in the country?"

"Probably about as often as you," I remarked.

"Actually," she said, holding a finger up, "my uncle owns a farm, and I've driven out there enough to know that if you get stuck in the muck, the only way you're getting out is with a tow truck."

I pushed my sunglasses up. "Fine. And what's with the use of big boy?"

"It's just a saying," she defended. "If you prefer big man though instead, I'd be more than happy to use that term."

Even though I glared at her, her gaze never dropped from mine. In fact, her eyes were so expressive, they were capable of swallowing a man whole. Again, I ignored that, too. "I prefer neither."

"Little boy, then" she giggled. When I glared at her this time, she quickly looked back down at her phone.

At least she sensed I had limits. Shaking my head, I put the car back in drive. Knowing she was right about spinning my wheels, I eased slower this time on the accelerator and rocked the Jag easily onto the mucky road.

"Woot," she catcalled, grabbing hold of her hair to keep it from blowing in her face.

Juliette, or Jules, as I was told to call her, had insisted we take the top down. Most of the time when a woman was in the car with me, I just left it up. The whole *my-hair-will-be-a-mess* thing got old after a while.

She wasn't like that.

Then again, she wasn't like anyone I had known.

Sassy, but sweet.

Funny, but a smart-ass.

Tough, but weak.

She was such a contradiction.

Back at the coffee shop, I had every intention of telling her to just do her job and leave me the hell out of it. And yet, as soon as she called me on my crap, I couldn't make the words come out.

The truth was I had been an asshole to her. Taking out my own shit on her. It wasn't right. It wasn't who I was. Or who I wanted to be. *It wasn't someone my old man would have been proud of.* So yeah,

I decided to cut her a break, and atone for my poor behavior by agreeing to participate in the planning of my sister's wedding.

Go figure.

Once we reached the bottom of the hill, all I could see were more hills and acres and acres of what looked to be vineyards and open fields.

"Well," I said, the sarcasm more than evident in my tone. *Hey, I was doing my best to go along with this thing, but I never said it was going to be easy.*

Jules unbuckled her seat belt and leaned back against the seat to stand. Her long, slender body was impossible not to look at. Shading her hand over her eyes, she pointed to the left. "I think I see the top of the barn right over that second hill."

Spending my time driving around a cow pasture wasn't exactly how I thought I'd be spending my first night off in ten days. I waited for her to sit back down and buckle up, and then I hit the gas. Again the wheels turned, but the ground was dryer down here, so I knew we wouldn't get stuck.

Climbing up the hill, I took my time, but when I reached the top and started down, I gave the Jag a little more gas. As soon as I did, Jules put her arms up in the air and closed her eyes.

"What are you doing?"

She glanced at me and opened one eye. "I love that feeling when the car shifts into first gear and the wind starts to blow on my face. It's like when you're on a roller coaster, you know?"

I shook my head and let that one just go without an answer.

She didn't seem to care that I didn't quite get it because she kept on doing what she was doing until we reached the bottom of the hill.

Minutes later we were pulling in front of the barn.

"Here it is!" Jules yelled, full of excitement. Hopping out of the car before I even put it in park, all I saw was she was there one minute and gone the next.

"Jules," I yelled, dashing out and around.

She was climbing up the car door before I reached her. "Nothing to worry about. Just twisted my ankle. That's all."

I helped her the rest of the way up and then pointed to the passenger seat. "Sit down and let me see it."

"I'm fine," she said as she waved me off.

I pointed. "I'm the doctor, not you. Now let me see it."

Begrudgingly, she sat and extended her leg.

"Can you flex your foot?"

She did.

"Wiggle your toes?"

She did.

"Move your foot in a circle."

She did.

There was no swelling. She was fine, and yet I didn't let go. With my hands firmly gripping the bare skin of her ankle, I couldn't stop myself from wondering how it would feel to have those ankles wrapped around my neck.

"Well, Dr. Kiss? What's your diagnosis?" she asked.

Normally I hated, no despised actually, when anyone called me that. Yet, hearing her say it in that saucy tone of hers zapped a bolt of electricity through my veins.

Confused by my reaction, I stood straight and put my hands in my pockets. "It's pretty serious."

Her eyes grew wide. "Why? What's wrong?"

I leaned in and fixed my gaze on her. "I hate to be the one to inform you of this, but you have a severe case of clumsyitis, and I suggest you stop wearing shoes you can't walk in."

She narrowed her stare at me. "Not funny."

I shrugged. "Hey, you're not the only one with a sense of humor around here."

Jules shook her head. "I hope you don't expect me to pay you for that diagnosis?"

The corner of my lips tilted. The answer on the tip of my tongue was anything but appropriate, so I kept it to myself and extended my hand. "Come on, klutz, let's check out this place so we can leave."

When she got to her feet, she gave me a slight shove and headed toward the barn. "Don't call me that."

I gave her a second to make sure she could walk without pain, and when she could, I quickly strode up beside her. "What's the matter, you can dish it out, but you can't take it?"

She snorted. "If that isn't the pot calling the kettle black."

This could go on all day, so I stopped and looked up at the barn. "Yep, that's a barn all right," I muttered.

It was old.

Weathered.

Big.

Old. *Did I already say that?*

And again, it was nothing I saw my city girl sister getting married in.

"It's charming," she remarked. "Not quite magical, but I can fix that."

A woman in her early sixties with gray hair and a blue dress came walking out. She looked surprised to see us. "Can I help you?"

"Yes," Jules said, "We're here to take a look at your venue."

The woman patted her hair and smiled. "George, come out here, we have a happy young couple who'd like a tour."

"I'll be right there, Ethel."

"No, you got—" I started to say, but was cut off.

"George and I just love when newly engaged couples come to visit. This hasn't happened in quite a while. Lately, it seems like we've had a parade of those snotty-nosed wedding planners from the city who want to change everything about our place to make it more sophisticated."

Jules, who I thought had been attempting to correct her at the same time I was, grabbed hold of my hand. "Yes, well, Jake and I wanted to see firsthand if this was the right place. Didn't we, honey?"

Honey?

No one had ever called me that. The shock on my face was hard to hide, especially when she batted her lashes at me.

A man, also in his sixties, wearing overalls and cowboy boots came rushing out of the barn. "This must be the happy couple."

"Yes," Ethel responded. "Aren't they darling?"

Darling?

He wiped his hands on the denim of his pants. "Looks like the picture of real love right here," he said. "And it just happens, we have a wedding starting in about an hour. Let me show you around first, and then, of course, you'll stay for the event."

Love?

Stay?

I felt a cold sweat coat my brow.

"Yes, you must stay. We insist," Ethel echoed.

"Ethel! There aren't enough mason jars for the punch," someone called. "The rest are up at the house," she answered. "I'll go get them."

Mason jars.

Punch.

My sister would go out of her mind. She was more of a *crystal and champagne* kind of girl.

George looked at his wife. "You go on, sweetheart. I'll take care of the lovebirds," he told her.

Lovebirds?

I thought my airway might be closing up.

"I'll see you two in a bit." She smiled and walked over toward an old Chevy pickup that was cherry red, and pretty damn cool.

I let go of Jules' hand. "I appreciate all of this, but—"

"We'd love to . . . stay," Jules spoke up, cutting me off. "I'm Jules, and this is Jake."

Fuck, that sounded so monogram.

So couple-like.

"Nice to meet you," George said. "Now, follow me. We don't have a lot of time."

I stared at Jules and consciously had to keep my jaw from dropping.

All she did was smile back and then she retook my hand. "Come on, sweetheart. Let's not keep George waiting."

Sweetheart?

What. The. Hell?

chapter 12

Don't Judge a Book by Its Cover

JULES

THE MENU WAS down-home southern barbecue-style. From ribs to chicken to coleslaw to biscuits, even peach cobbler.

I sat back in my chair and placed my red-checkered paper napkin next to the china-looking plastic plate. "I'm so full."

"Me too," Ethel said, setting her mason jar of non-alcoholic punch down.

I took a sip of my Pinot Grigio. Jake had gone up to the main house to get the bottle. George had insisted when he learned it was my favorite. He said a friend of his from California sent him a case, and it was the best wine he had ever tasted.

Turned out his friend was Steve Johnson, the winemaker for Cupcake Wines. *Go figure.*

Jake took a sip of his punch, and I could tell he was biting back the bitter taste with a grin.

He was larger-than-life.

Sitting beside me, he was talking rather animatedly with George about country life and how far away the nearest physician was. I was surprised how at ease he was.

Then again, we both had our fingers crossed that no one, especially the bride and the groom, asked any questions about our relationship.

Our fake relationship.

So far, other than what we did for a living, Jake and I had gotten off easy. He more so than me. He, at least, had told the truth. I hadn't exactly lied. I simply left my answer vague, stating that I worked for my uncle in his small business.

A sparkle of moonlight hit my wineglass just right, and it looked like fairy dust had been sprinkled from the ceiling.

I glanced up wondering if it had but knowing that was ridiculous.

Nope. No fairy dust, but still, the inside of the barn was beautiful.

Thirty-foot ceilings with twinkling lights strung across the rafters made the place seem right out of a fairytale. Round tables with white billowy covers and white chairs brightened up the parquet wood floors. The scent of water and rain and everything outdoors filled the air.

There were huge floor-to-ceiling windows in the back, which overlooked a river. A wooden fence ran along it with the most beautiful wildflowers growing all around it. I could imagine sofas placed here and there with overhead swaths of fabric as the perfect backdrop for photos . . . just not for Rory's photos.

Inwardly, I sighed, but then I smiled when I noticed the same wildflowers from outside were what filled the tin cans that served as centerpieces.

Ethel was quite the wedding planner herself. The perfect touches here and there proved this.

This place was magical. Just not Rory's kind of magical. And although I was sure I could transform it into anything, it was clear that George and Ethel took a lot of pride in what they had created, and changes were out of the question.

"Isn't that right, sweetie?"

An elbow nudged me, and it wasn't until then that I realized *I* was sweetie.

Sweetie?

Could he find something a little sexier to call me? *Sugarcakes. Honeypie. Cookie, even.*

"What's that, *Chocolate Cake?*" I smiled big and wide when I said it.

Jake draped an arm around my chair just as Shania Twain's "Any Man of Mine" came bellowing through the speakers.

When his fingertips brushed my shoulder, I wasn't listening to the beat of the music though because butterflies took flight in my belly, and this time they drifted even lower. I had to remind myself this was part of the show, but still, I found myself having to squeeze my thighs together to sooth the ache his touch had ignited.

"I was just telling George how much you love to dance. Especially square dance," he said.

I had been reaching for my water, and I practically spilled it when he said that. *Was he out of his ever-loving mind?* I didn't know a thing about country dancing other than the fact that the word *do-si-do* had something to do with it.

I tucked a piece of hair behind my ear. "Yes, *big boy*, I do like to dance, but you know I prefer to watch you line dance because you're so great at it. Besides, don't forget, I did hurt my ankle not that long ago."

His grin was beyond wicked. "You can be a klutz sometimes, but I seem to recall you assuring me your ankle was absolutely fine, and after I checked it out, I did concur with your self-diagnosis."

Ethel tapped George on the shoulder, and when he looked at her, she whispered something in his ear.

"Did you say you wanted to dance, Jules?" George asked me

over the music.

Before I could say no, George was on his feet and standing beside me with his hand extended. "Would you do me the honor of having this dance with me?"

Like I could say no now.

He really was so sweet. Dr. Kiss, on the other hand, well he was the devil incarnate. "I'd be delighted," I said and glared at Jake as I stood.

"Have fun, Sweetie," Jake grinned.

I bent to whisper in his ear. "While I'm gone, do you think you could come up with something to call me that doesn't make you sound like you might be George's age?"

He narrowed that blue-eyed stare at me.

Satisfied with that, I pivoted around and didn't look back.

The bridesmaids, in their short, peach dresses and cowboy boots, were having a blast stomping their feet and clapping their hands all while shaking their behinds and pressing their thumbs into their sides.

How on earth were George and I going to dance to this?

Thank God just when we reached the center of the dance floor, the music changed, and Tim McGraw's voice came overhead. As Tim sang about how no one ever made him feel the way she did, George and I stepped into position.

He took my hands and started to move, ballroom style. This type of dancing I knew how to do. "So," he said, "when are you and Jake planning on getting hitched?"

Up until then, I had been able to twist what I said so it didn't sound like a blatant lie, but this question was pretty straightforward. "We haven't decided yet."

Which was true. In fact, we hadn't decided a lot. Like, as a starting point, if we were friends or enemies.

"I noticed you ain't wearing a ring. He not gotten you one yet?"

"That's complicated," I answered.

And it was. He hadn't gotten me one and he never would because he didn't even like me, and after tonight, I was fairly certain he wouldn't be able to stand me.

"Well, he's a good man. Give him some time. He'll come around."

Yes, he'd come around all right. Come around to telling me I was fired, which reminded me of Finn.

Where had he gotten his information?

I leaned back. "Is Labor Day weekend available for a wedding?"

George started to laugh. "You'll give the man a heart attack if you make him move that fast."

"Oh, I know, but just in case, is it?"

"As a matter of fact, it might be. A lad called here today inquiring about it though, and I told him to come up and see the place before I reserved it for him. Since he ain't shown, I reckon it could be yours."

"Good to know." I winked.

He raised a curious brow.

I shrugged. "Just in case."

Yes, just in case I decided to come clean. And just in case I could figure out how this place was suitable for Rory. But even as I thought it, I knew it wasn't.

I nearly missed a step when I caught a glimpse of Jake leaning against the wall, watching us.

He threw me off, and I had to order myself to tune back into George for the remainder of the dance. My lack of focus had to cease right now because the bottom line was that at the moment I couldn't allow myself to be thrown off course.

When the music ended, I stepped back and curtsied.

"Thanks for indulging me." George gave my hand a squeeze. "You and the Doc are really quite a couple."

"Thank you," I told him, but I knew I should have been correcting him instead. I hated the lie, but I couldn't undo it now, nor could I stop what he was doing. George had signaled Jake over, and he had started to move.

All tall, dark, and handsome, he strutted my way with a cat-that-ate-the-canary grin on his face. I wanted to wipe it away—with my lips.

No, I didn't mean that.

"It's your turn," George told him.

"Oh, but he only likes to line dance," I said.

George laughed like it was a joke and strode toward his Ethel, who had started clearing the buffet table.

"May I?" Jake asked, all debonair-like.

"I don't know, may you?"

He shook his head. "Just give me your hands, will you? I'd hate to ruin George and Ethel's night by admitting this was all a ruse."

"Grrr . . . You are so frustrating," I said offering my hands.

He laced his fingers in mine and drew me close. "Did you just growl?"

With a frown, I placed my hands on his shoulders. "I did no such thing."

His hands fit my waist like they were made for me. "Yes, you did. And smile, they're looking at us."

Forcing myself to keep the corners of my mouth tilted upwards was very difficult because I could barely breathe when he slid his thigh between mine.

The crowd surged around us, and just like that, I forgot it wasn't real. We were aligned thigh-to-thigh, belly-to-belly. If I turned my head, our mouths would be close enough to kiss.

Silly thought.

We moved together, and when my hands slid from his shoulder to cup the back of his neck, the edges of his soft brown hair tickled my knuckles. The heat of his skin was almost too much, as was the feel of his body so close to mine.

When his fingers splayed against my back and lingered there, I could have sworn the music thumped in the pit of my stomach, my wrists, and especially between my thighs

"What are you doing?" I asked.

He moved closer to me. "I believe it's called dancing."

"Are you still acting? Because if you are, George and Ethel are no longer watching us," I whispered this in his ear.

"Does it matter?" he answered back, and when he did, his breath caressed my ear.

"Do you want it to?"

He pulled back to look into my eyes, his smile less bemused and his gaze bright. "Do you always answer a question with a question?"

"Only when . . . I'm talking to you." My hesitation sounded coy, but I hadn't meant it to. Scared of something, but no idea what of, I said, "This place isn't that bad. It just needs some sparkle."

"Sparkle?"

"Yes, like crystal chandeliers hanging from the beams."

He chuckled. "I don't think crystal chandeliers are George and Ethel's style."

"No," I said. "We should probably go. You were right to begin with, this place isn't appropriate for your sister's wedding."

All of a sudden the music ended, and before I could say another word, I was being pushed into a very grabby crowd of women.

Oh, no! The bouquet toss!

I had to get out of there. I bent down and crawled around, through, and practically under, a number of jumping cowboy boots.

"One."

"Two."

"Three."

Rushing out of the side of the crowd, I stood up, and I could hardly believe it when the bouquet landed at my feet.

Without thinking, I picked it up to throw it back into the crowd, but it was too late.

"Oh, Jules, you caught it." It was Ethel, and she was escorting me to the front of the room. When I saw George leading Jake there as well, I wanted to end this charade.

It was too much to handle.

Having him so close was too much to handle.

He was too much to handle.

George and Ethel pushed us both together, and all the girls started chanting, "Seal the deal. Seal the deal."

"What are they talking about?" Jake muttered.

"Kiss her, Doc," George clarified for me, and before either of us could step away from each other, George and Ethel were once again pushing us together.

I landed against Jake's hard chest. My mouth flew open in surprise, and a small sigh escaped.

My lips were so close to his.

Tantalizingly close.

The need to close the distance between us was strong.

He was breathing heavy, and I could see the muscle twitch at his temple, witness how tight his jaw was. Everything about him screamed he was holding himself back.

We were both losing that battle though.

Whether out of obligation, pressure, or need, his mouth came crashing down over mine in the hardest, heated, and most demanding way.

Oh, God, I wanted this.

Wanted him.

Especially when his tongue pushed inward, hot and sensual. It glided over mine as he licked at the roof of my mouth and swirled around my tongue in the most erotic dance.

His lips were so soft.

His mouth so hot.

His possession unlike any I'd ever experienced.

I could hear the catcalls, but ignored them all because he wasn't simply kissing me, he wasn't just sealing the deal, he was devouring me.

In that moment, any other man I'd ever kissed faded away.

No one had ever kissed me that way.

I became boneless. I became lost. I was lost. In him and his sinful mouth and full lips.

"Okay, okay, you two, that's enough. You're going to outshine the newly married couple." George was now pulling us apart.

Stepping back, I stood stunned and brought my fingers to my lips, which tingled from his kiss.

"We need to go," Jake said.

I swallowed hard and nodded. "Yes, that's a good idea. It's getting late."

In a trance-like state, I thanked George and Ethel. They were such a perfect couple. I promised to call them and then headed for the door. The barn door was opened and gave rise to the most star-filled sky I'd ever seen.

It was magical.

This place was magical.

Sighing, I walked away.

With his hands in his pockets, Jake waited for me to pass through the door, and when I did, I looked up at him. His expression was blank, but his eyes were filled with a kind of strange light I couldn't interpret.

I wondered if he was in some kind of state of shock, but then he passed by me without a word and took the lead.

Something was wrong.

Something was off.

On quick feet, I followed behind him, my wedges too high to

move at the pace I was, and yet I still managed.

The thick air filled my lungs. The light breeze felt too hot. And suddenly it was obvious this whole thing was one giant mistake.

He was already at the car and holding the passenger door open before I made it halfway there. Clearly impatient, he practically ushered me forward when I was within his reach. "Get in," he said, careful not to actually touch me.

It was a demand that I didn't care for, but my mind was in too much of a flurry of upheaval to argue with him, so I got in.

After he put the top up, he hit the gas, and before I knew it, we were turning onto the country lane. I looked out the window. The night was dark. The sky filled with stars. And the company in the car was dead silent.

It wasn't until we reached the main road that he looked over at me. "Are you cold? I can turn the heat on."

Was he serious? It was like ninety degrees outside. Just then I glanced down. I was hugging myself and trembling. "No, I'm fine."

Or I will be as soon as I get over that kiss.

"Jules?"

The sound of his husky voice had my heart doing a quick, extra thump. I looked anywhere but over at him. The knob on the radio was actually lovely with its sheen of silver. "You don't have to say it," I whispered.

"Say what?"

"That the kiss was a mistake, and it didn't mean anything."

He didn't respond, and the silence was deafening. Wanting to escape it, I turned the music on and stared out the window.

As the country faded into a blur, the bright lights of Atlanta seemed almost intrusive, and I was reminded of the first time I'd seen them twinkle. That was not a happy time, and one I always hated thinking about it.

Yet, as an odd sadness seemed to swallow me whole, I couldn't stop that time in my life from coming back, and I wasn't sure I even wanted to.

Sometimes remembering wasn't so bad.

Then again . . . sometimes it was.

chapter
13

Let Sleeping Dogs Lie

JULES

Seventeen Years Earlier

IT WAS A typical Tuesday morning in Brooklyn at the Easton household as I walked down the stairs. The dog was at my mother's feet waiting for a treat, and my father was on her other side waiting for a kiss.

I turned my attention toward the television, and the annoying newsman was talking about the election for Mayor.

Boring.

I grabbed the remote and immediately switched the station.

My mother was at the sink rinsing her teacup. My father was sipping his coffee. Almost in unison, they both yelled, "Hey, turn it back."

I rolled my eyes and nabbed a cereal bowl. "Sorry, I cannot watch another minute of that."

My father leaned back against the counter. He was in his neatly pressed uniform and highly polished shoes. As a K-9 unit officer in the Explosive Detection Division for the Port Authority, he could be very intimidating, *especially when he pointed his finger at me. "That is very important. That is the fate of New York City right there. It might very well change your future, Juliette."*

Just then, his trusted partner, Diogi, rolled over. I couldn't help but laugh out loud. Diogi was a golden retriever highly trained in sniffing out explosives, but at home, with us, he was just my dog.

I loved him.

Especially when even he knew what my father was saying was equivalent to, "Blah, blah, blah."

Grabbing the box of Frosted Flakes and carton of milk, I sat down and flicked through the stations. When I glanced up, there were four narrowed eyes on me, so I gave in and switched the television back to the sleeper news station.

Whatever.

"I might be late tonight. I have a meeting," my mother told me. "Will you be okay?"

I propped an elbow on the table. "Yes, Mom, I'll be fine."

My mother was wearing her very best suit and her pearl earrings rather than her favorite diamond stars. I knew the meeting had to be important. She worked for Silverstone Properties and was hoping to be promoted to senior executive. If that happened, she was going to get an office overlooking both New York Harbor and the Hudson River, and that really excited her.

I guessed it was cool.

"Call me when you get home, so I know you made it safely."

I shoved a spoonful of cereal in my mouth. "I always do, don't I?"

My father kissed me on the head. "I'm headed in early. I have rounds to make around the complex before going inside."

I looked up. "Bye, Dad, see you tonight."

He snapped the leash onto Diogi's collar. "Have a good day at school, and don't forget your lunch again," he pointed to the counter, "I made it, and that means there's something delicious inside."

"Josh Easton," my mother scolded. "You know she doesn't need any

more sugar. Next thing we know she'll be running into the walls."

Okay, so I walked into an open locker yesterday after I bought a brownie for lunch and broke my glasses. It wasn't like I'd done it before. And it wasn't like it was the brownie's fault.

"Rachael Easton, you know a little something sweet never killed anyone."

"But Josh Easton—"

"Rachael Easton, you know Juliette is perfect just the way she is."

"Well, you are right about that."

The whole using full names thing was vomit-inducing enough, but when he patted her on the butt, I thought I might have thrown up a little in my mouth. "Gross!"

They both laughed. "Some day you won't think so," my mother said.

"I doubt that."

"Lunch," my father pointed, more sternly, and then after kissing my mother, he headed for the back door.

"Bye Diogi," I called. "Love you, Dad," I added.

"Love you too," he said, and then he closed the door.

"You ready to go?" my mother asked.

Grumbling, I got to my feet. "I really hate school this year.

"No, you don't."

"Yes, I do. I think I'm having a panic attack over gym class today, and maybe I should stay home."

She jingled her keys. "Good try."

"Feel my forehead."

She handed me my lunch. "Let's go."

I grabbed my backpack. "Mom, you're supposed to be worried about my mental state. Suggest I see someone or something like that."

She shook her head. "Juliette, there is nothing wrong with you, now let's go."

Pulling at the sides of my old glasses because this old pair was way too small, I gave her an exasperated sigh and marched out the door.

After she dropped me off, I tried to figure out the best way to change for gym class without anyone seeing me. I was tall and lanky and flat chested, and I knew I was going to be made fun of.

School really did suck.

At eight thirty, the homeroom bell rang. Some of the kids lingered in the hallway, but I was sitting promptly in my assigned seat when the teacher came in. "Good morning class," he said.

"Good morning," some of us answered.

"Busy day today," he remarked.

I started to doodle on my notebook.

There was a crackle overhead and he stopped talking so we could hear the announcements. First, we were given a rundown on school elections. I couldn't escape politics. Then there was talk about the fall dance and blah, blah, blah.

I doodled a little more. This time I drew a heart and wrote Robbie's name inside. He was so cute, but he never even looked at me. I quickly scribbled through it.

Math was my first class, and I stayed put. Even though it was only the second week of school, Mr. Gilbert loved to give pop quizzes, and as he handed one out, there was a twinkle in his eye.

I breezed through the quiz and waited for everyone else to finish. When time was up, we exchanged papers to correct them. And then the new lesson started. I took notes and doodled some more.

Time seemed to be dragging until I realized it was past first period and the bell had not rang yet. Everyone else must have realized the same thing because they started to talk over each other.

"Well, class," Mr. Gilbert boomed, "perhaps the office is still working the kinks out of the new school year. Let's give it another minute."

It was less than thirty seconds later when the school principal's voice came over the loudspeaker, and what he had to say would change my life forever. "Two planes have flown into the World Trade Center."

Chaos broke out. The students were so loud I couldn't hear anything else, but I didn't move as my entire body stiffened.

My mother.

My father.

Diogi.

They were all there, but I knew they had to be okay. Just like I knew they would be coming to get me to assure me of that.

We were told to remain where we were. School would be closing, and parents had been notified.

Mine, too.

Girls were hysterical all around me.

Boys were milling around.

I stayed where I was.

Glued to my seat.

Then, not even an hour later, another announcement came overhead. "The South Tower of the World Center has collapsed."

Tower Two.

Something started to rise in my gut, but I pushed it down. My mother worked in Tower One, and my father, well he could have very well still been outside.

They were coming to get me.

They'd be here soon.

I couldn't stop myself from inhaling deeply and quickly.

I couldn't seem to get enough air.

I waited in my seat while most of the other kids got picked up, and then the principal's voice came over the loudspeaker again. "The North Tower of the World Trade Center has also collapsed."

Tower One.

I vomited all over Mr. Gilbert's floor, and then I raced to the bathroom to splash water on my face.

They were okay.

They were coming for me.

They'd be here soon.

I was feeling light-headed, and the dizziness caused me to sway as I walked down the crowded hall.

Back in the classroom, tears streamed down my face as I waited and waited and waited.

"I called your uncle," Mr. Gilbert said, placing a hand on my shoulder.

I shivered. I was so cold. "My uncle?"

"He's on your emergency contact list."

"But he lives in Atlanta," I told him, trying to blink the haze away and suddenly feeling so hot.

"I know. He asked me to take you home and find someone to stay with you until he can get here."

Uncle Edward was my father's much older brother and ran a wedding business in Atlanta. He came to the city twice a year, but other than that, I really didn't know much about him.

"My parents will be coming to get me," I insisted. "And my dog, too."

"Well, how about we wait at your house?" he asked, and I hated the grim look in his eyes.

"I don't feel so well," I told him.

He squeezed my shoulder. "Come on, I'll get you home."

I looked around to see an empty room.

Everyone left.

Except me.

Panic struck, or maybe it had long ago.

Is this what a real panic attack was?

I looked at the clock.

Hours had passed.

And still no word from my either my mother or my father.

I was alone.

And I'd be that way for a very long time.

chapter
14

Out of the Horse's Mouth

JAKE

THERE WAS A lot more to say than what she'd said.

It was that simmering, smoldering heat inside the aloof package that stopped me from trying to talk about what had happened between us.

Correction, what was *happening.*

She was so much like me in that way. Shutting down rather than risking getting burned. It was my MO, and apparently hers as well.

The garage was dimly lit, and my hands were gripping the leather of the wheel so tight that I practically jerked my car into the empty parking spot next to hers.

I knew I only had a matter of minutes to try to turn this situation around. Yet the problem was even after more than sixty minutes, I still couldn't figure out what to say.

That didn't change the fact that time was up.

As soon as I put the Jaguar in park and switched the engine off, silence rushed in. I didn't like it, and I turned toward Jules. "Look,"

I started to say.

She was already looking over at me, and the distance in her eyes made me wonder where she'd gone on the ride back. Momentarily caught off guard by the sadness I saw, I paused for a moment, and that's when she pounced. "I'm sorry I ruined your night off. I'll let your sister know she needs to find someone else to help her with her wedding. I'm not the right person for the job."

I opened my mouth to tell her that was bullshit and she knew it, but she bolted out of the car so fast, I didn't have time to utter a single syllable before the door slammed shut.

Without any hesitation, I jerked my door open and hustled around my car.

Obviously, she hadn't planned her escape out very well because she was still rummaging through her giant bag, which she hilariously called a briefcase, when I caught up with her. "Damn it, Jules, you're so frustrating."

She whirled around, and her features were locked and impassive as she stared coolly at me. "I'm frustrating. Are you kidding me?"

The space between her car and mine was tight at best, but still, I moved closer. "Look," I started again, "I know I'm not the easiest person to deal with, but you're no piece of cake either."

Her eyes were wide, her nostrils flaring, and I could see the pulse beating wildly at the base of her throat. "Grrr . . . you . . . you really—"

There she went again with the growl. I couldn't decide if she was more kitten or cat or maybe even lion, and I couldn't stop myself from throwing my head back in laughter.

Her eyes widened in surprise. She looked . . . shocked.

I sobered and glanced curiously at her. "What's that look for?"

She immediately dropped her gaze and remained silent.

"Jules?" I prompted.

She sighed, and then lifted her head, her stare almost rebellious as her chin thrust upward. "I've never seen you laugh. Or even smile, for that matter. You don't show your emotions much, other than the angry ones. I can never tell what you're thinking, and that's frustrating."

Seemed like we were both filled with frustration.

My features relaxed into an easy smile, and I noted again her surprise. "I've been accused of being an emotionless bastard by more than one woman, but we've usually had sex first."

The laughter she expelled was exhilarating and sent an electrical charge throughout my entire body, but more specifically right to my cock. "That just about says it all then, doesn't it?" she somehow managed to mutter through her laughter.

I shoved my hands in my pockets to stop them from streaking over that gorgeous body of hers. "Does everything have to be a battle with you?"

She stopped laughing, but her breathing remained hitched. "I could ask the same about you."

I shook my head. "What I was trying to say in the car, twice, was that I have some kind of thing for you, and I want to figure it out."

She said nothing for a moment, but then curiosity seemed to take hold, and she bit her lip. "All right. I'll bite. What does *figure it out* mean exactly? Be friends? Date? Screw?"

I quirked a brow. No woman had ever irritated me and turned me on at the same time the way she did. "What if my answer isn't that straightforward?"

The disgruntled look she gave me didn't get past me.

Nor did I let it daunt me. "But, I mean, if you'd rather cut right to the screwing part, I'm good with that, too."

Now she was laughing again. "You really are too much."

"Oh, you have no idea," I mused and stepped forward, pushing her back against the car.

I wanted more of what I had back at the farm.

I wanted her.

And so I took what I wanted.

Crashing my mouth to hers, the taste of her was both hot and sweet, and something I couldn't quite identify, but I knew it was satisfying.

Her lips parted on a whimper, and she gave me full access to what I wanted. What I needed. What I craved.

This time she kissed me back harder and clung to me in a way that had her fingers digging into my back.

Feeling like I needed more, I tugged her thigh up so I could press deeper between her legs. When my hand tightened around her neck, she pushed against me, and I groaned. The vibration of it causing only more heat to shoot through me.

As the kiss grew more demanding, it muddled my head and took me somewhere else entirely. The air crackled dangerously between us, and I let myself go. My hands wandering, my lips seeking, my tongue thrusting, and my body wanting.

When I felt my control starting to fray, I lifted my head, but didn't step back, didn't let her go. "We should talk first."

Breathless and panting, she was attempting to steady herself and placed a hand on my chest as if she needed the support. "Okay, you're the first guy to ever say something like that to me."

Firsts were all over the place tonight.

"It's just that jumping into bed, or anyplace, would be easy, and I'm not saying I don't want to." I glanced down at my raging erection, "I mean obviously, I do."

A smile feathered her lips along with a slight blush that coated her cheeks. "But . . ."

"Yes, there is a but."

"Isn't there always?"

I shrugged. "But, you are going to plan my sister's wedding."

She shook her head back and forth. "I can't. I don't have enough resources to pull it off."

"Yes, you can. And yes you are. Somehow, someway you will make that day happen because I'm not letting you quit."

She raised a perky brow, and I couldn't help but glance further down at her perky nipples. Fuck, I wanted to take them in my mouth. "Did you just say you're not letting me?"

I shook off the thought of putting her in my car and having her naked beneath me right this minute. "Yes, I'm not letting you quit. I'll sue you if I have to."

Her palms pressed harder against my chest. "Oh yeah, on what grounds?"

I smiled. "Misrepresentation."

"Of what?"

"Using that sexy body of yours to lure me into doing business with you and then not allowing me to sink deep inside you. Not allowing me to fuck you so hard and for so long that you can't even remember your own name."

I watched her eyes smolder with an explosive heat and had to order myself not to press her right back against the car and just take her right there. In a public place. She cleared her throat. Straightened her shoulders. Her voice was shaky when she finally spoke. "I never said I wouldn't allow that."

Triumph blazed in my eyes. "Good. Then the faster we can move past the business aspect of our relationship, the faster we can move on to getting naked."

"That's right to the point."

"I'm always right to the point. You'll figure that out soon enough, just like you're going to figure out where to have this wedding. And then once you do, you are going to plan the biggest event the country has seen in decades." I lifted her chin with my fingers. "Do you understand me?"

She nodded. Swallowed. Went to open her mouth, but I shut

it with a kiss.

"Don't even think of disagreeing," I whispered around her lips.

Ignoring me, she placed her hands on my face and leaned back. "What I was going to say is what happened to figuring us out? To being friends? To dating? You're skipping right to the sex part."

"Isn't that the best part?" I murmured.

Dirty blonde hair and big eyes framed an unexpected charm of twin dimples. "Well, yes, and no."

"No?" I asked in surprise.

"I mean, when it's good, yes."

"I don't know who you've been having sex with, but I promise you with me it will be more than good."

She rolled her eyes at my flirtation, but those dimples flicked in amusement on her cheeks when she went on. "You sound like Tony the Tiger by the way, and I'm waiting for you to say, *It's great.*"

An exasperated sigh escaped my throat, but so did a surprised smile. She knew how to dish it, that was for certain.

"Seriously though, Jake, dating is how you get to know someone."

I sobered. "Dating is . . . complicated, and expectant, and time-consuming," I ran my hand through my hair. "Three things I can't handle in my life right now, and besides, I have a job waiting for me in New York."

"New York?"

I nodded. "In the trauma unit at New York Presbyterian Hospital."

"When do you start?"

"That's open-ended right now."

She nodded as if she understood that it was dependent on my grandmother. Then she rose on her toes, linked her hands behind my head, and laid her mouth on mine. A jolt of pleasure shot straight through me. I had to fight the urge to grab her as I had before, because all I wanted to do was release even a small portion of that pent-up lust that was between us.

I could have just a little taste right here, and it would help do just that. I ran a hand up her body then down it again. Stopping at the loose waistband of her pants, I eased my fingers inside.

Quivering, she drew back, and a pretty flush tinged her tan cheeks pink. "How about this? I agree to plan the wedding—with your help—and you agree not to define us, to see where things go, regardless of the place."

All kinds of alarm bells went off in my head, and I pulled my hand back. That was dangerous right there because it meant she wanted more than I knew I could give.

Than I had to give.

"Look," she said. "I have a business to run that you must already know is floundering, and that is my first priority. I like you, and I want to figure this out between us, but I want to do so with an open mind."

I looked down at her. "Figure it out, that's all."

She removed her arms from around my neck and offered me her pinky. "Pinky swear."

I shook my head. "I am not doing that."

"Come on, please, it means we both understand the deal. We enter into a relationship with no expectations."

"But with sex?" *Hey, I was hopeful.*

She smiled. "Yes, with sex."

I offered my pinky and couldn't believe I was doing such a foolish thing. She just had a way about her. Part strong woman, part lost girl. She was both a kitten and a lion, and I was drawn to her. With my pinky wrapped around hers, I said, "Now, for the sex part."

"Yes." Her eyes were wide, and her lips parted.

However, before I could tell her we were going to my place in midtown because it was closer than Buckhead, and I didn't want to hear anything about it, my phone started ringing from my car, where I'd left it. I uncurled my pinky and held up a finger. "Give me one second."

She nodded.

Opening the door, I grabbed for my cell. It was late, so either there was an emergency at the hospital, or it was concerning my grandmother. "Dr. Kissinger," I answered.

"Dr. Kissinger, this is Matthew."

I stood and held my phone to my ear. My heart was clambering in my chest. "Yes Matthew, is something wrong?"

Matthew was my grandmother's night nurse. I'd hired him to take care of her at her home, and tonight was his first night.

"Yes. Yes. Everything is fine. And I hate to bother you, but she's asking when you'll be home."

Relief washed over me and I laughed. "Tell her I'm on my way and then will you please remind her that I'm nearly thirty, which means she no longer has to wait up for me."

"Yes sir, I understand sir, but I'd rather not if you don't mind."

"Sure thing, Matthew, I'll tell her myself when I get there."

"Okay, sir, goodbye then."

I shoved my phone in my front pocket and backed Jules up against the car. "I'm sorry, but I'm going to have to postpone things. My grandmother just came home today, and I told her I'd stay with her. Somehow she took that to mean I need to be home before she goes to bed."

Jules was giggling. "I heard you, and I think it's cute."

I thrust my hard cock against her. "Baby, I'm anything but cute. When you get home tonight, and you're touching yourself, thinking of me and what I'm going to do to you, I doubt the word cute will come to mind."

"I probably shouldn't admit this, but I've been playing with myself a lot since meeting you."

I groaned and thrust into her again. "That's something we have in common then because I've had an itch I haven't been able to scratch. But tonight when I get in the shower and grip my cock, this time I'll be thinking about you playing with your gorgeous pussy and the sounds you make when you come."

Her lips formed a perfect O. "When will I see you?"

Stepping back, I took her bag and immediately found her keys. "Me or my cock?"

"Don't they come together?"

Unlocking her door, I smirked. "Oh, they do. Trust me, they do."

"Seriously, when?"

I opened her door. "I'll call you tomorrow, but check your phone tonight."

"Are you going to send me a dick pic?" she asked, lowering herself inside.

"Not just a dick pic. Something better," I told her and stepped back to shut the door. "Now get going. I'll follow you out. If I don't get back to Rosewood, my grandmother won't get any sleep tonight."

"That's it!" she shouted with a burst of excitement.

"What's it?"

"Rosewood. We'll have the wedding at Rosewood and recreate the scene in that picture of your great-grandmother. A tea party in the garden before the ceremony during the day and the ball of all balls inside at night. It will be just like one of Gatsby's parties, only so much better."

I had to hand it to Jules; my sister would love the 1920's vibe. I wasn't so sure she'd love the Rosewood idea, though. Yet, I could sell her on that, especially since I knew Mimi would go for the suggestion the minute I repeated it. I tapped my knuckles on the hood. "Start planning, but Juliette, not before you make yourself come thinking of me."

She ignored me again. It was really starting to irritate me, and that only turned me on more. "I need to come over, but not tomorrow. How about Sunday?"

I raised a brow. "My grandmother will be home, but if you insist on having me, I guess I'll have to say yes."

"Not for sex," she scolded.

"I know," I said and closed the door.

She opened the window. "I'll be there at eleven."

I leaned in. "What about getting together tomorrow for the sex part?"

With eyes the brightest green, freckles alight, and dimples practically dancing, she shoved me back. "Oh, that will have to wait. I have a lot to do tomorrow. See you Sunday," she said, and then closed the window.

I watched her back out and then I watched the taillights of her little Miata fade. As she turned the corner, I wondered if this was all a big mistake because I couldn't wait to see her again.

And that was so unlike me.

So very unlike me.

Taste of Your Own Medicine

JULES

EXHAUSTION HAD LONG ago set in.

At nearly eight at night, I was finally able to relax. I had run a bath and was lowering myself into the water when I decided on lavender-scented oil and bubbles.

After adding them, I settled myself against the back of the tub and reached for my phone. I thumbed directly to my messages to play the video Jake had sent me last night for the hundredth time.

It wasn't of his dick.

It wasn't of him making himself come.

But it was still such a turn on.

It was of him eating a piece of chocolate cake. *"I want to come inside that hot mouth of yours,"* he whispered and then opened his mouth wide. *"I want to taste your pussy and make you come so hard,"* he moaned as he licked at the fork with his tongue. *"I want to bury myself deep inside you,"* he said in a guttural tone, and the way his eyes closed when he did, made me think he was orgasming right in front of me.

He knew this of course.

And he was acting.

He was trouble.

And I knew it.

The dirty talking doctor was a bad boy through and through.

And I liked it. Worse, I wanted more.

What I had responded with was:

Me: No dick pic

Him: How bad do you want it?

Me: Not that bad.

Him: Send me something first, and I'll consider it.

Me: Something like what? Me painting my nails?

Him: Something worthwhile.

I didn't respond to that text, and we hadn't spoken all day, but I'd spent the day contemplating what was worthwhile.

And I couldn't believe what I was about to do. I was going to give him a show, and it was one he didn't have to use his imagination for.

I'd never done anything like this before, and my hands were shaking.

Turning the video on, I angled my phone toward my sex, which was, of course, hidden by the bubbles, and then using my free hand, I ran my fingers down my belly.

Resting my chin on the water's surface, I found my clit and started circling. The bath oil made my skin slick and my cunt even slicker. Smooth. Soft.

For some reason, my arousal seemed heightened because I knew I was doing this for him.

Sinking lower into the deep tub, with my ears in the water, I was able to hear the wildly beating thump of my heart.

The pitter-patter caused by thoughts of him.

His mouth.

His lips.

His tongue.

His cock.

Spurred on by the sound, I took my nub and started pinching it between my fingers. I pushed myself back up and allowed a sigh to leak out of me as my pussy tightened and bucked.

Water splashed out of the tub, but I didn't care because his voice was in my head. *"I want to come in that hot mouth of yours."*

Needing more, I opened my legs wider and pushed my hips against the water when my fingers plunged inside me.

I bit my lip, the intrusion causing my hips to jerk toward the surface. Still, it wasn't enough. Not nearly enough. Not him.

Needing even more, I applied pressure and circled my clit. Over and over. My moans were real, and they were for him. The water supported me and lifted me, but not for long. Soon I was pushing my pelvis against my fingers, and my shoulder blades bumped the bottom of the tub.

I held the phone up higher.

His hands.

His big, callused palms.

Rough and soft.

His long, strong fingers.

That's what I wanted to feel. That's what I pretended I felt.

Sliding two fingers inside, I tried to make believe it was okay that it wasn't his thick, hard cock fucking me. And for a minute, it was okay. My clit swelled. And my body opened with an ache to be filled. But then I realized it wasn't him, and I forced myself to keep pretending.

I imagined it was him in here with me. Fucking me. Telling me to sit on his lap. To ride his hard cock. And we were all tongues, hands, and hot explosive kisses. And then, and then, I exploded in a small whirlwind of tiny sparklers.

No fireworks.

No stars or other galaxies.

And surely no earth moving under my feet.

I mean, I was alone. But I came hard, and I came for him. I may not have known what it was Dr. Kiss was making me feel, but I did know for absolute certainty that I wanted to find out.

I turned the camera off and thought about deleting the video, but what did I have to lose by sending it?

Just then my leg slipped from the tub and bubbles blew all around me and landed on my screen.

It was a sign.

So, without overthinking it any further, and before I could totally chicken out, I brought up my contacts list and hit send without attaching a message.

He'd figure it out.

I relaxed back in the tub and closed my eyes. Oh, how I wished I could be there when he watched it.

Five minutes passed and nothing.

Ten minutes passed and nothing.

At fifteen, I stopped counting.

The caustic bastard wasn't going to respond.

He was waiting for me to come begging.

Well, he'd be waiting a long time.

chapter
16

Off One's Rocker

JULES

I HAD TURNED into a prune, literally.

My skin was all wrinkled and my toes shriveled by the time I finally emerged from the tub. Grabbing a towel, I dried myself and noted that my skin might have been clean from the hot water, but my arousal was not nearly satisfied.

As I wrapped a robe around my naked body, I knew that I would give in and call him to invite him over. Now. Tonight. The simple truth was—I wanted him. His mouth on me. His hands on me. Him.

I wanted to feel him lick the soft, wet slit of my pussy. I wanted to coax a smile on his lips when I came hard under his tongue. I wanted him to fuck me with his hands and his cock and his mouth until I came. I wanted to make him come and beg for more.

And I couldn't wait any longer.

When my phone rang, I lunged for it. It was him. I was sure, and I was going to order him to come over right now.

Before I could get to it though, I slipped on the wet floor and landed on my butt. With my rear throbbing, I got on my knees and crawled across the tile to grab for my phone, and then I hurriedly pressed answer. "Hello."

"Is this Jules Easton?" the gruff voice asked.

I glanced at the number. I didn't know it. "Yes."

"I have a guy in my back room that gave me instructions I was to call you if anything happened to him."

"What happened?" I asked in alarm.

"He got knocked out, and he's in pretty bad shape."

"How bad?"

"I'm not a fucking doctor, lady, but he doesn't look good, or I wouldn't be calling."

"Can I talk to him?"

"He's out cold."

"Can you take him to the hospital and I'll meet you there?"

He said nothing.

My nerves started to flutter. "Where are you? I'll call for an ambulance?"

His laughter was almost sardonic. "Look, lady, we don't take nobody to no hospital, and we don't call for no ambulances. You got that?"

All I could do was close my eyes. "Yes, I got that."

There was some crinkling of paper. "I was about to throw his ass out on the street when I remembered he told me if I called you I'd get $200."

"How did he tell you that? He's out cold."

He sighed. "When he came in he gave me your number. And in case of an emergency, I was to keep him with me until you got here. If I did, I'd get $200 bucks. And I did, so are you coming to get him, or what?"

I got to my feet. "Yes. I'll be right there. What's the address?"

"Lady, I ain't no phone book. We're at the AX. And when you

come, don't forget the money."

"No, I won't."

After hanging up, I got dressed as fast as I could. Once I slipped my sneakers on, I googled the AX. I gasped as I read posts about the underground fighting ring, or rather the cage fights. They were illegal. That much I knew. According to the internet, the referees weren't trained, the fights weren't monitored, and the rules weren't set in stone. There were also no medical personnel there to help with injuries.

It sounded barbaric.

Why was Finn there, of all places?

No time to think about anything, I had to move fast. In a rush, I scrambled down the stairs and rifled through the kitchen cabinets for the coffee can where my uncle had once kept money when we were kids, in case we needed it. Luckily, there was still some in there, and I grabbed it all. I was fairly certain Finn didn't have that amount of cash on him. And I didn't have much, either.

Combining what I had with the money from the can, it totaled two hundred and twenty dollars. I tossed it in my purse.

In my car, I plugged the address into my GPS and then headed downtown.

What had he done?

In the past, I'd cleaned and bandaged Finn's cuts, but he'd always come home and then asked me for help. Things had to be pretty bad if he couldn't even get to the house.

Finn liked to fight, sure, but he was training with someone that was helping him get ready to apply to the UFC.

I had no idea where I was when my GPS told me I'd arrived. The building didn't have a sign on it, but it looked like an old abandoned factory.

Cars, trucks, and motorcycles filled the parking lots, and when I got out, a man that had been loitering around whistled at me.

"Hey, over here, pretty thing."

I didn't know why I even looked his way, but I did. He had leaned against a building and was unzipping his pants.

"Help a guy out," he smiled.

My heart started to pound.

Luckily, I'd thrown on a pair of jeans and a tank top, along with my Converse, and I was able to move fast.

Throwing open the door, I could hardly believe what I was looking at. Hundreds of people filled the space. Stepping inside, I was nearly blinded by the fluorescent lights and the music was so loud, the floors were shaking. I felt there was a subway running beneath me.

This unsanctioned event was utterly rampant.

Pushing my way in through the throng of people, I ignored the smell and the heat. I had no idea where I was going, but I just kept moving. Even as the sweat beaded on my skin, I didn't stop.

Up high, windows were open, and fans were blaring in almost every corner. I don't think the place had air-conditioning.

There were sweaty men and women everywhere, most of them drunk or high. To my surprise, some of the men were dressed in suits and some of the women wore expensive high heels.

When I got close enough to the center, I could see the cage. People were screaming as they huddled around it. "Rambo. Rambo. Rambo."

Their attention was on the fighter covered in tattoos who was pushing through the crowd with his corner men and three half-naked ring girls leading the way. He was huge. Big and ripped with biceps so large they had to be bigger than my thighs. Blood was dripping from his eye down to his mouth, and I prayed to God he wasn't whom Finn had fought.

Scurrying away from the hustle and bustle, I spotted a sign that read, "Office."

Finn had to be in there.

Weaving around and through the crowd, I reached the door and knocked on it.

"Go the fuck away," came an angry voice.

I closed my eyes and took a deep breath. Stupid. This was stupid. I should have called my uncle. "I'm here to pick up my cousin."

The door flung open, and his eyes raked over me. "You got my money?"

I nodded and took the money out of my purse, tossing one of the twenties back in before I handed it to him.

After he took it, he shoved it down his pants. He didn't have to worry—it wasn't like I was going to try to get it back, but if I were, there was no chance of it. "He's over there. Now get him out of here."

My eyes darted to the heap on the floor. "Finn," I cried out as I rushed over to him. He was shirtless and lay lifeless on the floor. There was dried blood on his face and hands, and he was coated in a sheen of sweat. "Finn," I said again softly.

The burly guy turned up the wall unit, and a blast of cold air hit me in the face. I felt my nipples pebble and cursed myself for wearing this shirt.

The manager sat at his desk and picked up his sandwich.

"What happened to him?" I screamed.

With a hunk of food in his mouth, he said, "Like I already told you, he got knocked out."

"By who?"

He wiped his mouth with his sleeve. "Rambo."

"Why was he fighting a guy so much bigger than him?"

"Why do you think, girlie? Money."

I looked back down at Finn. "How much money?"

"Ten grand. Any more questions?"

I shook my head. Finn knew I was in dire straits and when he said he'd help me out, I thought he meant with his time, not by trying to raise cash through fighting. I fought back my tears.

"Then get him out of here."

With my ear to Finn's chest, I could hear him breathing, and sighed in relief. "I need help. I can't carry him alone."

He sipped his beer and then burped. "That will cost you another hundred."

I pushed Finn's hair away from his eyes and saw how swollen both were, and by the amount of blood around his nostrils, it looked like he'd broken his nose again. "I don't have another hundred."

"Then come back when you do. I'll be here all night."

Tears fell hot from my eyes. I didn't have a hundred dollars in my account. I wasn't even sure I had ten dollars. "I have twenty dollars left in my purse. If I give you that, will you please just help me get him to the car?"

The guy had turned his attention to the porn he was watching on the small television. "I told you. That's gonna cost you a hundred."

"Finn." I tried again to lift him. I couldn't. I just couldn't. "Please Finn, get up."

The guy turned toward me, "He's out cold, girlie. There ain't no way he's getting up on his own, but I'll take that twenty and a blowie if it helps you out."

Disgusted, I got to my feet. "In your dreams."

He shrugged. "Just thought I'd offer."

I pushed the hair that had fallen loose from my ponytail back into the elastic. "You'll keep him in here until I get back?"

His eyes were glued to the screen. "Like I said, I'm here all night, and he sure as hell ain't going anywhere."

Straightening my shoulders, I headed toward the door. "I shouldn't be very long."

He didn't respond.

He didn't care.

Outside his door, I pulled out my cell, but I had no reception. The place was concrete—everywhere.

Sighing, I made my way back toward the entrance. Fluorescent lights from overhead flickered as I weaved through the crowd once again. Hands touched my ass, my breasts, and tugged on my ponytail, but I did not show any fear. Instead, I just moved faster, and faster still.

Gasping for air out in the humid Georgia night, I pushed away the feeling that I couldn't breathe and that I wasn't quite steady on my feet. There was no time for that nonsense.

Knowing it would alter the dynamics of our relationship, but having no other choice, I pulled out my cell once again and called the only person I could think to call.

When he answered, I started to cry, and I hated myself for that. "I need you. Can you come?"

"Where are you?"

I told him. I told him everything. It just came out.

"I'll be there as soon as I can."

"And can you bring a hundred dollars in cash, please?"

"Yeah, sure," he said without question. "And go where I told you, and don't move from there."

"I won't."

I hung up and clung to myself.

How had things gotten this bad?

"Hey, pretty thing," said that same gruff voice.

I tried to back away, but the brick way got in my way.

He grabbed my arm with his huge hand. "Did you change your mind?"

I felt it coming, but there was no way I could stop it.

PANIC.

And once it started, there was no stopping it.

I'd learned that many years ago.

Take With a Grain of Salt

JAKE

THE PLACE WAS a fucking mob scene.

Without hesitation, I pushed my way through the crowd and shook my head when I looked in the direction of the cage. One guy had the other on the floor, and his fists were pummeling down without mercy.

AX was one archaic place.

Bare-knuckled fights without protection. Choke holds, eye gouging, groin attacks, the only rule was there were no rules. Over the past few months, I'd seen these guys come through the ER claiming they'd fallen or gotten into it with a buddy, but the bruising around the neck and bloodied knuckles always gave it away.

Whatever, I wasn't there to judge. My job was to keep them alive. Nothing I did could stop them from wanting to kill each other.

The volume of people inside was unreal. Those who weren't watching the fight were either drinking or smoking or looking for a good time. It smelled like piss and vomit and cigarettes everywhere, yet hands were exchanging hundred dollar bills like it was a fancy casino in Las Vegas.

I searched for the sign she'd told me to look for, and then strode past it down the hallway she'd mentioned.

It was where the restrooms were located. It was dark, and water dripped from copper pipes above. There was no doubt the place had once been condemned and was now occupied for the sake of off-the-grid illegal activity only.

A payoff here and there must be what was keeping them open for business. With any luck, not for much longer.

There were a few dudes in leather loitering about halfway down the corridor. This set me on edge. It could be a drug deal going down, or perhaps a plan was being hatched to inspire a good time.

Who the fuck knew or cared, so long as it didn't involve Jules or me. To help ensure that, I pulled the hoodie of my sweatshirt up and started down the yellowed linoleum. Drawing attention was the worst thing I could do in a place like this. Invisible was what I wanted to be.

Christ! Jules would be anything but invisible with that bold dirty blonde hair of hers and those big green eyes.

Every muscle in my body tensed and my hands made fists so tight my knuckles ached when I thought about what an easy target she was.

These guys were all hyped up, one was bouncing on his toes, and another was throwing punches in the air. They did, however, seem in their own world. Exchanging stories of fights they'd seen go down, they barely appeared to notice me. I kept my cool and made casual as I breezed by them. Giving the only one guy who looked my way a slight nod, I then quickly averted my gaze.

I wasn't a chicken shit, by any means.

In fact, I was a black belt, and I could probably take all three of them if I had to.

I just didn't want to have to.

I had to find Jules.

The women's restroom was where I'd told her to go. I had no idea how safe it was or wasn't, but it was better than anywhere else I could think of since she'd refused to leave.

It was just ahead, and I glanced over my shoulder to see if any of the guys I'd passed were watching me, but no one was. They were too caught up in the insanity of this place to displace their attention for long.

I huffed in a huge breath and pushed inside. It was hotter than hell in here. I glanced around and saw only one small window opened for ventilation.

The room was quiet despite the open window. Having no idea if anyone was in there, I peered down like a peeping tom to look under the stalls. Only one was occupied, and by a pair of red Converse. Uncertain if it was her or not, I whispered, "Jules."

The door opened slowly with a creak that seemed way too loud, and there she was standing in the opening staring at me with wide green eyes.

"Are you all right?" I asked.

"I'm fine," she answered, her voice low, shaky and her hands gripping the edges of the stall frame.

I wasn't convinced.

"You shouldn't have come here alone," I barked, taking a step forward to inspect her.

She came closer to me. "I had to, Jake. I didn't have a choice. I already told you that guy said he was going to throw my cousin out on the street if I didn't come get him."

I looked her up and down, and not because I was turned on, but because I was concerned. The blood had drained from her face, her breathing was slightly labored, and she seemed unsteady on her feet. As my gaze rose, I noticed a large red blotchy spot just above her elbow. "What happened to your arm?" I asked, gently taking her wrist to lift her limb.

"It's not a big deal."

"What happened?" I asked again, a little more sternly this time. Upon examination, the redness didn't appear irritated or punctured in any way, but more like a hand mark, like someone had grabbed her.

She tugged her arm away before I could finish looking at it. "I said I was fine."

"And I said, tell me what happened!"

She stared up at me wide-eyed with resolve. "Fine. When I was outside calling you, some drunk creep approached me and took me by the arm, but I took care of the situation."

There was no way to explain the surge of adrenaline that spiked through me, the need to put that motherfucker in his place. I wanted to find him and tear him limb by limb.

It was crazy.

No, it was insanity.

Acting out irresponsibly in that way could cost me everything I'd worked for.

With a muttered curse, I shook off the white-hot rage that was threatening to consume me and focused on Jules. "How exactly did you take care of it?"

She smiled a bit, and right away that put me mildly at ease. "I kneed him in the balls and marched back inside."

Fuck, yeah.

Smirking at her, I pulled her against me like it was the most natural thing in the world, and then I stroked my hand over her cheek. "What are you, some kind of ninja?"

She leaned into my touch for just a moment, but then she pulled back and looked up at me. "How did you know?"

The comedy she found in the situation wasn't really funny.

However, the fact that she could find it so fueled an insanely crazy need to kiss her. I couldn't right now, though. *Focus. I had to focus.* "Other than being slightly delusional, where'd you learn to do that?" I asked instead, thinking it would be a great skill for my sister to learn.

"Finn taught me. And we should probably go get him, he really didn't look good."

"He's in the office at the end of the hall, right?"

She nodded. "That creep said he'd keep him in there until I returned."

Creep. The term probably wasn't that far off the mark . . . for either of the men.

Looking at the way her tits filled out that tank top like half oranges, I unzipped the beat-up navy sweatshirt I was wearing and handed it to her. "Speaking of creeps, put this on, and pull the hood up. We'll draw less attention that way when we leave."

To her credit, she might have wanted to refuse, but she said nothing. Instead, she surprisingly held her arms back for me to help her into it. From behind her, I reached around and zipped it. She smelled like sunshine in a place that smelled anything but. I had an urge to hold her for a moment, and I had no idea why. Hugging was definitely not my thing. Besides, my sister did enough of that for the both of us.

I took her hand. "Come on, stay close to me."

Back in the hallway, the group of guys had cleared, and it was empty. With quick strides, I was knocking on the closed metal door that read, "Manager," in a matter of seconds.

Manager.

That was a joke.

More like human janitor.

"Go the fuck away."

I raised a brow as I looked over at Jules. "I got this," she told me. She put her face close to the door. "It's Finn's cousin, I'm back to get him."

When the door swung open, I had to admit I was clearly impressed. "He's awake now," the burly dude with lettuce stuck in his beard, grumbled.

He looked me up and down. "Who the fuck are you?"

I looked around the shabby office and wondered what the hell her cousin was doing in a place like this. "A friend."

"Friends ain't welcome."

Jules stepped forward and breezed right past him. "He's here to help me get Finn to the car. And don't worry, you'll still get your money."

Those beady eyes of his narrowed on me "Fine then. Saves me the trouble," he muttered, and then he held his palm out. "I'm guessing you're the ATM."

I wanted to shove the twenties up his ass as I pulled them out of my pocket, but I wasn't stupid either. Getting into it with this prick wasn't going to make getting out with a defeated fighter in tow any easier. Besides, by the looks of the heap of a body in the corner, it was already going to be tough enough.

I held out the money though, he could take it himself.

"Finn, are you okay?" Jules asked her cousin.

He mumbled something that at least gave me hope he was alert enough to ambulate.

She looked over at me. "He says he's fine."

Without appearing to be overly worried, I strode over toward Finn and Jules and then squatted down. "Do you know your name?" I asked him.

"Finn," he mumbled. "Finn Easton."

I tracked his pupils. "Do you know what day it is?"

He looked over at Jules, and she nodded at him. "Saturday," he answered.

"You know why you're in here on the floor?"

"I was knocked out," he said, his lip more than a little swollen and impeding his speech.

"What the fuck are you, a doctor or something?" the human janitor asked.

Finn was alert at least, and I felt comfortable enough that getting him out of there should be the first priority.

The sound of shuffling feet was quick, and huge boots were beside me. "Cause we don't allow medical attention to be given in the building."

I glanced up. "Do I look like a fucking quack?"

It wasn't like I denied who I was. I simply asked a question.

For some reason using the term for a sham doctor seemed to satisfy him. "Just get him out of here," he fumed, and then he turned and stormed out of the room.

"Come on," I told Finn as I hoisted him up.

Jules went to his other side.

"I'm good," he told her.

I pulled his arm over my shoulder. "I need that sweatshirt back," I told Jules.

She removed it, and I couldn't help but watch the way she moved. The shape of her body. Her slight curves. Once she handed it to me, I put it on Finn and pulled the hood up. If the crowd saw him, there was a chance he'd get heckled. This way we might slip out somewhat unnoticed.

Before I opened the door, I asked him, "Have you vomited?"

He shook his head no.

"You know, you should go to the hospital for a scan."

Again, he shook his head no. "I don't have any insurance. It'll be too expensive."

"Finn!" Jules admonished, "Don't worry about that."

"No," he said firmly.

I nodded. "How about I examine you first, and we decide after?" To that he said nothing.

As soon as we stepped outside the office and into the hallway, he broke free of me. "I need to walk out of here on my own."

The main room looked even more crowded than when I'd arrived, and the crowd sounded even rowdier.

It wasn't a bad idea.

"Jules, stay between the two of us. I'll lead the way." I told her.

Jammed wall-to-wall with bodies, even though I had her hand, and she had Finn's hand, it was hard to weave through the mass and stay together.

Jules wrapped her arms around my waist to stay close. I tensed and sucked in a breath, realizing the shaking I felt was a physical response to her body. And the feel of her front to my back had me wanting to do very bad things to her. I couldn't recall a time any woman had sent a shiver racing down my spine.

Outside, she let go of me, and I didn't like it. I wanted to keep her cocooned in safety until we could get out of there. After taking another few deep breaths to shake off whatever this was, I turned to check on Finn.

"My vehicle is over here," I said, "Let me get you back to my place, and I'll take a better look at you."

"We can't go to Rosewood!" Jules exclaimed.

"Not Rosewood," I said. "My apartment in mid-town."

She nodded. "Do you want me to follow you?"

"No. I want you to ride with me. I'll bring you both back here tomorrow to get your vehicles. They'll be fine until then."

"But your car is too small."

"I didn't drive my car. I borrowed the night nurse's Explorer."

"Matthew's?"

I nodded. She remembered.

Finn was quiet but keeping pace. The air was humid, but still so much better than inside. I wiped my brow and kept moving. When we got to the truck, I opened both the passenger and back doors. Jules slid in, and I closed her door, and then helped ease Finn down. As he slowly sat, he stopped for a moment to say, "You must be the infamous Dr. Kiss I've heard so much about."

Normally, I would have cringed over the use of Dr. Kiss and what he'd said, but tonight I found myself grinning. "Don't believe all the bad shit your cousin says about me, I'm actually a decent guy."

He nodded. "I know you are. She told me."

"Finn!" she exclaimed. "Shut it."

I laughed as I closed the door. He might have been banged up pretty bad, but at least he was talking and tracking.

The rear window was jammed open about an inch, and as I walked around the vehicle, I heard Finn say, "Relax Jules, it wasn't like I told him you think he was made for you."

Made for her.

What the hell did that mean?

Burn the Midnight Oil

JULES

I PRESSED MY fingers to the cool glass.

Atlanta was never dark, but it looked more alight than ever from the forty-fifth floor of Jake's apartment. Painted in a silver and gold wash, everything down below appeared almost magical. The streetlights resembled twinkling lights, and Lake Clara Meer seemed more similar to a reflective mirror than a body of water.

Yet, the reason I was there was about as far from magical as you could get. I was in way over my head. That was becoming clearer and clearer by the day. As if running Easton Design & Weddings into the ground wasn't bad enough, now I had Finn risking his life to help me build it back up.

Things couldn't go on like this.

I hated to admit it, but maybe I wasn't cut out to run a business of such large scale. I loved planning weddings. I loved the parties. It was the business dynamics I sucked at.

Expenses. Invoicing. Checks and balances.

It was all too much.

The sound of a door closing had me whirling around. Jake had been in his guest room with Finn for over an hour, and I was a nervous wreck.

Barefoot and looking exhausted, he came down the hallway, running a hand through his damp hair. In fact, his entire body looked damp.

"How is he?" I asked.

Jake started toward the kitchen. "He's going to be fine. Nothing broken. And as far as I can tell, a few bruised ribs and a mild concussion is the worst of it. I helped him take a shower and gave him some clean clothes. He's sleeping now."

Relief washed through me, and I sagged back. "Jake, I don't know what I would have done without your help tonight."

With his bottom lip in that state of semi-permanent pout he wore so well, Jake stopped at the small bar in the kitchen. "He shouldn't have been there."

I swallowed the lump in my throat. "I know that, and I'm sure he does as well. He was doing it to help me."

Lifting the whiskey bottle, Jake gave me a knowing nod, and then he started to pour the amber liquid. "I told your cousin I'd introduce him to a friend a mine whose father is the general counsel for the UFC. If he wants to fight because he has demons to slay, that's his business, but he needs to be smarter about it."

I started for the sofa where I'd left my purse and phone. "You'd do that for him?"

Setting the bottle down, he looked up. "Sure, if it will help him out."

My eyes found his but dropped a little when I noticed the way his shirt was sticking to the sculpted muscles of his chest. "That's really nice of you."

Jake smirked a little and cupped his ear. "Say that again, I don't think I heard you."

I grinned at him. "You heard me."

He reached for a bottle of wine. It was Pinot Grigio, and of the Cupcake variety. This made me smile. "I didn't buy this for you."

"Oh, I didn't think you did," I quipped. "I mean it fits so well among your bottles of vintage varieties, it's like it belongs right where it was on your shelf."

Looking up at the fine bottles of wine that obviously he had collected over a long period of time, he shrugged. "I figured I'd help the company out."

When he started to open it, I stopped him. "I should probably call for a ride and go home. It's late."

Ignoring me, he poured the wine into a glass. "You can't leave. You have to help me check on your cousin throughout the night."

Alarm shot through me. "What do you mean? I thought you said he should be fine."

With a glass of whiskey in one hand and wine in the other, he started toward me. "Finn needs to be woken up every couple of hours to make sure he's alert. Nothing to worry about. It's standard practice for concussions. And then he needs to be watched for the next three days as well."

Suddenly, I felt nervous. He'd rejected me by ignoring my text. Oh, God, the text. Obviously, I'd gone overboard. "Yes, of course. I can sleep on the sofa."

His lazy gaze drifted over me, warming my skin as if he'd touched me. When he handed me the wine, he said, "You do have other options, you know."

Setting my purse back down, I took the wine and sipped at it. "Oh, and what might those be?"

He lifted a thumb and pointed to the hallway opposite of where Finn was. "I have a really big bed in there. I'm more than willing to put myself out and share it."

I frowned at him. "Why didn't you respond to my text?"

He finished sipping his whiskey. "I didn't get a text, or unlike you, I would have responded."

My expression turned to confusion. "You didn't get the video I sent from my bathtub?"

A half smile curved his lips upward. "No, but I'm more than intrigued. Were you naked in the bathtub?"

Pulse racing, I tripped over the coffee table leg when I went to set my glass down and landed face first on the sofa. Crawling across the leather the few feet I had to go, I dove for my phone in my purse as soon as I reached it.

Jake sunk onto the sofa beside me, his gaze more than intrigued as he watched me intently bring up my messages.

Still on my knees, my heart was pounding against my ribcage when I saw what I'd done. "No. No. Nooooo!"

It hit me like a brick.

I'd searched the letters Ja and never noticed I hadn't selected Jake Kissinger.

Instead, I must have tapped on Jaxson Cassidy.

Oh, my freaking God, Jaxson!

Quickly, I typed out a message.

Me: Jaxson, I'm so sorry. Please disregard the video.

Him: You have some explaining to do.

Me: I will. Later. Promise.

Without asking, Jake took the phone from my hand and looked at the screen. "Who's Jaxson?"

Deflated, I answered in a pathetically sad tone. "My ex-fiancé."

Jake's eyebrows climbed. "You were engaged? What happened?"

I looked down at him. "Yes, but Jaxson and I weren't right for each other, so I broke it off."

"How long have been broken up?"

"Almost a year."

He was quiet for a moment.

When I couldn't take it, I tried to snatch my phone back.

Jake held it just out of my reach. "Oh no you don't. I'm going to watch this."

"No way!" I reached across him, but his hold on it was too tight.

His gaze met mine. "I'd think after everything I did tonight, you'd be more than willing to let me watch something that was meant for my eyes to begin with."

Resigned, I flung myself back on the couch and covered my eyes. With my feet on the sofa, I peeked through my fingers just enough to see him.

How was this even happening?

He set his empty glass down and then angled one leg over the other as if settling in for a movie—of the porn variety.

As soon as the sound of running water filled the quiet, sparse room, I felt my cheeks flush.

My on-camera moans were loud, and I had to fight my physical reaction to his response. His pupils flared as if a raw hunger had ignited inside him. When he watched me climax, he sucked in a breath. Thinking about what it would feel like with his very real, very thick cock inside me, an uncontrollable shiver worked up my spine.

The sound of the water lapping mixed with the noises of my climax filled my ears, and I knew the video was almost over. By the time it ended, Jake's chest was rising and falling at a very rapid pace.

He was turned on.

I could see it in the way his jaw tensed. The way he bit his lip. The rigidity of his body. *The outline of his erection.*

It only took Jake a moment to look away from the screen. When he did, his gaze was hot and heated, and on me. "Fuck, you're so hot. Show me your pretty pussy."

I blinked. Did he just ask me to show him my pussy?

He did.

I know he did.

Was it like *you show me yours, and I'll show you mine?*

I looked down at his thick erection.

I wanted to see it. Touch it. Feel it. I wanted to own it.

And yet I didn't respond. I couldn't. But my body did. My nipples hardened and pressed against the silky material of my bra causing arousal to shoot through my body in a blast of heat.

He untied my Converse. "That was a tease."

"In what way?" I managed to ask.

"You made yourself come for me but never showed me so much as a glimpse of what you were touching. I want to see it. Show me." His voice was so husky it sounded like gravel.

My entire body was trembling. "Right here?"

His nod was slow and seductive. "Right now. I can't wait another second."

I was still on my back, and I was looking at him through my spread thighs. Like this, he had a bird's eye view of my denim-covered pussy and would have the same view of my naked one. "But what about Finn?"

Pulling both of my sneakers off at the same time, he let them drop to the hardwood. "He's asleep, and won't wake up for hours."

"You mean until we wake him up."

"Yes, until we wake him up, in *two* hours."

Two hours.

It didn't get past me that we had two hours of time to occupy.

With shaky fingers, I unsnapped the cool metal. Was I really going to strip for him? *I was.*

The small noise that eked out of his throat convinced me I made the right choice. My panties were already damp. They'd been that way from the first moment I saw him, no matter how many times I'd changed them.

I wasn't telling him that.

Pulling on my zipper, it ratcheted apart tooth by metal tooth. I could feel the cool air whoosh over my skin when my fly opened. I hooked my thumbs in the sides of the denim to push them down.

Jake's features had turned almost primal as he watched me slide the fabric over my hips and thighs. The jeans were tight, and I had to lift my hips to ease them down.

Slow.

Slow.

Slow.

I kicked out of them.

"Take off your panties," he whispered in a voice rough-edged with need.

My breath was coming in short, harsh pants as I easily slid the tiny piece of lace down and then kicked it off.

I gasped when he got to his knees and circled his fingertips around my ankles. "Spread your legs, Jules."

Automatically, my legs went slack, falling open and baring myself to him.

With just his fingertips he brushed over my smooth pink flesh. "Fuck, you're perfect," he groaned.

Nobody had said that to me in a very long time.

Using a single finger, he dragged it along my folds in a teasing manner. "You're so wet. I can't wait to taste you, to be inside you, to make you come."

I couldn't stop the hitch of my breath or the thump of my heart or the smile on my face.

The tease was over, and he withdrew his soft touch and then rested both of his hands on my knees. "Take your top off, and your bra as well." This time I didn't have to think twice. With the way he was looking at me, I would have done just about anything.

Without waiting another second, I lifted the hem of my tank and pulled it over my head and then reached behind and undid my bra. Once I'd pulled my arms out of it, I tossed the pieces to the ground. And then hesitantly, I raised my gaze, holding my breath as I looked back up at him.

"Fucking perfect," he said again, but this time his voice was a low growl of appreciation that sent a jolt all the way to my toes.

There was a discernible bulge between his legs straining at the denim fly, and I wanted to reach and unzip him.

"Do you even know how sexy you are?" he asked.

His question stunned me. "I know the way you're looking at me right now makes me feel sexier than I ever have."

And it was true, under his needy, heated gaze, I don't think I'd ever felt this desired.

Ever.

The only way I could describe the intensity of the moment was to say it was like being brushed with fire every time he raked his hot stare down my body and back up.

I was completely naked now, and yet he didn't pounce. His approach was slow. My toes curled into the couch cushions with the anticipation of what he'd do next, but he made me wait.

Of course, he made me wait.

Then he was crawling. Coming up and over me, his body was strong and looming. When his face was directly above mine, he began to lower his head. I tilted my chin upward and placed my palms against his chest. I ran my fingertips down to his abs, and he flinched beneath my touch, his muscles going tight and quivering. I hastily withdrew, but he caught my hands with one of his and guided them back. "Don't stop."

I didn't.

And then all at once, his warm, sensual mouth was moving exquisitely over mine and one of his hands was sliding up my body, and I couldn't move. The feel of his skin on mine was pure bliss.

I sighed into his mouth.

The kiss deepened. His lips moved strongly over mine, demanding, taking, owning, and his urgency bled into my mouth. "I can't be the only one feeling I'm going to die if I don't get inside you."

The statement was filled with warmth, and seeped into my blood, traveling through my body. "You're not."

He dragged his lips away from mine. "Tell me," he demanded.

"I want you. All of you. I want to taste you, touch you, feel you, have you. All of you," I said breathlessly, my heart surging as adrenaline spiked through my veins.

His eyes were brimming with lust and arousal. "Wrap your arms around me."

I smiled and did just that. As if I weighed nothing, he hoisted me up. His hands slid beneath my bottom to hold me as I hooked my ankles around his waist. He strode out of the living room and down the hall to his bedroom. I clung to him and captured his mouth to give him a wild and hurried kiss.

A kiss to remember.

A single light from the bathroom shone into his bedroom, and it, like the rest of his apartment, was sparse and barren of any color, but the air in the room crackled like electricity ran through it as soon as we entered.

Wasting no time, he leaned over and landed me softly on the bed with my head on a stack of pillows that made me feel like I was floating on a cloud.

Just as quickly as he'd set me down, he stepped back and started tearing his clothes off. As soon as he pulled his shirt over his head, I felt dizzy. Dizzy with exhilaration, lust, and need.

I grew impatient at the sight of him half-naked. His strong

shoulders, muscled biceps, and hard sculpted abs had me licking my lips.

I lifted my head as he unfastened his jeans and yanked them down his hips. His desire for me was right there to see in every inch of his tightly coiled body. He was hot. So freaking hot.

Standing there, his erection was straining, and his eyes burned over me with blazing heat.

My pussy throbbed and ached for *him*.

Him.

His muscles bunched as he crawled up the bed. My heart never pounded so fast. Grasping my legs, he spread my thighs open wide. I had never been so vulnerable and so turned on at the same time.

"Oh God," I whimpered.

Those eyes flared and then his head dipped.

"Oh God," I cried out again when his hot breath blew over me, and he kissed me there. Right there. When he licked me, his tongue flicked and teased. I drew in a breath. It had been so long since a man had gone down on me. Too long.

His lips worked my clit as he pushed a finger, then two, then three, inside me. Rough, but not harsh. He found my G-spot, and I think I convulsed around his fingers. Pleasure took my voice away.

I could feel my climax building, the muscles in my thighs trembling and tightening. He sucked and licked at me and slid his fingers in and out. I pushed my hips upward, and he fucked me with his mouth and hands and tongue until I gasped and trembled. I was heading for the cliff's edge. Fast.

Trembling, I looked down at him nestled between my thighs. Passion hazed my vision, but everything became crystal clear when he paused to look up at me.

"Don't come yet." His breath drifted over my wet flesh mercilessly.

"Jake, please," I protested.

He moved up my body and captured my wrists with his hands as he pushed mine over my head. "No touching yourself."

It was a tease of course, but it felt more like torture. "Jake," I whimpered.

His head surged down, and he kissed me, his tongue moving against mine in such hard, quick strokes, it was almost punishing. "Patience," he chuckled.

My fingers curled around the headboard to fight the urge to touch myself just for a respite of relief, and I watched him as he fumbled in his nightstand for the package of condoms and slid one on.

When he moved back over me, he positioned himself between my thighs. "I can't go easy, Jules."

"I'm good with that," I breathed out, my voice a husky whisper.

With one hand on his cock to guide it inside me, he stared at me with those intense blue eyes, and then I felt the tip of his cock push into me. He paused only for a moment before surging fully into me.

The shock of his entry nearly sent me over that same edge I'd come so close to moments ago, but I didn't want to fall. Not yet. This was too good to end so fast.

My eyes closed as he filled me. When he moved, I moved with him. His fingers dug into my hips, and then he slid his hands up my belly to my breasts, palming them and tugging at my nipples.

Unable to stand it, I let go of the headboard and slid my hands up his arms to settle on his shoulders. He was so strong, and I reveled in the idea of touching him everywhere, all night long.

His palms went flush against the mattress as he fucked into me faster. Then he was back up on his hands and driving his cock deliciously deeper. He withdrew and thrust forward again, jolting my body with the force of his reentry. "Did I hurt you?" he rasped.

I couldn't even draw a breath. I was lightheaded from the exhilaration and anticipation. "No. Don't stop," I cried out when he slowed.

His gaze seared into me, so intense that I shivered. "I won't."

My gaze was riveted to him, to his mussed up hair, his hard body, his soft touch.

He reached down, grasped my legs and pushed them both upward to wrap around his waist, and then pulled us both into a sitting position. Oh, God. Like this I was so tight around him, I wondered how he could possibly even move.

"Jake," I cried out at the same time he cried out, "Juliette."

Juliette.

It sounded so right coming from him.

Our gasps mingled, and the sounds of passion filled the room. Like this, I lifted my body and slammed myself down on his cock.

This was raw. Real. Primitive. We fucked hard and fast. No boundaries. The thrill of the next surge only driving me higher and higher than I had ever climbed.

The brink of orgasm was right there, but I had to keep chasing it up the mountain. I closed my eyes to stop myself from reaching the top. I wanted to see just how high I could go. Just how good it would feel.

"Keep your eyes open." He thrust deeper into me. "Fuck," he whispered, "keep your eyes open."

With my hands in his hair, I found his heated gaze and lowered my mouth to his.

"You feel amazing," he grunted against my lips.

I moved faster against his thrusts, my heart racing out of control. "So do you."

"Juliette." His grip on my hips tightened. "Juliette."

"Jake," I whimpered back as he thrust at just the right angle and I knew I had reached the top.

"Fuck." He started to pump even harder, faster.

I was shuddering against him in tiny jerks trying my best to stop the fall and stay on top for just a little longer. The feeling was almost surreal. *One I never wanted to go without.*

His eyes glittered. "Come for me, Juliette," Jake commanded, his voice gruff with need. "You're so tight. Come around me. Let me feel you go wild around my cock."

He was deep. So impossibly deep that I could feel nothing but the pulsating hardness of his cock as it drove inside me.

I let out a sharp cry as my orgasm flashed, explosive and intense. The fall into oblivion was higher and longer than I'd ever experienced, and it was with an intensity that I never could have imagined. Suddenly all those clichés I'd made fun of seemed so real. The earth shifted. The ground moved under my feet. I was on cloud nine.

As I floated back to earth, Jake held me to him and his rhythm increased. A few seconds later, his face pressed against my neck, his hips jerked, and I felt the release of his climax.

I shuddered.

He shuddered.

We held each other tight until our bodies stopped trembling.

And when our gazes met again, we both fell to the mattress in a heap and laughed.

Jake moved to get rid of the rubber in a nearby garbage can and then slipped beside me. He rolled to the side with one arm and laid one leg over my body.

I looked at him. Watched as his hand moved lazily up and down my body in smooth, flat strokes.

"Jules."

"Yes," I said.

"That was—I don't even know how to describe it." His hand centered over my pussy, his fingers dipping into my wet folds.

I opened my legs wider, loving the feel of his soft touch, and craving more, even though we'd only finished having each other a moment ago. "Out of this world. Amazing. Fantastic." I threw a few words out there.

He stroked my pussy. Up. Down. Soft. Softer. "Yeah, all of that," he laughed.

"I like it when you touch me," I told him.

A wicked grin crossed his lips, and he dipped his finger inside me. "I like touching you."

"I like it when you call me Juliette, too."

His breath puffed hot on my shoulder and he kissed me. His lips pressed to my skin. His fingertips settled on my clit, and he circled lightly. "Why don't you let anyone but Monty call you that?"

I was on my back looking up at him with my legs spread wide. He was on his side looking down at me, stroking me. And yet I found myself sucking in a breath and saying, "I tell everyone it's because I was teased so much in school about the whole Romeo and Juliette thing, but that's a lie."

He stopped his stroking. "Why is that a lie?"

I took his hand and started to move it for him, telling him in my own way I wanted to feel his touch when I divulged the truth, and he figured it out because he dipped his fingers inside me and then started circling my clit in slow, even motions. Not enough to get me off, but enough to make me feel that tingling sensation a woman wished she could hold onto forever. "I think it's because it reminds me of my parents, and sometimes I don't want to be reminded."

Jake didn't stop playing with my clit, but he looked down at me with such intensity I felt like he knew exactly what I meant. "Do you want to tell me about them?"

I arched up, letting the good feeling in and trying to push out the bad. "They were perfect. More in love than anyone I've ever known. And then they died, and I had to leave New York and come here to live with my uncle. That was sixteen years ago, and I still miss them."

He drew in a breath and his hand stopped.

"Don't stop. Please, Jake, don't stop. Let me feel this instead of the pain."

And he did. He brought me to orgasm. Taking his time in a slow and steady motion, and although I didn't climb the highest mountain, the fall was equally intense.

When I settled against him, I took his straining cock in my hand and started to stroke it. He shivered under my touch. He was big and thick and beautiful, and his skin was so soft. I wanted to touch him forever.

He reached for a picture on his nightstand and brought it back to show me. The light was poor, but I could see it enough.

I stopped my stroking.

It was of an older man in a doctor's coat and a young man who, although much scrawnier and smaller, was still the spitting image of the older man, and there was no doubt who the younger man was.

He set the picture back down and took my hand and started moving it. "Don't stop."

I didn't.

I found his gaze. "Was that you?" I asked, already knowing it was.

He nodded and let his legs fall open. "With my father, before he died," he said, and then he closed his eyes as if wanting to block out the pain that accompanied the memory with the pleasure of my touch.

I understood.

I stroked up, circled his tip, and back down to circle at his base, and then lower to cup his balls.

His mouth fell open.

My heart pounded. He was silk and steel in my palm. I moved a little faster. Up. Down. Circling his width, stroking. I wanted to make him feel good. To help ease the pain of what he had yet to tell me.

His mouth parted on a small gust of breath when I moved faster. He fucked into my fist, and then he was crying out, short and rough, as his orgasm jetted onto his belly.

I watched the rise and fall of his chest, and then he opened his eyes and looked at me. "How did your parents die?"

My lips trembled, but I held myself together. "They both died in the World Trade Center attack. They both worked there. My father was a K-9 unit officer in the Explosive Detection Division for the Port Authority and my mother worked for Silverstone Properties."

Jake sucked in a breath, and then he was silent for so long, I wasn't sure he hadn't fallen asleep with his eyes open. "My father died there that day trying to pull people out. He wouldn't have even been there if it wasn't for me. It's my fault he died."

"Jake," I gasped, rolling onto him, not even caring that his sperm was still on his belly. "Don't say that."

His gaze was distant, and I knew he'd gone to that place I'd been to so often. That place where the hurt was so intense, you thought you couldn't survive it.

The thing was, I'd been there too, and because I had, I knew how to bring him back. "Tell me what happened," I whispered, knowing if he did it was going to open old wounds that had never healed.

Jake wrapped his arms around me and rolled us onto our sides. I was facing him, and we were close, so close, and yet he moved closer. It wasn't until we were a breath apart that he opened his mouth to speak.

I braced myself.

I heard my pulse start to race.

What he was about to tell me was going to hurt both of us, but this time we had each other to help ease the pain.

And I knew it would make a difference.

It had to.

chapter
19

Drastic Times Call for Drastic Measures

JAKE

Sixteen Years Earlier

IT WAS TUESDAY.

I hated Tuesdays.

Hated them ever since my father moved out three years ago and used his day off as his visitation day.

Rory was too young to know the difference. She thought it was fun when Dad came over and took us to school and then picked us up and brought us out to dinner.

I hated it.

Hated him.

For leaving us.

For leaving us with her.

Monica Alexander Kissinger.

Our mother, and completely incompetent.

My father worked at New York Presbyterian Hospital in the city and *recently moved from Connecticut to the city to be closer to work. He also refused to let us come live with him. Well, he hadn't exactly refused. He was working on that, but the laws regarding custody weren't that easy, or so he'd said.*

And then there was the fact that Monica was a well-known socialite with connections and was fighting him tooth and nail.

Whatever.

All I knew was that Monica was passed out in her bedroom, and I was the one getting Rory ready for school.

So he could fuck himself!

Pissed off that Monica wouldn't even get out of bed and I had to deal with all the shit that was his responsibility, I texted him a message and told him not to come. That Monica had insisted on taking us early to meet the teachers since school had just started back up and didn't want to have to see him.

That was a big, fat lie. Not the not wanting to see him part. Monica loathed him. But the part about school. I didn't even think she'd ever set foot in either of our schools or knew what grade we were in, or even where our schools were for that matter.

I looked around at the mess in the kitchen and heard the stumbling on the stairs. Monica had come down looking peaked and a mess. She rushed to the sink where she vomited. Looking over at me, she said something I couldn't understand.

I didn't care enough to ask her to repeat it. "I can get us both to school," I barked, and walked away, assuming she was apologizing again for her bad behavior.

The thing was I'd been covering up for Monica my whole life, and I was tired of it. I'd been filling in, doing what she was supposed to do, and keeping it to myself. Which was why I was in the place I was.

I got Rory on the bus, and then walked to school. I was early and hit the basketball court for a not so friendly game of pick up.

When the bell rang, we all hustled inside.

I glared at the teacher when she returned my paper with an F. "See me after school, Jake. I want to discuss this with you."

I flung the paper onto the floor. "Don't bother. I really don't give a shit."

She stood with her mouth opened and pointed to the door. "Principal's office, now!"

Whatever.

I took my time walking to the office and realized what a dumbass thing that was to do. She would just call my mother, who wouldn't answer, and then she'd call my father, who would. He'd be pissed off, disappointed in me, and give me the lecture about how if I wanted to be a doctor like him, I had to do better in school.

I

Did.

Not.

Want.

To.

Be.

Like.

Him.

"Wait outside," I was told when I arrived.

I sat on the bench with my head down and pondered what to say.

I could come clean and tell her I was drowning.

That I couldn't take care of my sister and my mother and do my homework and come to school and lie to my father and get good grades.

It was all too much.

That my mother had now started bringing strangers home at all hours of the night and waking me up with the noises she made while banging them.

That in order to make sure Rory didn't wake up and hear her, I'd carry my sister out to the car until the dude or dudes would leave.

The door opened, and when I looked up, I saw the horror on Principal Mears face. "Jake, go back to class."

I blinked. "But I was sent down here."

"I know." She was crying. "Please go back to class."

Okay, I thought. That was easy, but why was she crying?

I didn't have to wonder for long.

Her voice came over the PA. "Students, there has been a great tragedy. A plane has flown into the World Trade Center. The reason is unclear, but we are canceling school for the day."

Unclear?

What did that mean?

Canceling school had to mean it meant something bad.

My blood went cold.

I had to get to Rory.

I ran as fast as I could out of the main doors and all the way to Rory's school. Mass chaos was taking place there as the news had broken. I didn't care about protocol or signing her out or that I was authorized or not.

I went to her class and called her into the hallway through the glass. She came out, and I told her we had to leave. She cried that her favorite pink bracelet was in her desk.

"Leave it," I told her.

"I can't. Daddy gave it to me and told me when I wear it to think of him."

"Why did you take it off?" I gritted through my teeth.

"It's too big. It keeps falling off."

I waited for her to go get it, and then I took her by the hand and brought her home.

As soon as I got there, I turned the television on. A plane had flown into one of the towers, and they no longer thought it was an accident.

It was an attack.

We were under attack.

I tried to call my father.

He didn't answer. He always answered when I called. I left him a message. "Dad, call me please, we need you."

Monica stumbled down the stairs with a bottle of vodka in one hand and a cigarette in the other. "Aren't you two supposed to be in school?"

"Mommy," Rory ran to her. "Look at the television. New York City is under attack."

She puffed on her cigarette and blew it out. "Oh, good, maybe it will wipe out the whole city and your father, too."

Rory clung to the silk of Monica's robe. "Don't say that, Mommy. It isn't nice."

My mother pulled her back and slapped her across the face. "Don't ever tell me what to do and not to do."

The hatred I felt for Monica at the moment was unlike anything I'd felt in my life. "Rory, come over here."

"You're just like him," Monica muttered. "Always the do-gooder."

"I'd rather be like him than you," I answered.

"Oh yeah, what do you think I am?"

"A drunk."

Just then news of a second plane flashed across the screen. I held Rory tight and prayed for the first time in a long time that my father was on his way here.

But as the hours passed, I heard nothing from him. I kept trying to reach him. I didn't understand why he wasn't answering his phone. It was around nine at night when the phone rang.

"Hello?"

The voice was rough. "Can I talk to Mrs. Kissinger?"

"This is her son, she's out, can I help you?"

"Yes, Jake, this is Dr. Peter Wright."

"Dr. Wright, have you heard from my father?" He was my father's friend and colleague.

"Listen, son, I really need to talk to your mother."

I looked around the room, and then down at Rory who was asleep next to me. "She isn't here. Is this about my father? I can't reach him, and it's not like him not to call."

He ignored me. "Can you ask her to call me?"

"She won't call you, Dr. Wright, come on, you have to know that. Please just tell me where my father is."

A pained sound emanated from deep in his throat. "Son, your father went to the World Trade Center today to help with the victims, and—"

My world turned black.

I tuned the rest out.

He was dead.

Later that night, when I was beside Rory in her bed, I heard Monica come in the door, and even on a day like this she wasn't alone. The music turned on and I smelled smoke and heard her drunken voice.

I didn't have the energy to carry Rory out to the car tonight.

Anger burned through me, and I stormed downstairs. I found my mother and some young guy dancing around the living room. I went over to the stereo and turned it off.

My mother's head jerked in my direction. "What the hell do you think you're doing?"

"Rory's sleeping. Do you think you could keep it the fuck down for once?"

Monica was scratching her thin arms, and her pupils looked smaller than I'd ever seen them. I had no idea how drunk or high she was, just that she was out of control. She practically leaped toward me and slapped me so hard, blood leaked from my mouth. "Don't you ever talk to me like that!"

With a shake of my head, I turned my back on her and walked away. I was so done with her.

Upstairs, I heard Rory sniffling. I rushed toward her, and when I did, she sat up and looked at me. "Jake," she cried.

"I'm here," I said.

She took her little fingers and wiped the blood from my lip. Then she lifted her wrist and looked at the sparkly pink bracelet she was still wearing that was way too big for her before slipping it off. "I want you to have this."

"It's yours," I whispered.

"But you need it right now."

I took it from her. "I'll keep it safe for you. Now, go back to sleep."

"I can't. I'm worried about Daddy. What if he never comes to get us? Who will take care of me?"

"I will," I told her.

"But you're not a grown up."

She was right.

I might have felt like one, but I wasn't.

That's when I grabbed my phone. Rory couldn't grow up like this.

"Hello?"

"Mimi, it's Jake. You have to come and get us."

And she did.

chapter
20

Through the Dark, I See the Light

JULES

THAT DAY MARKED our entry into an exclusive club—a club no one would ever, ever wish to join.

We were the children of those tragically killed. There were over three thousand of us under the age of eighteen.

Each of us suffering through the never-ending DNA tests, the endless phone calls, the personal items identification process.

I'd blocked it all out.

Never talked about it.

This was, in fact, the first time I had shared my story or listened to another.

When Jake opened his eyes, they were the saddest, bluest eyes I'd ever seen. I knew I could drown in them, and I also knew I could pull him out of the water.

Tears fell from my eyes, but I forced myself to keep it together. For once I stayed strong.

I gazed down at him and threaded my fingers through his hair to push it from his handsome face. "Jake," I whispered, "I'm so sorry for what you had to go through, but your father's death wasn't your fault. You have to know that."

He shook his head. "A part of me does. A part of me knows my father would have made it to the World Trade Center even if he was in Connecticut, because that was just who he was. Helping people was in his blood."

I stared at him in wonder. "And you followed in his footsteps. I'm sure he's looking down at you with pride."

His own eyes filled with emotion and his voice was hoarse when he said, "I never really hated him. In fact, I think I always wanted to be like him, I was just afraid I'd end up more like her."

I pressed a sweet kiss to his lips. "You are a strong, kind, and giving man. And you are you."

With a laugh, Jake rolled us over and looked down at me. "I'm not sure if you see me differently than the world or if you're just blinded—"

Cupping his face in my hands, I cut him off. I didn't care what he thought I was blinded by. His good looks. His arrogance. His brooding personality. His alpha tendencies. It didn't matter. "I see you the way you are. I see you perfectly."

He shook his head and then he lowered it, stopping just before my lips. "We have thirty minutes before I have to check on Finn. Let's not spend any more of it talking."

"But we're not done—"

His mouth met mine like a fever, and the flashpoint of heat melted me. Like this, I forgot what I wanted to say.

All I knew was that we were connected through tragedy, and somehow that made this kiss even more intense than any of the others.

My head fell back as his teeth nibbled at the curve of my throat. He let his free hand roam, over my skin, my angles, my slight curves.

Had I ever been kissed like this before?

In that way that the meeting of lips, of tongues, of teeth, vibrated through my entire body.

Dazzling.

Hot.

Sweet.

Seductive.

I knew I hadn't.

So I kissed him back.

And he kissed me.

And then we kissed some more.

I wanted him to kiss me forever.

When Pigs Fly

JAKE

THE INTIMACY OF the night had thrown me for a loop.

As the sheet covered our bodies from head to toe, I didn't want to think about the same heartbreaking pasts we shared. Instead, I thought about her, and touched her, and then touched her some more.

Caressing my hand down her back, I lightly nipped at her shoulder with my teeth. She giggled, and I swore the oddest thing happened to me—my heart skipped a beat.

What the hell was going on with me?

She laughed from inside our cocoon. "That tickles."

I buried my face in her neck and sucked on the spot behind her ear I'd already discovered didn't tickle her as much as drove her wild.

Her breathing picked up the minute I applied pressure there with my lips. She might not be ticklish in that spot, but it definitely turned her on.

"Does this tickle?" I murmured in her ear, knowing already it didn't. Knowing the more I sucked, the wetter she would get. The hotter she would get. The more she'd beg.

"No," she said, and her voice sounded breathy.

We'd spent most of the night exploring each other's bodies. I checked on Finn every two hours, and he was doing fine. Irritated. Sore. And in need of sleep, I'd decided to give him three hours before waking him again.

When Juliette and I had finally fallen asleep, it was almost dawn. With the light streaming in my room now, I wasn't sure what time it was, just that it wasn't early morning anymore. I didn't really care either.

I nipped at her earlobe, and she giggled. The sound was one I was beginning to really like.

The soft chime of my alarm told me exactly what time it was. I rolled over onto my back and pulled the sheet from our heads.

"What are you doing?" she asked.

"Going to check on Finn." I sat up.

She burrowed out of the sheet and crawled up to lay her head on my thigh. "Is it time already?"

"Well, I do have ten minutes." I reached for my phone to see if I had any messages, but then I looked down at her. Her grin was wide and her hair was a beautiful mess of tangles. As soon as I saw that smile, I unclenched my hand and left my phone where it was. "You know what, ten minutes can be a really long time."

"It can be," she grinned, "but we should probably use that time to shower."

"Together," I added.

Just then her stomach rumbled.

"Are you hungry?" I asked.

"A little." Her eyes seemed to light up at the thought of food.

"Okay, tell me what you want."

"You," she whispered and nipped at the skin of my thigh.

With a growl, I lifted her chin to look at me. "I meant what food do you want, but I like your answer better. Let's go ahead and shower, right now."

She looked away and then covered her face with her hands.

"Why are you acting shy all of a sudden?"

She lifted her fingers from her eyes. "I'm not, but I have to tell you something before we get in the shower."

I raised an eyebrow. "And what might that be?"

Her cheeks flushed. "The day I went to Rosewood to meet with your sister, I saw you masturbating in the shower," she confessed.

I bit my lip. "I know."

She bolted up. "You know? How do you know?" she asked horrified.

The grin on my face had to be priceless. "I saw you in the reflection of the mirror."

"Oh God! Why didn't you say anything, or close the door, or tell me to get lost, or . . . or . . . or stop."

I took her face in my hands. "I didn't want to. It was hot watching the way you reacted to seeing me touch myself."

"Hot? That was not hot. Well, I mean, you were hot. You were really, really hot, but—"

The things she got flustered about were sexy as fuck.

Did she even know that?

"I'll do it for you again sometime, if you want." I offered her a cheeky grin.

Her eyes hooded and her lips parted. "Okay, I'm good with right now."

Laughing, I got out of bed. "Well, I think we could probably do something together."

"That works, too."

When I turned to take her hand and lead the way, her earrings glistened in the sunlight the exact same way they had the first time I saw her at the bakery, but I realized right then that wasn't the first time.

The enormity of how I knew her, where I knew I had seen her before, hit me hard, and I sat on the edge of the bed.

She wrapped her arms around me. "What is it, Jake?"

I twisted around. "Your earrings."

It didn't make sense, I knew, but I had to catch my breath.

Touching one of them, she said, "What about them? They were my mother's favorite pair. I wear them all the time."

I shook my head. "No, that's not what I mean. You attended the circle of honor at Ground Zero in 2002."

It wasn't a question.

I knew she had.

She nodded. "Yes, just before the candlelight ceremony in Battery Park. President Bush and the First Lady attended," she said, and then swallowed. "How do you know that?"

"I saw you there," I said my voice going low. "You were talking to the Mayor. I saw your blond hair and the way your earrings sparkled in the sunlight and the sadness on your face. It was something I knew I'd never forget."

Her stare remained blank as if she'd gone off to that far off place that was filled with nothing but darkness.

"I came up to you right before the air filled with the solemn sound of "Amazing Grace" and gave you a single white rose."

"Oh my God, that was you? That was you!"

I nodded. "I saw you looking around at everyone holding a flower."

She smiled a sad smile. "And you said, "here you don't have one, and you should," and you handed me one."

At the same time, I said, "And I said, here, you don't have one, and you should," and then I handed you mine."

Juliette crawled onto my lap and pressed her forehead to mine.

"You were my hero that day."

I shook my head. "The heroes were those we were there to mourn."

She cupped my face in her hands. "Yes, they were, but to me, you were also one."

I wrapped my arms around her, and held her tight. I didn't know what I was feeling or how I felt, but I knew it was something I'd never experienced before.

I was no one's hero.

chapter 22

Your Guess Is As Good As Mine

JULES

THE WEEK PASSED by in a flurry.

Jake had worked eight nights straight. I had worked eight days straight.

Him, at the hospital.

Me, on Rory's wedding.

I'd only seen him once, and that was four days ago. It was the Friday afternoon I'd spent at Rosewood to meet with the potential caterer, and he had woken up early and brought me to the pool house.

That didn't mean we hadn't been in touch though. Talking on the phone and texting had occupied a good portion of my days this week. We'd seemed to climb some wall, and what was on the other side held no barriers. He told me about what it was like when he moved into Rosewood, and why he went to medical school in New York City. In turn, I was able to tell him about my parents and Diogi, and smile at the memories, not cry.

It was a first for me.

The air just felt lighter with him on the line.

I sighed.

We talked about everything. I asked him why he worked as much as he did and he told me because he was good at his job. That he liked helping people. Liked learning what he didn't learn in medical school. That in his first year out of residency he was putting in his dues. And that working nights allowed him to stay away from the administrative rules he found suffocating. It allowed him to take care of the patients.

He had me at the confident way he told me, *"I'm not just good at my job. I'm great."*

"Tony the Tiger," I'd snickered.

Work wasn't all we talked about.

We talked about sex.

Boy, did we talk about sex.

From everything to first times to past lovers. About limits. About sex drive. About our positions on using condoms or not using condoms. Since I was on birth control, I wasn't opposed to not using condoms as long as both parties were tested. We'd agreed to both be tested and go from there.

We also talked about stupid things like if we could only eat one food for the rest of our life, what it would be. Mine was spaghetti and meatballs. His was grilled steak and potatoes.

The list went on.

Favorite colors, sports teams, movies, games, and exercise routines were also discussed.

Jake was fun to talk to. Our conversations were easy. His texts were flirty and sometimes dirty. They made me smile and made me blush.

"What's that grin for?" Finn asked, dumping a pile of folders on my desk.

The business space we occupied was small—one office, one conference room, and a lobby where Finn was temporarily located, and not exactly thrilled about it.

I picked up the files and glanced inside. They were the measurements for each of Remy's twelve groomsmen. "I'm not wearing any grin, and great job on gathering this information so quickly. I'll get it over to the tailor today."

He rolled his eyes. "Emailing a bunch of dudes for their measurements isn't exactly rocket science."

I raised a brow and slid the list of twelve women his way. "Good, then contacting the bridesmaids should be a piece of cake."

The bruises on his face had faded but were still evident. "Come on, Jules, you're killing me here. I'm going to look like some pervert."

"Or a Casanova," I winked and waved him along. "The faster we get this information, the faster we can order the dresses. And as you know, time is of the essence."

"How much longer are we open for business?"

I shot him a look. "Don't forget to close the door on your way out."

He threw me the bird.

"Very mature, Finn. Very mature."

Once the door closed, I glanced around my uncle's office. Nothing had changed since he'd left. Nothing had changed in twenty years either. It was looking tired and old and in need of a facelift. That would be for the new owners to decide though.

Uncle Edward hadn't returned yet, so I had called him late last week and confessed the dire situation of the business. Needless to say, he was shocked. Then again, I had infused all my savings into it, so there was very little for him to suspect. Still, I think he breathed a sigh of relief. Me holding onto it meant him holding onto it, and he was more than ready to let go. It was time to sell.

And hopefully, after Rory's wedding, the business would be worth even more than before.

I had my fingers crossed.

As for me, I would have to find a job with another consulting group, which I knew wouldn't be that difficult.

I was crap at finances, but I was good at planning weddings.

At least I had that going for me.

Pulling up the announcement for the Harrison/Kissinger wedding, I gave it one last read before hitting send and sending it to the social media expert I'd hired and all of the appropriate Crawford Media outlets.

In a matter of minutes, it would be world news.

This part of the job was what I lived or. There was nothing like the thrill of seeing all the hard work start to come together.

I glanced at my phone. I had texted Jaxson days ago and told him we needed to talk. He said he'd call me, but I had yet to hear back from him.

I decided to call him.

"Hey, Jules," he answered, sounding distracting.

"Hi Jaxson, I was just calling to make sure you received the information I sent you for the Kissinger wedding. Sorry it's on a holiday weekend."

I heard him tapping the keyboard. "Yeah, I got it, and that works out great. I didn't have anything booked."

I looked at my own computer screen and the screensaver of the picture he had taken of me on my uncle's farm. I loved it out there. "Okay, great, I was just checking," I said. "So, about that video," I added.

He laughed. "Right, that video. I have to say, I don't remember you ever doing anything like that when we were together."

I went silent.

He laughed some more. "I'm teasing you, Jules. I'm glad you

found someone who brings something out of you that I couldn't."

"It's not that," I started to say but he cut me off.

"It's all good, and I've already forgotten you even sent it to me."

"So we never have to talk about it again?"

"Never," he said. "Listen, I have to run, but we'll talk soon."

"Bye, Jaxson," I said.

"Bye," he replied, and then hung up.

I stared at the picture on my computer. It was taken on a beautiful fall day a couple years ago. Red, yellow, and orange leaves were everywhere, and I was sitting in a chair out near the barn, researching an upcoming wedding I was planning. He'd snuck up on me and called out my name. I glanced toward him and he snapped my picture. We were happy together, but even then, something was missing. Whatever it was had always been missing, I supposed.

The shrill of the old dial phone beside me rang. "Easton Designs & Weddings," I answered. "How can I help you?"

"There are at least ten different ways I can answer that, three of which require you to get on your knees."

It was Jake, and for whatever reason, there was *nothing* missing between us.

My nipples peaked in arousal at his innuendo, and I had to force myself to play it cool. "Who is this?"

"Who else talks to you like that?"

"Let's see," I tapped my chin. "There's the butcher, the baker, and the candlestick maker."

"Not funny."

Amused by myself, I tsked. "Why are you calling me on my business line?"

"Pretend to answer again, and I'll tell you."

"Okay, I'll play along." I cleared my throat. "Easton Designs & Weddings. How can I help you?"

Heavy breathing filled the line. "I just got back from a run. I'm in the shower touching myself and wondered if you wanted to come watch."

A blush heated my cheeks in the most schoolgirl way. With a quick glance out the door, I looked at Finn, who thank goodness was hunched over his computer typing away and paying no attention to me. "Stop that, Jake," I admonished in a whisper. "I thought we already settled that issue."

His chuckle tickled my eardrum. "We did? Refresh my memory—exactly how did we do that?"

"Remember the whole *why watch when you can touch* thing," I purred. It was so unlike me.

"Then come over and do just that." He got right to the point.

I sank back into my chair. "I can't. It's three o'clock in the afternoon, and I have work to do."

"Come over." His voice had turned husky, low, filled with desire.

My whole body zinged from just the thought of it. "Jake, stop it. I can't."

"My grandmother wants to meet with you to discuss the wedding."

I bolted up in my chair. "She does? Why didn't you say so to begin with?"

He laughed. "Yes, she does. And I'm going to ignore your comment."

"When?' I asked.

"Today."

"What time?"

"Six."

"Okay, I can be there, but don't you have to work?"

"Yes, I do. I think the two of you should meet alone. It will make her feel like she's a part of this."

"Okay, but she's your grandmother."

He laughed again. "Juliette, put on your big girl panties and come to the business meeting with Beatrice Crawford Alexander."

I sneered through the phone line. "I'll put on my big girl panties all right."

"Good, and after you do, as your client, I'm requesting you come early."

I smirked.

My client.

I was 'doing' my client.

That sounded kind of naughty.

I cleared my throat. "That can be arranged. Will we be discussing the flower arrangements or the wine selection?" I asked with a smirk on my face.

"Juliette, I'm about to stroke my hand down my cock."

Lust whooshed in my lower belly. "I'll be right over," I said and hung up.

It was ninety-five degrees. With the high humidity, it felt even hotter. My car barely had time to cool before I was inputting the gate code Roger had given me, and then pulling through the iron bars. I parked next to the vintage Jaguar that Jake had told me belonged to his father.

The car made even more sense.

I could tell he wanted to be like the man, and I was fairly certain that was why taking the trauma unit in New York City was so important to him.

It was like he had something to prove . . . to himself.

I grabbed my bag and got out. Steam practically simmered on the brick pavers, and I felt myself melting before I even reached the front door.

Fanning myself, I pondered what to do.

Hmmm . . . did I ring the bell and tell Roger the man of the house was expecting a booty call? Or did I just go on in and up the stairs?

At least I didn't have to figure that quandary out.

The door swung open before I had to make a decision, and Jake's searing gaze washed over me immediately with a hunger that ate me up. I'd dressed comfortably thinking I was going to be in the office all day—a knee-length cream slip dress with strappy sandals. The dress was nice enough with its chiffon overlay that I didn't have to change before coming over to meet his grandmother, everything but my undergarments, that was. The underwear and bra I'd picked up on super sale during lunch, so they came in handy.

Jake's eyelids lowered in such a smolder you would have thought he could see them with x-ray vision, and that wicked look sent off a rush of tingles between my thighs.

"Hi," I said.

In gym shorts and a T-shirt, with his trademark fresh out of the shower wet hair, he looked so freaking sexy. He leaned forward and his hot breath whispered across my lips. "Let's go up to my room."

My whole body tightened at the thought of what he'd do to me once we got there. I sounded a little breathy when I replied, "Shouldn't you say hi first and invite me in?"

Bowing like Roger, he ushered me forward. "Hello, Juliette, would you like to come inside so I can fuck your brains out?"

A smile tickled my lips. "I suppose I would."

That was when he grinned at me—a huge, wide smile that made my heart flutter. "You're too much," he said, and then he picked me up and tossed me over his shoulder.

I kicked my feet. "Jake! Put me down!"

Ignoring my pleas, he carried me all the way up to the third floor and marched into his room. I lifted my head to look around. I was in his boyhood room. There were plaid curtains, and posters on the walls, and basketball trophies on the shelves.

Closing the door with his bare foot, he stopped just before his bed, his small double-sized bed, and smacked me on the bottom.

I yelped in surprise. "What was that for?"

"For being such a smartass," he said, as he tossed me onto the mattress and followed. We were a tangle of arms and legs and laughter, but it didn't take long for the laughter to get swallowed up in a deep, hot, heart-stopping kiss.

I wound my arms around his neck and curled my fingers into his hair as our tongues stroked, and our teeth clashed, and our mouths crashed.

There was a desperation between us that hadn't been there before. Four days suddenly seemed like way too long to be apart. Hungry for him, I pulled at his T-shirt, and he quickly jerked it over his head, finding my mouth again just as quickly.

We kissed and kissed and kissed until we both needed air, until our lips tingled, until we couldn't stand not being naked.

Rising up on his knees, he slowly pushed my dress up past my thighs, up over my stomach, my breasts. His touch was warm, searing, and inviting. I reveled in it for a few short moments, but then I raised my arms above my head so he could pull the fabric off me easier.

His eyes devoured me, raking me over as I lay under him in my hot pink lace bra and panties. "Hot pink, I like it."

I shrugged. "It's old."

"Liar."

With wide eyes, I balked, "Excuse me."

Reaching down, he pulled something from my bra, and it snapped.

"Ouch," I yelped.

He held the tag in his hand. "Old, huh?"

Oops.

Forgot about that.

I grabbed the tag from him. "I got it on super sale, so it was old merchandise in the store."

Shaking his head, he ran his fingers over the lace of the cups and licked his lips. "It's sexy as fuck."

Sexy.

He was the sexy one.

My skin tingled where his fingers were caressing it, and the rise and fall of my breath was so fast that I dropped my gaze. It landed on the thick arousal stretching across the fabric of his gym shorts and my breath hitched even more.

When I looked up, our eyes met, and I knew lust had overtaken us. I lifted my head and he lowered his and then our lips met again.

Fireworks.

There were fireworks in the middle of the day.

His hand flattened on my stomach, and he smoothed it upward between my breasts, where he unclipped the front clasp and eased it off. "You're so fucking beautiful," he murmured.

Cool air rushed over my breasts and they swelled under his admiration. The goosebumps on my skin came naturally as he stroked me softly, his thumbs brushing over my nipples in a gentle circular motion.

When he bent to take me in his mouth, his erection pushed against my belly. I sucked in air and fought the dizzying sensation that swarmed me.

Jake started to move down my body, but I stopped him by pulling on his mussed up hair. He looked up. "Ouch."

I was shaking my head. "It's my turn."

The wickedest grin crossed his face, and he flung himself onto the bed like an eagle. "Have at it."

Okay, that was way too easy. Maybe he really had been touching himself earlier and was even hornier than I thought, or maybe he just really wanted this.

Rising up on my knees, I straddled him, and his cock sprung up between us. It was like a steel rod of heat on my belly.

Deliciously hot.

I tried to ignore the fact that Lebron James was reaching out to me from the Sports Illustrated poster over the bed that read, "THE CHOSEN ONE."

The chosen one.

It almost felt like a sign.

Of what I had no idea, but I did know that his skin was warm where I'd put my hands on his chest and that I could feel his heart thump steadily beneath my palms.

Reaching up for me, he cupped my face and brought my mouth to his, and our lips locked instantly. I pumped my hips against his erection, and a lustful and needy throb bloomed between my legs.

It wasn't until I was breathless that I broke away from his mouth. When I looked into his blue blue eyes, they were gleaming, like the sky through the window and shining just like the sun.

I paused for a heartbeat just to look at him. He really was beautiful, if you could say that about a man. Not pondering on his looks for long, I bent to lick down his neck with my tongue.

Inch by inch, I inhaled the fresh, clean scent of him. I was going to take my time. Trailing my tongue down his body, I outlined the hard muscles of his shoulders. When his body went taut under my touch, I couldn't think of anything but him and what I wanted to do to him.

I wanted to go slow.

Take my time.

I wanted to tease him.

Torture him.

While my lips glided down his body, his hands were caressing me—up my back, down and around to my sides, up to my breasts. It was as if he wanted to touch me everywhere.

I liked that.

Really liked that.

With a smile on my lips, I licked at his nipple, and he sucked in a breath. And then I counted his ribs with my kisses, and he chuckled. When I reached his sculpted stomach though, his belly muscles quivered beneath my touch. That was when my smile faded. I found myself dizzy for air. As I went even lower, I felt him quake, and I couldn't go slowly any longer.

I did that to him.

Made him shake and tremble and gasp for air.

With deft fingers, I pulled down his bottoms and kissed the bare skin of his cock. My hands and my mouth worked in tandem down his length to his balls, and back up.

For the very first time with him, I took his cock in my mouth, and the mewing sound he made had me closing my eyes in wonder.

What was this thing between us?

We hardly knew each other.

We were both at crossroads in our life.

And yet, knowing that didn't seem to change this chemical reaction between us. It should have. It should have been a warning. I didn't understand it. All I did know was that I wanted to be with him as well. I wanted to touch him. To feel him. Every beautiful inch of him. For as long as I could.

"Don't stop," he groaned. I hadn't realized I had. I didn't hesitate to pick up from where I'd left off.

He shifted on the mattress with a sigh that sounded so erotic it made my own body tremble.

I pushed my hands under his ass to lift him closer to my mouth and then I took him all the way in.

"Oh, fuck, Juliette, that feels so good. Take me as far as you can. All the way."

I did as he told me and took his cock down my throat as far as I could. Over and over. Tip to base, my mouth sucked him, my fingers stroked him, my lips and teeth and tongue moved together.

Soft words and louder groans told me how much he liked it and I kept going. I wasn't going to stop until he was overtaken by pleasure.

When I sensed he was close, I asked him, "Do you want to come in my mouth or inside me?"

His hips thrust upward. "I want to come inside you," he whispered.

More than ready for that too, I sat up and pulled him up with me. "That's good, because I need you to be inside me," I whispered.

He had a condom on and me on my back before I could blink the sun out of my eyes. And he was sliding his cock in me within moments. "You're so wet for me."

I ran my nails down his back. "It's because you have me aroused all the time lately."

He grinned. "Oh yeah, tell me more. Do you think of me when you're getting into bed at night?"

I nodded.

He moved in and then out. "Do you touch yourself when you're talking to me on the phone?"

I nodded again.

He moved faster and changed position.

"Oh God," I screamed out.

"Do you make yourself come with my name on your lips?"

"Yes," I cried.

That electric shock of connection we shared was the first thing I felt followed by a sizzling awareness that, all joking aside, maybe he really was perfectly made to fit me.

"You're so tight, and you feel so good around my cock. And I can't stop thinking about being inside you," he confessed.

Sex.

That was what this was.

All this was.

Good sex.

Great sex.

Feeling his body all over mine was all I needed to expel my silly notions of anything else.

He was leaving.

I knew that.

Yet, it didn't mean my heart did.

A swell of emotion bubbled through me. I forced it away, and then I let go of everything except making sure my hips met his over and over. When his pace picked up, so did mine.

Flesh on flesh.

Frantic.

Grasping.

My moans couldn't be contained. It felt way too good.

"Do you like that?" he asked.

"Yes. Don't stop," I pleaded and then, out of nowhere, trembling spasms of pleasure started to sweep over me. My fingers clutched his shoulders as the tremors kept coming.

Over and over, like electric shock waves that felt way too good for any one person to be able to enjoy.

Jake groaned at the slight gouge of my nails in his flesh.

I couldn't help myself.

The sound only tipped me farther over the edge. My orgasm continued, and my entire body began to shake.

He drove himself deeper, moved faster, and my pussy responded by clenching around his cock.

"Oh, God, Jake. Don't stop." The sweet pleasure rippled through me again as he pounded harder, faster, harder, faster.

"Fuck!" he cried in a shout that matched my own cry, and I knew then that he, too, was coming. He murmured my name, over and over, a little louder each time.

"Juliette."

"Juliette."

"Juliette."

Hearing my name, my full name, made me feel like my blood was singing.

Once we were both spent and gasping, he shifted his weight off me. After tossing the condom in the wastebasket, he rolled onto his side.

I turned to face him, and we stared at each other for at least five minutes.

My hand caressed his cheek. "Talk to me," I said. "What are you thinking?"

He kissed my fingers, each of them, and held my hand tightly. "I'm thinking about how I could fuck you a million times, and it wouldn't be enough."

I wasn't sure that could possibly be true, but bedroom talk was bedroom talk for a reason.

He slid his lips lower and murmured, "I want you to sleep here tonight."

"Here?" I breathed, "like in your room with your grandmother in the house?"

When he looked up at me, with the sun shining through the windows, he looked so much younger and more carefree than he had when I first met him. "Yes, here, in my room."

"Jake," I tried to protest.

His hand reached between my thighs. "I want to slide in next to you when I get home."

I arched.

He circled my clit. "I want to feel how wet you are for me all the time."

I moaned.

His finger dipped inside me. "I want to taste you."

I sighed.

He parted my swollen, slick folds with his thumbs. "I want to be inside you."

I rose onto my elbows. "I'm pretty sure you'll be inside me again in a matter of minutes."

He found no humor in my words. "It's not enough. I already told you, I can't get enough of you."

The air whooshed from my lungs. This was coming from the man who wanted to make sure I had no expectations. But I said nothing about that. There was no way I was going to ruin the moment. If this was what no expectations felt like, I'd gladly take it and more. "Okay," I acquiesced. "I'll spend the night, but I have to go to work tomorrow."

"Good," he murmured. "I'm off for the next three days, so I can join you."

"You want to come to work with me?"

He nodded and removed his hands from their pleasuring of me to hop out of bed and grab for another condom. "You've been asking for my attention."

I stared at the way his cock was jutting straight out and tried to still my racing heart. "Yes, I have been, for the wedding," I clarified.

He rolled the condom on and then his gaze went molten. Need sizzled over my skin when he indicated I should roll over. His instruction would have been laughable if I weren't so caught up in the haze of desire. "I know," he said silkily. "You want my opinion on the flowers, the food, the wine, and the music, right?"

On my belly, I looked over my shoulder. "And the napkins and favors and cake and photographs." I had to add those.

He pulled me close to the edge of the mattress. "Yes, those things as well."

Instinctively, I rose on my knees and planted my palms forward. "Good,' I quipped.

The blunt head of his cock nudged against my opening. I couldn't believe it. I'd just had him, and still, I was crawling with need.

He slammed into me. "And I plan to give it to you."

Oh God . . . he sank deep inside me, his cock fitting in my cunt in the most perfect way.

His thrusts were quick.

They felt so good.

His kisses rough.

They felt so good.

His grip tight.

It felt so good.

Moving together, we fucked hard and fast. And all the while, incredible bursts of pleasure crested through me, making my entire body shake.

My orgasm struck fast and shut my mind down. Tiny explosions behind my eyelids were all I could see, and in that moment there was nothing else that mattered but he and I and the way our bodies responded to each other.

Jake started to come in the midst of my orgasm. I could feel his body still and felt that one last deep penetration before he called out my name.

My name.

I loved how it sounded groaned in ecstasy.

It was the perfect ending to an incredible union.

With my clit pulsing around his cock, I wanted to stay like that forever. It was strange, but at the moment, I didn't care about what could never be, or what might be.

This feeling was what I had been searching for.

"And oh, how I plan to give it to you," he repeated.

Oh. My. God.

He wasn't talking about directing his attention to the wedding details. He was talking about this. Sex. Fucking. Raw. Dirty. Animalistic fucking.

The promise slid over me like silk, warm and inviting, and so sinfully sexy.

Bring. It. On.

chapter
23

Cross That Bridge When You Come To It

JULES

THE HALLWAY WAS longer than a football field, and my sandals clacked down every foot of it.

I swear the sound was so loud I would have woken the house if anyone was upstairs, and if it weren't six in the evening.

As I proceeded down the back staircase, I could feel my muscles twitch and my heart pound.

Calm down.

Jake had to leave for work and left me to shower upstairs. And let's just say seeing Dr. Kiss in scrubs and a lab coat was hot. Like really, really hot. I had to practically fan myself.

At least after he kissed me senseless, he told me how to get downstairs without using the formal staircase. Thank goodness. The thought of his grandmother seeing me coming down the stairs, and then me having to explain to her that I was up there because I was banging her grandson's brains out had me wanting to flee out the front door.

When I passed Roger in the kitchen, he was standing at the counter with seven sterling silver bowls in front of him.

He glanced up.

I hoped he hadn't heard Jake and me upstairs.

We had both been quite loud.

I smiled at Roger, who was more than just a butler, and gave him a small wave. In response, he gave me a discreet nod. "Good evening, madame."

My cheeks flushed. "Please, call me . . ." I hesitated. "Juliette."

"Very well, Miss Juliette."

I smiled some more. "It's just Juliette."

Filling the last of the bowls, he bowed. "As you wish, Juliette."

I curtsied. *Yes, curtsied.* "Thank you, Roger."

And believe it or not, that made the corners of his mouth quirk up, just a little, but still.

Yah!

Okay, it was on to meet the woman of the house.

Adjusting my posture as I walked, I thought I was all calm, cool, and collected. However, by the time I reached the parlor, a tiny bead of sweat had formed at the base of my neck, and my heart was pounding even faster. That's when I knew there was a very good chance I might end up in full-on panic mode.

Wishing my anxiety away, I drew in a deep breath as I stared at the wooden panels.

One breath.

Two.

Three and four.

Exhaling the air I'd taken in, I shook off any residual anxiety and raised my fist. Mrs. Beatrice Beau Crawford Alexander had summoned me to the parlor to discuss her granddaughter's wedding. This was nothing out of the ordinary.

I'd met with clients at their homes all the time.

It should have been business as usual.

Still, it felt like anything but normal.

From what I'd already known and the research I'd recently done, Beatrice Beau Crawford Alexander didn't like to speak to outsiders. Known for being ruthless, she'd fired more people than she'd hired, however that could be.

According to the old newspaper clippings, she was a homebody who'd never really let the world know who she was.

Unless you took the time to look at the charities she'd funded, the clubs she belonged to, and the places she'd gone. She'd funded a number of local charities, especially those for underprivileged kids and traveled to third-world countries up until five years ago when she was first diagnosed with cancer.

Ironically, the media outlets she didn't own called her a bitch. Perhaps it was the competition that was the bitch. Fingers crossed that was the case.

I knocked lightly and waited. No one answered. I knocked again. This time a little louder.

God, my heart was pounding.

What if I looked at her the wrong way?

What if she hated me?

Fired me on the spot and ordered me out?

Oh, God.

Just as I was about to knock one more time, the front door swung open and a wave of heat blasted through the foyer followed by a trotting noise. I glanced over my shoulder expecting to see Roger with the dogs. However, it was not Roger.

It was her!

A cold sweat coated my forehead, and as I turned, I discretely wiped it away. Southern women never sweat, they glistened, and I couldn't have her seeing me as the Yankee I was.

This was Beatrice Beau Crawford Alexander.

The Beatrice Beau Crawford Alexander.

The media mogul.

And Jake's grandmother.

His beloved grandmother.

A famously private millionaire who fought to run her family business in a time when females didn't often take the helm of large enterprises, and then went on to become the most successful female CEO in Atlanta.

Mrs. Alexander was a woman to admire.

The older woman was in a wheel chair and being pushed inside by a man in black scrubs. Five dogs flanked either side of her, with Mr. Darcy in front and Daisy on her lap.

She was small, petite, and had big blue eyes. It was evident her genes were strong because Rory looked just like her. Her red headscarf was silk, and she was wearing a cream kimono with red cherry blossoms printed on it. Her slippers gold and the pearls around her neck were beautiful. When she smiled brightly at me, she said, "Juliette, I'm so glad we could finally meet."

There was a real possibility my knees were actually knocking together, and it took me more than a second to find my voice. "Mrs. Alexander, it's a pleasure."

The man I assumed to be Matthew had stopped to unleash the dogs, and as I rushed over toward her so that I could greet her with a handshake, I was literally stopped in my tracks.

Mr. Darcy insisted on his greeting first and got right up on me. Losing my balance, I was knocked backward and landed on the third step of the grand staircase.

"Mr. Darcy!" Mrs. Alexander scolded. "Leave Juliette alone."

"I got him," Matthew called, rushing toward me.

"Mr. Darcy," I cooed, letting my bag fall to the ground in a clamor to free my hands. "I think you want my attention."

"Yes, well, he is an attention whore," Mrs. Alexander said as she laughed.

Giggling, I waved Matthew away, who was on Mr. Darcy's heels to retrieve him. "It's okay," I said.

"Matthew, please help her out. Mr. Darcy has to learn some manners," said Mrs. Alexander.

Now seated, I was at the same height as Mr. Darcy, and I allowed him to say hello to me with a lick before I took his face in my hands. "Well, hello there, I'm happy to see you, too."

As Matthew pulled the giant dog off me, Daisy barked, and the other dogs joined in. It was rather chaotic, but I could see how much Mrs. Alexander loved her dogs as she attempted to appease each of them.

Roger must have heard the commotion because he was on it. Standing in the dining room doorway with a bowl in his hand, he clanked a spoon against the silver and called, "Dinner time, my loves."

In an instant, all the dogs went charging toward him. I couldn't believe it. I also couldn't believe the manner in which the proper English man addressed them. My heart swelled a little. It showed how much he cared for them.

Turning my head, I found Matthew wheeling Mrs. Alexander toward me. "Are you alright my dear?"

"Yes." I grinned, getting to my feet and fixing my dress. "I'm fine."

Her eyes twinkled. "My babies have taken to you just as my grandson has, and I can see why. You're simply a delight."

With no time to process her comment, I extended my hand. "Mrs. Alexander," I said, "it's a pleasure to meet you."

Wait, I already said that!

"Nonsense," she opened her arms and reached for me. "Call me Mimi, and I insist on a hug."

As I embraced her, I couldn't believe how frail she was. "Mrs.

Alexander—Mimi," I corrected, and then pulled back.

She looked up at Matthew. "This is Juliette. Isn't she beautiful?"

With a flush, he extended his hand and I took it. "Nice to meet you."

I smiled at him. "Nice to meet you, too."

Neither of us said anything about the AX and the fact that Jake had to borrow his truck last week and then never got home in time to return it because he was in bed with me. I'm pretty sure Matthew didn't care though since he got to take the Jag in exchange.

Taking hold of my hand, Mimi gestured toward the dining room. "Come, my dear. Eat dinner with me, and we'll talk all about the wedding and Jake."

Dinner wasn't the plan, but how could I say no?

Besides, I had told Jake I'd spend the night, and now all I had to do was go home and pack a bag. I didn't have to worry about cooking, which I really hated doing.

Speaking of eating, back in the same dining room I had taken breakfast in almost two weeks ago, things felt so much different.

Lighter.

All that panic I'd felt then for not, and all the panic I'd felt just minutes ago was for nothing as well.

I had to learn to calm down.

This woman, who had been dubbed an eccentric recluse in everything I'd read, was nothing like she'd been described. Maybe like Jake, she was all bark and no bite. Or perhaps there was never even a bark. Just rumors she never bothered to set straight.

And that takes a strong woman.

I hoped I was maybe just a little like her.

The chair at the head of the table had been removed so Mimi's wheelchair could fit in its place, and I sat to the right of her. Matthew left us alone.

The table was set exquisitely, and it was apparent she was

expecting me for dinner, something Jake had obviously decided not to mention. This oddly made me smile. He knew me already. Knew I would be even more nervous at the prospect of dining with his grandmother, not just meeting with her.

Still, he was going to get an earful from me.

Mimi lifted the bottle of wine from the table, and my eyes darted to it. The bottle of Cupcake Wine was Pinot Grigio.

Did Jake buy stock in the company or what?

Bottles were popping up everywhere.

"So." Mimi poured wine into the gorgeous crystal glass in front of me. "Tell me about yourself."

A delicate pattern of roses lined the rim, and I found myself staring at it.

"It was my grandmother's. She had two of them sent all the way from France. They were handmade for her."

I looked up. "They are exquisite," I told her holding the glass up to the light.

She smiled at me. "Jake told me you were curious about everything around you. Curiosity is a very good trait to have."

Oh, if only she knew, she wouldn't say that. I snorted. "What else did he tell you? Some good things, I hope."

She shook her head, eyes bright with affection. "All good, my dear. He really adores you."

Practically choking on my wine, I coughed a bit and then managed to say, "Adores might be pushing it a bit far."

"Well, you did throw cake in his face," she smirked.

I was horrified. "He told you about that?"

The glass in front of her was filled with water, and she took a sip from it. "He tells me everything. Although he never used the word *adore*, I can tell he is falling for you, and it's not just because the sex is great."

This time I did spit my wine out all over the place setting in front of me. "He told you we have great sex?"

She chuckled. "No, there are some things Jake refuses to discuss with me. Even though he's my grandson, he's still a man though, and I can see it written all over him."

I covered my face with my hands, knowing my blush must have gone from pink to crimson red in that instant.

"It's okay, Juliette, you don't have to be embarrassed. Good sex can sometimes lead to even better things, but great sex can lead to that *once in a lifetime love* that not everyone gets to experience."

Using my napkin to wipe the wine away, I reflected upon what she said, and how she'd said it. "My parents had that," I commented. "Was your husband a once in a lifetime love?"

I knew very little about the man she'd married. There wasn't much printed about him other than he had been a famous Italian racecar driver and that they had divorced.

She waved her hand through the air. "That bastard. Oh no. Lorenzo was a good for nothing husband who couldn't keep it in his pants. The day he left me was one of the happiest days of my life. But before him, I had fallen for someone that my father absolutely forbid me to marry and then he arranged for me to marry Lorenzo to be certain I didn't disobey his wishes."

Shocked, perhaps even intrigued, I leaned forward. "Who was the man you loved?" Just then Roger came through the door with a plate in each hand and set them down in front of us.

The grin on my face was so wide, I thought my mouth might split open. Spaghetti and meatballs. "This looks delicious, Roger," Mimi said, giving Roger a grateful look.

"Yes, it does," I agreed.

"I'm glad you're both pleased," he said with a bow, and then left the room again.

I stared down at the food.

Jake.

She wasn't kidding. He really did tell her everything. I flushed at the thought as I put my napkin on my lap.

"Eat," Mimi insisted.

I twirled some pasta around my fork and tried to eat it as gracefully as I could. While I chewed, I watched as Mimi moved her food around.

"I hope you like it? Roger was worried the meatball recipe might not be right," she said.

Grinning, I looked over at her. "They are delicious, this is my favorite dish."

She dabbed the corner of her napkin to her lips. "I know, my dear. I know."

"You seem to know a lot," I joked.

"That's because I make it my business to know," she winked. "Now, tell me about Rory's wedding. I have a few requests of my own."

We spent the rest of the meal discussing the wedding and the budget since Jake refused to set one. Even then I had to ask twice. Mimi did have some requests of her own, all of which I mentally noted.

Once we'd finished eating, or once I'd finished, Mimi ate very little, Roger cleared the table and brought coffee, tea, and chocolate chip cookies, again my favorite kind—without nuts.

I was eating my second cookie when Roger came back in the room. "Madame, I hate to disturb you, but Miss Monica is on the phone, and she is insisting she speak with you about Rory."

Mimi held her hand out. "Very well," she said to him, taking the phone. "Give me a minute, please, Juliette?"

I nodded. "Of course."

She glanced up at Roger. "Do you mind helping me out to the garden?"

"Not at all. It would be my pleasure."

Facing the French door, I noticed the sun had begun to set. Its golden rays penetrated the glass and made everything in the room sparkle bright.

The doors were left open, and the garden was fragrant as a warm breeze traveled inside.

Monica was Mrs. Alexander's daughter fathered by Lorenzo Alexander, the famous Italian racecar driver killed on the track the year following his divorce from Beatrice Crawford. The details of the divorce had never been disclosed, just as her estrangement from her daughter had not either.

I, of course, knew her estrangement from her daughter had something to do with Jake and Rory. Other than that, his mother was one topic Jake steered far away from.

"Monica, absolutely not. I forbid you from attending the wedding." Mrs. Alexander's voice was loud. The news must have broken about Rory's engagement.

"There is nothing further to discuss. Do not come here, neither Jake nor Rory wish to see you."

There was a pause.

"I'm sorry, but neither do I."

Another pause.

"How much will it take to keep you away?"

The silence seemed longer this time.

"I want to believe you."

She sighed.

"I hope so, Monica. And it isn't that I haven't taken that into consideration, but Jake and Rory haven't seen you in sixteen years. I can only hope you will give them their space to grieve once I'm gone."

There was more silence.

"Monica, I think you should know that once I'm gone, I have informed Roger that if you renege on your promise to maintain your distance, he is to call my attorney and immediately stop the monthly stipends. Then you will truly be cut off."

There was a long pause.

"I wish things were different, too."

I could hear her sniffling.

"I hope that's true. Goodbye, Monica."

Silence filled the space, and I tried to occupy myself by looking at my phone. Jake had texted me.

Him: Hope dinner is going well.

Me: Thank you for heads up.

Him: Didn't want you to be nervous over nothing.

Me: Well, I appreciate that, but still paybacks are a bitch.

Him: You can pay me back any way you want. When you go to bed tonight, you can touch yourself, but don't come.

Me: You are so bad.

Him: You have no idea. And if I didn't mention it before, be naked for me.

Just then Mimi wheeled herself inside, and I jumped, my phone flying face up on the Oriental rug beneath the table.

Oh, God, if she reads that I will die a thousand deaths.

Practically lunging for it, I had the phone in my hand and back in my bag in a matter of moments. "Oops," I said, looking over at her.

She now looked tired and worn. "Can I help you?" I asked.

"Yes, if you don't mind Juliette, I'd like to go into the parlor for a bit before bed."

"Not at all." Rushing over to her, I wheeled her out into the grand foyer and across to the parlor. The doors were open, and all of the dogs were lulling around inside as if waiting for her to join them.

As soon as Mimi entered the room, they all came scurrying toward her. I continued toward the center of the room and locked the brakes. Daisy was whining, and I helped her onto Mimi's lap and then sat on the couch beside her chair to pet Mr. Darcy, who believe it or not was patiently waiting for my attention.

"Did you hear my conversation?"

I nodded. "Part of it. I'm sorry, I didn't mean to eavesdrop."

"It's okay. Has Jake spoken of his mother to you?"

"Not that much. Just that he called you when he knew his father had died because he was worried about Rory."

"Yes, he did," she concurred, "and I'm very thankful he did. I had no idea my daughter was so very much like her father until then. I mean, I had an inkling she wasn't doing as well as she'd tried to convince me she was. But if I had known, I would have never allowed it."

I glanced over at her. "Rory and Jake were lucky they had you."

She started to slowly pet Daisy. "Jake and Rory haven't seen Monica since I brought them here. Rory was so young, I don't think not having her mother around impacted her the way it did Jake. For the longest time, he thought he was like her. He isn't, of course, but no matter how hard I have tried to make him see that, he still feels the need to prove he is more like his father than his mother."

"The job that is waiting for him in New York," I said, having already figured that out.

Daisy closed her eyes in contentment and purred like a kitten. "Yes. He thinks if he follows in his father's footsteps, it will make up for something that doesn't need to be made up for."

I nodded. Clearly, she knew Jake had told me about how his father died.

Mimi sighed. "Guilt manifests itself in many ways. It is why I continue to give money to Monica even after all these years."

"But what do you have to feel guilty about?" I asked.

"I should have known that she was incapable of settling down. Conrad thought he could change her. I knew he couldn't, but I wanted to believe he could. That he was her *once in a lifetime*. He wasn't, of course, because people like Monica and her father don't have *once in a lifetimes*.

"After Conrad and Monica divorced, I should have paid more attention to what she was doing. I should have seen what she was doing to her children. The way she was ignoring them. Neglecting them. Conrad was blind when it came to her. He only wanted to see the good. And I was busy building my empire. It's Jake and Rory who suffered. Now by paying Monica, I am assuring she stay out of her children's lives. After all, it was how I got them away from her, to begin with."

Mr. Darcy licked at my fingers. "What do you mean?"

Mimi wiped a tear from her cheek. "All I had to do was dangle a trust over her head in exchange for full custody of Jake and Rory. You see, Conrad wasn't entirely blind. His will left everything he had to the kids. Monica got nothing, not even the house. So she took what I offered without hesitation. And the kids were much better off with me."

I looked at her with compassion.

"I wasn't heartless like the papers reported. I tried to help Monica, but she didn't want help."

My heart ached for all of them. I was sure it was hard.

Mimi took my hand. "My grandson is a wonderful man, and I hope one day he sees that about himself. And you have no idea how much I wish I could be around for that day, but sadly I won't be. Please don't think I'm trying to rush things between the two of you, but you do care for him, don't you?"

I nodded.

"Then you should know, you make him happy."

I scrunched my brows together. "How do you know that?"

She squeezed my hand. "Through his laughter."

I laughed. "What do you mean?"

"I have never heard him laugh so loud and so much as I have since you came into his life. The way it echoes through this house brings tears of joy to my eyes. And it makes me feel like with you in his life he just might be okay when I'm gone."

I wiped my own stray tear away. "I really do care about him, a lot."

"I know. I didn't really have to ask. It's evident, Juliette." She smiled at me. "Promise me one thing."

"I'll try."

"Once I'm gone, he'll be leaving for New York to take the same job his father held."

I nodded, very aware of this.

"When he goes, don't let him slip away as easily as he will want to. He's not good with goodbyes, and he's terrible with relationships. Show him the way."

"To what?" I asked.

"To love, my dear, show him the way to love."

Uneasiness moved through me. "But what if I don't know it myself?"

Just then Matthew came into the room. "I'm sorry Ma'am, but it's time for your medication."

I lowered my head and put it on top of Mr. Darcy's. Mimi gave my hand one last squeeze. "Then gather the strength to find it, for the both of you," she whispered.

Find the way.

It sounded so easy.

Too bad it would prove to be anything but.

chapter 24

Keep Something At Bay

JAKE

TIPTOEING INTO MY own room wasn't something I was used to.

I'd worked much later than I'd planned on, and it was almost six in the morning by the time I'd showered and was finally headed toward my bedroom.

Although I was in desperate need of sleep, it wasn't what was on my mind. There was an itch under my skin I couldn't alleviate.

And it was Juliette Easton.

Who just so happened to be in my bed. Waiting for me. Naked, I hoped.

Opening my door, I smiled when I saw her curled in the middle of the mattress. With the covers to her chin and her head resting on my pillow, she was sound asleep. Slivers of the early morning sunlight bled through the blinds and cast a golden glow on the wall behind her. She looked like a princess the way the waves of her dirty blonde hair fell onto the pillow, all mussed and sexy.

Fuck, how my fingers twitched, because damn it, I really wanted to touch her. So much so that my cock was already rigid and straining. And yes, making things all the better, it was now standing at full attention. "Down boy," I murmured to myself as I circled the bed and set the test results down on the nightstand.

Too bad my dick didn't pay attention to my command. Hey, it knew what it wanted. But who could blame him when what he wanted was so close.

Ignoring the urge to wake her, I carefully pulled the covers back and slid in beside her. And yes, she was naked.

I might have fist pumped.

Closing my eyes, I felt the corners of my mouth tip up as I settled against her. This wasn't what I had in mind, but it wasn't a burden either. Besides, these twelve-hour shifts had worn on me.

I'd just nodded off, or maybe not, when she whispered, "You aren't really going to sleep, are you?"

Hell no.

My body leaped to life at just the sound of her voice. I couldn't tell if she was being a smartass or serious, but either way, I'd show her just how awake I was. Sliding one arm under her and wrapping the other around her, I pulled her tight against my body and allowed my erection to prove my intentions. "Good morning, Juliette," I murmured into her ear.

At that, she couldn't form a coherent response.

"I didn't understand you," I goaded. "But I'm fairly certain it sounded like, "Good morning, Jake," I said, and then I plunged a finger deep inside her. "Am I right?"

"Yes," she cried out.

"Oh, fuck," I groaned. "You're so wet. Did you touch yourself last night and think of me?"

There was a slight nod from her as I nuzzled her neck and then nipped her earlobe.

"Did you come?"

She shook her head no.

Anticipation licked up my spine at how ready she was for me. All I had been thinking about was sinking my bare cock into her sweet pussy. I circled her clit. "But you wanted to, didn't you?"

"I did," she moaned.

"Do you want to come now?"

She ground herself against my cock. "Oh, God yes."

"Good thing, because it's all I've been thinking about." I captured her mouth and consumed her. It was inexplicable, the urge that came over me whenever I was near her. I'd gone without sex for months, but now having her was all I could think about.

Suddenly, she pulled away from me. "Let me jump in the shower really quick."

I shook my head, which was still wet from my own shower. "I'm hungry for you right now, and I don't want to wait."

Juliette turned to fully face me. Her naked body was soft and warm against mine, and when she gazed up at me, her eyes were glowing with that heat that made me weak. There were times when she looked at me I could have sworn I saw something else in those eyes, and this was one of them.

I felt a distant chill wash over me.

That look, what it conveyed, it was dangerous.

Love?

I wasn't sure.

But if it was, I wasn't looking for it.

Didn't want it.

From everything I knew, what came out of it was nothing good.

Heartache.

Despair.

Even death.

Who the hell would willingly sign up for that?

So yeah, love definitely wasn't part of my plan. Besides, the notion was crazy. People didn't go from hating each other to falling in love in a matter of two weeks.

"Are you sure?" she asked in a soft voice. "I haven't even brushed my teeth, and you're so clean and fresh."

Whereas the daytime version of Juliette was sassy, the morning version of her was sweet and adorable. I liked this side of her. Really liked this side. Then again I really liked the other side, too.

With a grin, I smoothed a hand down the side of her hair and stared at her beautiful face. Suddenly, my gut ached in the strangest way. "I'm sure, baby. You're perfect just the way you are," I whispered, my breath catching on the words in a way that I wasn't familiar with.

Her own breath stuttered across her lips, and her pupils dilated rapidly as desire seemed to devour her.

Unable to stop myself, I kissed her again. The angle was wrong, and she shifted a little on the pillow to meet my mouth. Gone was her soft that molded against my hard so nicely. I didn't like the space she put between us.

When I slid my tongue into her mouth to taste her, she gasped. And I realized what I did like was the way she swallowed her breath. The way I breathed the same air she expelled. There was something almost erotic about taking the air she gave, sucking it into my own lungs, and savoring it before returning it back to her.

It made me feel more alive than I could ever remember feeling.

My thoughts were bordering on crazy now, and I shook them off. "You're too far away. Come a little closer," I ordered in a gruff voice.

Scooting up on me, she huffed, "You're very bossy when you get home from work."

Light.

The light was back.

Relieved, I went with it. "I'm worked up," I grinned, pushing the hair from her eyes.

"I can see that."

Holding her chin in my hand, I leaned in closer to her. "Ask me why."

She raised a brow. "Why are you so worked up, Dr. Kiss?"

Dr. Kiss.

I really disliked that, but from her lips, I could tolerate it. It was even growing on me.

After nipping at her bottom lip, I reached over toward the night-stand. "Because I want to fuck you bare, and I brought you this to ease your mind about it."

She looked at the folded piece of paper. "And that would be what? A recommendation from that nurse you work with on how skilled you are with more than just your stethoscope?"

There was a slight hint of jealously in her tone that I chose to ignore. Instead of easing her mind though, I swatted her bare ass with the document and then handed it to her. "Don't be a smar-tass. It's my test results. I'm clean, and you're on the pill, so we're good to go."

"But I don't have my results with me. They're at home."

"Were you all clear?"

She frowned. "Yes, but you should still see them first."

I shook my head. "I don't need to."

"Are you su—?"

The information on these kinds of tests was cut and dry. You were either clean, or you were not. Cutting her off, I leaned down and fused my mouth to hers. It seemed that kissing her was something I also couldn't get enough of.

All of the anticipation of the night snapped like a band that had been stretched too wide, and it collided with the need that had so tightly spun up in me. And this kiss, this hot, damp, electric kiss was just a glimpse of what was to come.

Frenzied.

Filled with need.

Bordering on desperate.

As our tongues met and slid sensuously over one another, the need to join was suddenly all that mattered.

The covers were piled in a heap all around us. Unwilling to break our kiss, I shoved them out of the way with one arm while the other supported her back as I laid her down.

When Jules looked up at me with the most innocent eyes I had ever seen, I felt something crack inside me.

A shield.

My armor.

My reserve.

Who the hell knew?

I grasped her perfect face between firm hands, my hold just as commanding as my mouth.

She moaned, and I knew she liked it.

Bewitched by her, I pressed the length of my body against hers, blanketing her as my forearms fell to the mattress to support my weight.

I wanted to possess her.

Take her.

Fuck.

I wanted all of her.

With our mouths no longer moving roughly, but soft and slow, the mood had seemed to change.

Jules threaded her hands in my hair and murmured something in between our desperate bid to bring the other closer. The beating of my heart was so loud in my ears that her words got lost in translation. "What did you say?" I panted.

"Nothing," she moaned, tugging hard on the wet strands of my hair.

Growling, I pulled back slightly, but I still kept her close.

Spreading my fingers out over the back of her head as my thumb rushed along her delicate jaw, I looked at her.

Just took the moment to catch my breath.

We were face-to-face, nose-to-nose, and it was impossible to differentiate between the harsh gasps of air I drew into my lungs from those she drew into her own.

Unbidden, words scraped from my throat. "You don't have to worry about anyone else. I only want you."

Those big, doe-like eyes darkened, and as they did, she hinted of her fears. "And I only want you, but that doesn't change anything. You're still leaving Atlanta."

My heart skidded, and the frenzy that had wracked my body stilled as I nodded my head in agreement. That was true. I was leaving. I had to. And I was a selfish bastard for even saying what I had. Saying anything more about us, about how I was feeling, would be ruthless.

Trying to ease the sting of our reality, I ran my thumb along her collarbone and smiled softly at the girl who had captured my attention. "We have some time, and we should use it wisely."

Her eyes searched, possibly begged for more. And even though my chest squeezed in response, I couldn't give her anything else.

I just couldn't.

"Juliette," I whispered before I brushed my lips across hers and repeated, "Let's use our time wisely."

Her fingers gently fluttered across my face. "You're right," she whispered. I smoothed the back of my hand down her cheek and her mouth dropped open as she leaned into my touch.

Gone was all the banter. The playfulness. And somehow what had emerged in the morning sunlight was deafening and blinding and way too much to handle.

An odd feeling teased down my spine, quivered, but then it disappeared. Unsure as to what it was, I was ready to move past all this emotion.

I shifted to my hands and knees. Bending my elbows, I dropped my shoulders down to capture her mouth and kiss her softly, slowly, sweetly.

With my lips on hers, I closed my eyes and tried to block out the white noise in my head that was screaming danger. *Proceed with caution. Roadblock ahead.*

But then Juliette cupped my face, lightly scratching her nails through the stubble coating my jaw, and her warm touch erased any bit of reluctance I should have had about moving forward.

Lust spread through my veins as gentle hands roamed over my shoulders, down my back, to my sides. Her movements mimicked our kiss—unfrenzied, unhurried, and so unlike us. Or the us we had been only minutes before.

I sucked in a ragged breath when she ran both of her hands down to my hips. Flames scorched my already heated skin. God, she set me on fire. Sweet, kind, sassy, funny, and the sexiest thing I'd ever seen.

"Jules, what are you doing to me?" It wasn't meant to be a question. Then again it wasn't meant to be spoken aloud.

She nipped at my lip before she ran her fingers a little lower. "The same thing you're doing to me."

I lowered my weight to my elbows and stared down at her. "You really are always a smartass, aren't you?"

She giggled lightly and shrugged, but everything about her was still soft. There was something so beautiful about her smile. It had me reeling. It sent me over the edge. And I kissed her again. It seemed I couldn't stop kissing her. Soon, I took it a little further and pressed my bare chest against her breasts.

My palms were busy wandering down her sides, and hers had been traveling lower down to my groin, but the whole time our faces were no more than a breath apart.

This time she broke our kiss, searching for air, and taking mine.

There was a bond between us that I didn't want to acknowledge. She felt it, too. So, in the dim light I gazed down at her, not allowing myself to say anything else, and she stared up at me with her throat moving as she swallowed down whatever she wanted to say.

Her shaky fingers reached out to caress my bottom lip before allowing her arms to fall in a relaxed motion behind her. "Jake, take me."

Without breaking eye contact, I went to my knees.

Deep inside I knew all of this was fucking wrong. That ending things now would spare a lot of heartache. But with all the bad in my life, I just wanted a little good. And she was it.

Tempting.

Tasty.

Delicious.

She was licking her lips, her chest rising and falling in rapid measure, and her gaze intense. "Jake, it's okay."

"I know," I whispered. And I believed it was, or wanted to believe that, anyway.

With her arms draped over her head in a way that her dirty blonde hair was fanned out, she bent her knees and planted her feet firmly on the mattress,

It was a picture I knew I would remember forever.

There was no doubt she was the most beautiful thing I'd ever seen, but today something felt different.

I didn't like the feeling.

Nudging her knees apart wider, I settled between her thighs and kissed her slowly. With hungry fingers and lips, I traced the slope of her neck, the swell of her breasts, the curve of her hips.

She arched her back as if giving herself to me, and all the while my body screamed to hurry up and take her already. "Please," she begged as she lifted her hips.

With my arms caging her, I pushed inside her. "Ah, baby, you undo me." My voice was little more than a ragged grunt.

Her fingertips dug into the bunched muscles of my shoulders, and she quivered beneath me as she exhaled a shaky breath across my face. "I can feel you."

And fuck, how I could feel her, too. I pulled back before I thrust even deeper. In response, her legs trembled as she tightened them around my hips.

My knees were shaking like it was my first time, and in a way it was. I'd never gone bare inside a woman before. Everything felt the same with her, just a thousand times more intense.

She was so tight I could barely breathe as I pulled out and then thrust again. My elbows dug into the bed as my hands fisted in her hair. "Juliette."

A smile trembled at her mouth. "Jake."

My thighs shook as I moved above her slow and steady. The need to fuck completely gone and replaced by this, whatever this was. "Fuck, Jules, you feel so good."

In response, she rocked into me again and again as her fingers cut into my skin with the need to hold on.

Our bodies burned as we moved in an erotic, tantalizing, rhythm.

Up.

Down.

In.

Out.

Gasping my name, her gaze was solidly fixed on me. "I'm going to come, Jake. Are you close?"

"Yes, I'm right there with you, baby," I groaned and pushed inside her one last time, holding myself at the deepest possible point.

As pleasure knotted at the base of my spine and spread down the back of my thighs, I could feel the start of her orgasm. It rippled along the length of my cock and then squeezed me so tight that if

I hadn't already been on the brink, I would have been then.

It was like being turned inside out. The rush nothing I'd ever experienced before as I throbbed and ecstasy hit. Spasms jerked through my body, and every single one of my nerves felt electrified.

With my face buried in the crook of her neck, I cried out her name. As she cried out mine, I shuddered from head to toe.

Her arms circled my shoulders, and her hands rubbed up and down my back, her nails biting into my flesh there as well.

They would be scars that would always remind me of her.

Still inside her, I lowered my body on top of hers and gasped for air. She took my breath away, in so many ways.

This had been birthed from a silly conversation about sex. A game of would you or won't you. I'd simply asked, *"Would you ever consider having sex without a condom?"*

Her response had been as sassy as ever. "Since I don't wear condoms, I guess I would."

And I took the lead from there. Discussing the pros and cons of having sex without protection and the precautions that needed to be taken first.

Who knew the result would be anything but a game.

That it would be so fucking real, it hurt.

Best Of Both Worlds

JULES

SUMMERS IN THE south were always a bitch.

It meant dealing with blaring heat and pouring rain. Cursing the fact that I'd chosen to run a few errands at lunch without taking my umbrella along, I shook off what I could of the remaining drops of water and glanced at myself in the office window.

My hair hung sodden against my forehead and cheeks. My clothes clung damp and heavy and were now chilled in the frigid air conditioning Finn had taken control of.

Closing my door, I stripped off my carefully selected dress and grabbed the jeans and tank I'd thrown in the back of my car last week when I'd spent the night at Jake's midtown apartment.

After pulling my hair back into a messy bun, I wiped under my eyes and reapplied my mascara.

Ouch!

I'd stabbed myself in the eyeball, and in the process, my contact came tumbling out. Crap. On my hand and knees, I searched for it, but to no avail.

Scrunching the other one out, I tossed it the trash and opened my desk drawer, where I kept a spare pair of glasses.

They were cute enough. Made me look smart instead of geeky, but still, I hated wearing my glasses.

Glaring at my reflection this time, I sighed. I looked . . . unprofessional. Yes. That was the right word. Unprofessional. Unprofessional when I should be looking like one top dog wedding planner.

It was ironic that I looked the way I did since the cliché *money is no object* was about to take on new meaning with this wedding. The two million dollar budget meant an astonishing display of opulence had yet to be planned. And the riveting guest list would have every news outlet in town itching to not only catch a snap of the bride and groom but the venue as well.

Slipping my kitten heels back on, I opened the closet door in the corner that kept props for display. In there I found one of my uncle's suit coats hanging on a hook. I put it on and rolled up the sleeves.

Not bad.

Then I opened a few of the boxes and found a strand of pearls and some pieces of lace.

Perfect.

I wrapped the pearls around my neck and slid the lace in the suit pocket.

So I was rocking the Madonna look.

It was coming back in style. I'd read about it while checking out at the supermarket a few weeks ago.

With my outfit crisis put at ease, I had a lot of important choices ahead of me to make. And Jake would be here soon to start the selection process.

The thought of spending time with him working on the wedding details during the daylight hours of the next few days, and then going out to dinner and maybe even the movies at night had me positively giddy.

My breath hiccupped as I reached for the list of things we had to accomplish in the next three hours. Jake, of course, had needed to get some sleep after working all night, and I had to come to work. It was the whole passing in the night routine that had become our norm. But it was about to change. And even as I looked at the perfect dress I had selected in a heap on the floor, I was still smiling.

Shrugging it off, I sat down and scattered the photos I had Finn print off the Internet over the table. They were from the garden party scene of *The Great Gatsby* and were my inspiration for Rory and Remy's wedding.

Closing my eyes, I could practically see it.

The explosion of lavish hothouse orchids, stems of cymbidium, blankets of dendrobium. There would be a mix of cut blossoms, ferns, and potted orchids on the tables.

All in shades of white.

This would create a cream and soft green color palette. I could add crystals for sparkle and silver for shine. A dash of blush for the whimsy romantic effect. The cake. The cake would be blush in color. In the end, the garden would become a fairytale wonderland perfect for wooing true love.

It was going to be amazing.

There was a knock on the door, and I practically leaped out of my seat. "Come in," I called in excitement.

Jake was here.

As the door to the office opened, giddy nerves danced down my spine, and then . . . Jaxson walked in.

My smile remained, although not as brightly, and I took my seat again. It wasn't that I wasn't happy to see him. He just wasn't the man I had been expecting.

Jaxson, dark hair tousled from the wind and rain, raincoat open over faded jeans, and as handsome as ever, walked into my office.

His tranquil green eyes were downcast, and he was glancing at a handful of his own photos. "Good afternoon, beautiful. Lose a contact again?"

Jaxson oozed charm. It was in his nature. He was a natural born flirt, even with his ex-fiancé. "Hi handsome, this is a surprise, and as a matter of fact, I did."

He kissed me on the cheek, and his casual smile warmed me like sunlight. "Yeah, well, that's nothing new. I hope I'm not interrupting anything too important, but I wanted to get your opinion on these." He waggled the eight by ten glossy photos in his hands

Embarrassed, I pushed the pile of inkjet-printed photos in front of me aside in a rush. "Sure. What are you looking at?"

He looked me up and down, and then made an inquisitive face when he saw my wet dress on the floor. "Don't ask," I told him. He gave me a nod.

He knew me too well.

Perching himself on the edge of the table, he looked at me with the most serious expression I think I had ever seen him wear, and then he scratched his head. "Remember a few months back when I sent you that text with the link about Sports Illustrated restructuring?"

I relaxed back in my chair. "I have a vague recollection of it."

He laughed. "Yeah, well, it wasn't as eye-opening as the one you sent me."

I shoved him. "Jaxson, you promised to never bring that up again."

His smirk was wicked. "Yes, I did. What was I thinking at the time? It's way too good not to have in my pocket."

I rolled my eyes. "Get to the point before I kick you out."

"Right. Right. The point. That article discussed the Digital Department's reorganization. Now the print department is doing the same. They cut staff photographers by almost thirty percent and removed the chief photographer from his role. This created a huge hole for SI, and they did pictures. Good pictures. So they are holding a photo contest for professional photographers, and I'm entering it. The winner gets the chief photography position for a three-month trial."

I clamped my hand over my mouth. "Are you serious?"

This time his smile was genuine. "I sure am."

"What about your business?"

"Well, there is a sick amount of photographers entering so who knows if I'll win."

"You will," I assured him. "You're so talented."

He shrugged. "Says the girl who thinks inkjet-printed photos are acceptable to look at."

I scrunched my nose. "You caught me, again."

He shook his head. "Oh yeah, like that was getting past me. Anyway, putting your bad habits aside, if I don't win, I think it's time for a change."

I couldn't stop my frown.

"But, Jules," he beamed, "if I do win this gig, it could open a shit ton of doors for me either at SI in one of their regular segments or at some other magazine in the Time family."

I pointed to the stack of photos in his hand. "Are those the ones you're using to enter the contest?"

He bit his lip in reluctance. "I can only submit one, but these are the ones I have to choose from."

Excitement of a different kind than I was used to from the past few days brought a smile to my face. "Let me see," I said anxiously.

Leaning toward me, he carefully set the pictures down on the table one at a time. When he did, my eyes nearly popped out of my head. The photo shoot he had done at The Bride Box wasn't of brides wearing wedding dresses. It was of brides with no dresses on! They were in veils, or sexy lingerie, or wearing jewelry and nothing more. Each pictured a soccer ball or a football or a baseball somewhere in the photo, but the focus was on them sitting on the counter, or in a chair, or standing near the sink eating cake.

I glanced up at him. At the guy that had been such a huge part of my life for so long. How had I never seen his sensuality? It was written all over these pictures. In the way he posed the models. The angle of the picture. The faces the women were making, for him. "Montgomery mentioned you had done a shoot in the showroom, but conveniently left out the part about the brides being naked."

He pointed to one of the pictures. "She isn't naked."

It was a sideways view. "She's sitting on the counter wearing a blue garter and eating cake. Luckily the soccer ball under her arm covers up her boobies."

His head fell back in laughter. "It wasn't luck, Jules. I planned it that way."

"Whatever," I scoffed.

"Seriously," he said, "don't you think they're edgy and hot and just the kind of photo SI would be interested in if they ever wanted to put a bride on their cover?"

I had to give it to him, he was right. "Yes, I do," I admitted, and then I pointed to the bride wearing a cameo choker with tons of pearls around her neck. "This one is my favorite."

"Why?" he asked.

"I'm not sure. It's in the way you captured her expression. It's soft but sexy. The way a bride should look on her big day. Like she's in love. And with the blurred background, she could be anywhere. It's mysterious and romantic and eye-catching. She makes me want to be her."

Jaxson scooped me up and whirled me around. "I knew I could count on you."

Just then a husky throat cleared.

It was Jake.

There was a dip in my belly as Jaxson set me down. Feeling anxious, I tucked a piece of fallen hair behind my ear and slowly raised my gaze toward the door. "Hi, Jake," I said, adding a friendly laugh to help ease the tension I was feeling.

His hair was styled. He was cleanly shaven. He looked edible. He looked like sex. He looked like sin.

Looking at him made my toes curl.

In a pressed white shirt, unbuttoned at the top to reveal a smooth expanse of skin, paired with dark slacks, he looked like he belonged on the cover of *GQ*.

My knees went weak.

Under his white shirt, I could see the impressive muscle tone of his arms and chest. And his eyes, they were bright and wide, and for the first time, he didn't look at all tired.

His eyebrows rose and his lips curved. "Hi, Juliette," he said in return, and just as casually as I had addressed him.

Awkward.

"Jake." I nudged Jaxson back a bit. "This is Jaxson. He's ummm . . . he's . . . he's going to take the photos at Rory's wedding," I finally managed to say.

Jake strode into the room and held out his hand. "How's it going?"

Casual. That was good.

Not at all jealous. That was even better. Especially since he had nothing to be jealous about.

"Good." Jaxson shook his hand. "And just to help clear the air, I'm the guy Jules sent the video that was intended for you. Oh, and I'm her ex-fiancé, but we're just friends."

Jake smirked at him. "The first part I knew, and the second is good to know. I appreciate that."

I glared at Jaxson. Did he really have to make that the first thing he said?

Out of nowhere, Jake swooped down and kissed me, right on the mouth. He might have taken me by surprise, but his lips were always welcome on mine.

Jaxson started to gather his photos.

I stared at Jake, unsure whether he was upset or not. But then his eyes roamed my body, and I felt whatever it was whirling in them between my thighs.

Something magnetic.

Irresistible.

Erotic.

Jaxson patted me on the shoulder and jolted me out of my daze. "I'm headed out. It was nice to meet you, Jake."

Jake gave him a nod. "Same here, man."

Jaxson looked at me with a curiosity I knew I would be expecting a call about. "I'll be in touch about the wedding."

"And the contest," I called as he walked out the door. He waved a hand in acknowledgment.

Jake strode over to the old wooden desk so full of power goose bumps rose to the surface of my skin from the slight breeze he created in his wake. Casually, he picked up the picture that was on it. "Is this you?" he asked.

I nodded, my cheeks flushing in embarrassment. "I was seven."

"Nice veil," he commented.

"Yes, it was a pillowcase," I laughed.

"And the flowers?" he asked, genuinely curious.

"They were dandelions from the garden. My father insisted on taking the picture because he knew my uncle would love it."

Jake set the photo down and stared at me. "I bet he did."

Just then Finn came into the office. "Hey Jake, how's it going?"

Jake looked at him from head to toe, but for a completely different reason. "Good, really good, and you? You look much better."

Finn set a box full of fabrics, silverware patterns, china dishes, and glass vases down. "Never been better," he said with sarcasm. "Being the errand boy is the highlight of my life."

"Finn," I sighed. "You know I really appreciate the help."

Regret coated his face. "I know, Jules, Sorry. Here's the first batch of samples you asked for," he said. "The rain slowed me down. I should be back with the rest within the hour."

"That's fine."

Finn redirected his attention to Jake. "I made that call."

"And?"

Finn smiled widely. "He'll be in Las Vegas next month. He wants me to fly out and meet him at Moon's Fight Club when he's there."

Jake fist pumped in the air. "Excellent. Let me know if it works out."

"I will. And thanks, man," Finn said as he headed to the door.

"Finn," I called.

He turned.

"Vegas? You didn't tell me that? Are you sure you want to go back there?"

He shrugged. "It will be fine."

I stared at him for a long while. Until he gave me a nod, and then turned back around.

"Everything okay?" Jake asked.

"I hope so," I answered, and then gave him my attention. He was standing there with his hands in his pockets and looked so incredibly sexy.

Feeling butterflies flutter to life in my belly, I strode over to the table and pushed my glasses up before I began to look through the box Finn had brought in. "Should we get started?"

Jake strode over to me. He pushed my chin up to look at him. "I like your glasses. You look like a sexy librarian."

Those butterflies went crazy at the mere closeness of his face to mine. "Librarians aren't sexy."

His eyes blazed with heat. "Then you haven't been going to the right libraries," he drawled lazily.

I held his gaze for a few moments and that burn of desire started to pool in my belly. "Yes, well, clearly we have different interpretations when it comes to sexy."

He smiled slowly at me. "Oh, I think we're on the same page. And just to be clear," he said, using the phrase Jaxson had used, "I'm really fucking jealous that he had you in his arms."

I blinked in surprise. "You know you have no reason to be. Jaxson and I broke up for a reason, and now we are just friends."

"Yeah, I know. You've both told me. That doesn't change the facts."

"The facts, what do you mean by the facts?"

He shook the question off.

I didn't press him about it, but I did step a little closer. "If I promise to bang your brains out tonight, will that make you feel better?"

Features etched with determination, he yanked me roughly to him. "Then you better get started before I take you right here on the table," he said, and then he crushed his mouth to mine.

I made a noise of surprise in the back of my throat and sunk into his kiss.

When he finally let me go we were both breathing hard. He smoothed his thumb over my cheek and his eyes went alight with passion. "For the record, I want you wearing those glasses when you fuck my brains out."

My laughter exploded and Jake's did as well. With my arms wrapped around him, I hugged him tightly. It wasn't the first time I realized that I loved him, but it was the first time I wanted to say it out loud.

I did not.

Instead, I turned around and sat down at the table to get to work. Jake sat as well, easing back and crossing an ankle over his knee.

God, he was so sexy.

Work. It was time to work. I pulled my agenda from the stack of file folders beside me. "Let's start with type of service, time of service, and roles."

"That's easy," he grinned. "Non-denominational and I've already asked the Chaplin from the hospital to officiate, and he agreed."

I clapped my hands together in excitement. "Why didn't you tell me that?"

He smiled ruefully. "I just asked him last night, and you and I didn't really do much talking this morning."

Chewing my lip, I remembered vividly what we did. "Right," I said with a flush. "So, what time do you have in mind for the actual ceremony?"

He shrugged. "Two?"

I shook my head. "Since we are having both the ceremony and the reception at Rosewood, I wouldn't make it too early."

"Five then, and I'll walk her down the aisle," he said decidedly.

"Both work." I made some notations in my planner.

"See how easy I am?" he remarked.

I gave a huff of laughter. "Right. Easy. That's how I'd describe you."

"You wouldn't say I was easy?" His voice was gruff, deeper than usual, and the sudden smile on his lips was absolutely sensual.

I shook my head. "And moving on."

He moved his chair closer to mine. "What would you say I am?"

A prickle of nervousness tightened every inch of my body as he turned me toward him and stretched his arms on either side of me, caging me in. He was so close, and he smelled of soap and him. And I felt that dizzying sensation slide over me.

"Smart," I started with.

"Okay, go on."

"Strong."

He took my fingers within one warm hand and laced his fingers between mine. "Go on."

"Sexy."

His lips curved as if he was amused. "Would you say I'm a good lover?"

"I would," I answered, giving nothing else away.

He let go of my hand and eased back in his chair, although he didn't move it away. "I'll settle for that, for now."

Picking up a binder, I handed it to him. "Caterers are next. We have to decide what we are going to serve, and that will help narrow the choices."

Perusing it in five seconds flat, he shut it with a grunt. "Can I just close my eyes and put my finger on the menu and be done with it?"

"Jake," I held my tone confident. Right now he was my overwhelmed client, not my lover, not a sex god. I squeezed my thighs together at the last one. He was better than good in bed. That was for certain. "You could. But what you should do is look them over and see which one offers the foods that appeal most to you."

He opened the binder again and began reading the menus. After about five minutes, he pointed to one. "This one, but why exactly was I looking for what appealed most to me?"

I smiled at him. "Because it was the only way I could get you to read the menus."

He shook his head. "Always a smartass."

"On the bright side, we've checked one more thing off the list. Only ninety-nine to go."

He dropped his head to the table and sighed. "I have no idea how you do this all day."

"Because like you, I love my job, and I'm good at it." I got up and went over to the bookcase to pull down the invitation samples I'd had Finn get earlier during the week.

When I got back to the table, I set the samples down. Before

I could sit down, he grabbed me by the hips. "Let's take a make out break."

"We really should get through some of this," I whispered, resting my hands on his shoulders and leaning down.

His eyes started to flutter closed, his eyelashes dark on his cheekbones as his lips came within a breath of mine. "Okay, what's next?"

When I tried to move away, he dragged me onto his lap. "Jake?" I questioned looking at him over my shoulder. "What are you doing?"

"Making this fun," he grinned.

And fun it was.

Two hours later, I was still on his lap, and we'd accomplished very little, but the tension between us was thick with knowing and sparking with electric chemistry.

"Okay," I finally conceded, turning myself to straddle him. "Let's go to dinner so we can get back to your place."

His eyelids lowered slightly in an unconscious smolder that sent off a rush of tingles between my legs. "That sounds like a really good idea. We'll drop your car off and you can grab a bag. We'll stay at my apartment tonight but at Rosewood tomorrow night."

I curled my fingers in his hair. "I can't stay with you every night."

He pressed his fingers into my hips. "Sure you can."

"Jake, I have to work."

He ran his palms between my thighs. "Which has nothing to do with where you spend your nights. Besides, I plan to do two more days of this with you . . ."

All I could hear was my heart banging in my chest and my pulse ringing in my ears. He was talking, but all I heard was *take it slow.* Being around him made me feel a thousand different things, and the need to be guarded seemed to easily slip away. "Okay," I said. "I think that sounds like fun."

He placed a little kiss on the corner of my mouth. "I can promise you, it will be much more than fun."

I closed my eyes and told myself there was nothing wrong with letting this thing between us go on for as long as we had together.

Fun.

We were having fun.

When he kissed the other side of my mouth, the feeling that washed through me was something much more than fun, though. Butterflies swarmed my belly, my throat tightened, and when he full on kissed me, I felt like he was my home.

It was a feeling I hadn't felt in a very long time.

And right then I knew nothing would ever be the same in my life when he left.

chapter 26

Method To My Madness

JAKE

THERE WAS A very good chance that if I saw another piece of satin, silk, or lace, and I don't mean of the sexy underwear type kind, I was going to implode.

Who the hell knew everything had a sample? Napkins, tablecloths, place settings, even silverware for Christ sake.

After a solid week of looking at wedding this and wedding that, I was pretty much over it.

It was tedious.

It was tiresome.

And yet, it was also exhilarating.

Yes, exhilarating.

Not the selection process—that I never wanted to do again. But Juliette. She had a fire about her when she worked that was an incredible turn on. She was focused, competent, and at times even commanding.

I scooped up a handful of nuts and watched Juliette lose one last time at Gin Rummy against Mimi.

She'd stayed here every night over the past week, and while I was at work she ate with Mimi, and they spent time talking about God knew what.

She was . . . fucking amazing.

Not just the sexy, doe-eyed, full of life, golden-skinned, shiny blond hair, soft, full-lipped kind of amazing. That was killer enough. But you had to add in the heat and light she just seemed to emanate. And when you did, she was impossible not to fall for.

Not that I had.

I popped another handful of nuts in my mouth and took a sip from my beer.

Jules, as I had taken to call her at times, had taken to Mimi, and even though tonight was my only night off this week, she had insisted we spend it with Mimi. I wasn't going to argue. I wanted to spend as much time as I could with my grandmother, and Jules. I enjoyed seeing them both smile and laugh.

"Rummy," Mimi said, her voice was hoarse, and her coloring seemed paler. It was nearly nine, and she should have been in bed, but she insisted she wasn't ready.

I got to my feet and strode by the two of them sitting at the card table. All the dogs were lounging in their places, and of course, Daisy was on Mimi's lap.

When I squeezed Jules's shoulder, she looked up. Her eyes were bright with happiness and contentment. "I'm going to grab another beer. Do you want anything?"

She shook her head no. "I'm good, thank you."

"Mimi?"

She also shook her head.

"A guy is willing to wait on you and neither of you want anything, go figure." I grinned at the two of them.

As I walked out of the room, I heard Mimi whisper, "You're

doing a good job, sweetheart."

I had a feeling she wasn't talking about the wedding planning or the card game, but rather me, and I rolled my eyes. Who the hell knew what she had said to Jules, but I was surely going to find out as soon as I returned.

In the kitchen, I grabbed another bottle from the refrigerator and was just sinking a lime into when I heard Jules scream. "Jake! Come here, hurry."

Alarmed, I rushed back into the parlor.

Jules was beside Mimi holding her hand with Daisy on the floor beside her. Mimi had slouched down in her chair. She'd gone even paler and her eyes were squinted like she was in pain.

"Mimi?" I kept my voice even. "Are you okay?"

She looked up at me and gave me a smile I failed to believe. "I think I'm tired. That's all. I should probably go to bed."

I nodded and called for Matthew to assist me. He was upstairs getting her medications ready, and I could hear him already descending the staircase.

Mimi's head dropped again.

I lifted her chin. This time she was unresponsive and I calmly started checking her over. Her face was clammy, and her forehead was damp with sweat. Her pulse elevated.

"Let's get her to the couch," I directed Matthew.

He grabbed the blanket that was draped over her lap and headed that way. She looked so frail. Having lost even more weight, I lifted her easily and carried her to the plush cushions. Mr. Darcy came trotting over and put his head down with a whimper.

Jules gave him a pet. "It's okay, big boy. She's going to be fine."

When I put a hand to Mimi's chest, it was dry and hot. "Mimi, talk to me."

Nothing.

I searched as best I could for signs of irritation. Distress. I bent to run my hands up and down her legs, straightening them.

"What was her last red blood cell count?" I looked up and fear tried to steal my voice. I forced it aside.

"I don't have the exact number, but it hadn't changed significantly from the previous one."

"Increase or decrease?"

"It increased," he said.

Fuck!

"Mimi. Look at me."

Her head was drooping, and her eyelids started to flutter. When her whole body started to tremble, I pulled out my phone and dialed 911.

"Please state the nature of your emergency."

"This is Dr. Kissinger," I said. "I need an ambulance sent to 321 West Paces Ferry Rd, stat."

Terror was trying to crash over me. I was trained for situations like this. I dealt with them every day, and yet I had to stop and center myself, but then Mimi started gasping, and I went on autopilot.

"Grab her oxygen tank," I told Matthew.

He took off and ran up the stairs.

"What's wrong with her?" Jules asked, her voice scared and small.

"Hypoxia."

"Stay with me, Mimi," I murmured over and over while I worked on giving her rescue breathes until I could administer the oxygen.

Matthew came running into the room. He set the green tank down and together we tore open the sterile packages of tubing.

Her lips had already turned blue. Slowly, I cranked the dial on the tank and brought the mask to her face. "Give me your stethoscope and hold this," I told Matthew.

He took hold of the mask, and I put the rubber tips in my ears to listen to her heart rate. As soon as I did, panic gnawed at me.

Just then Mimi opened her eyes and smiled at me. "I love you,

Jake," she said softly.

"I love you, too. And you're going to be fine," I assured her.

The 911 operator had said she'd have someone here right away

Right away couldn't come soon enough.

chapter 27

In The Heat Of The Moment

JULES

AFTER SPENDING THREE days at the hospital, Jake brought Mimi home with around-the-clock hospice care.

The cancer had metastasized into the lungs. She didn't have long, and I prayed she made it until the wedding. Not for me, but for her, and Rory, and Jake.

With Mimi settled in her room, Jake and I had eaten and showered and next on the list was sleep, but neither of us could fall asleep.

It was seven in the evening, and the sun was still shining way too bright.

I looked over at him stretched out on the bed as he stared at the ceiling. There was so much I wanted to say but didn't know where to start. There was so much I wanted to be able to do for him, and nothing I could. Nothing except be here for him.

"Tell me a story," I whispered.

Jake put an arm behind his head. When he did, his shirt lifted. I wanted to lick the smooth stripe of skin exposed between the hem of the material and his belt, but I settled for running a finger along it.

He had been quiet for most of the day, and I knew he had a lot on his mind. Between organizing Mimi's care and also calling Rory and telling her she should think about coming home very soon. I understood why.

At my touch though, he shivered and moved a little closer. He turned to look at me, and the circles under his eyes conveyed his lack of sleep. "I've told you all of them."

I spread my fingers flat on his firm belly and rubbed in slow circles. "You can't possibly have. Tell me the craziest one."

Jake's sigh sounded annoyed, but I knew he was anything but. He loved telling me stories about the ER as much as I loved hearing them. There was no patient confidentiality violation, as he never mentioned any names.

I rested my head in the palm of my hand and studied him. The way his chest rose and fell as I stroked his stomach, the way his eyes seemed to grow a little less dim, and the way his frown lines eased.

Slowly, tentatively, I tugged his shirt a little higher to bare him to me. "One more," I pleaded. I wanted to take his mind off Mimi, and right now this was all I had.

"Fine," he sighed again. "Once upon a time, there were three little doctors . . ."

"Stop!" I protested with laughter in my tone. "Don't go any further."

His brow rose. "What? You don't want to hear about doctors, only patients?"

"No, that's not it."

He turned to face me and mimicked my pose. "Then what? You don't think doctors are sexy enough for once upon a times."

My hand went to his belt buckle, and I slipped the leather from it. "As a matter of fact, I think they're very very sexy. It's the little part that I disagree with."

He glanced down at his manhood. "Oh," he said. "You have a valid point. Then how about this: Once upon a time, there were three big doctors . . ."

"Jake, don't go any further with that or I'll have to turn that opening line into a nursery rhyme, and I guarantee you won't like my ending."

He gave me two raised brows.

I started to lower his zipper and raised my own brow. When he said nothing, I went on. "Once upon a time there were three big doctors, they were sooooo big one couldn't fit in the ER, one couldn't fit in his scrubs, and the one named Dr. Kiss . . ."

"Okay, okay," he halted me. "Stop right there. I'll tell you a real one. This might not be the craziest story, but it's one I've never told anyone about."

Intrigued, I stopped lowering his zipper. "Keep going."

He looked down at my hand. "I will when you do."

With a grin, I slowly eased the rest of his zipper down, and I could feel his cock pulse from outside the denim.

He flipped onto his back and resumed his position with his hands behind his head. Clearly what I had in mind was more than acceptable. "It was my first week of residency when a woman in her late twenties came in the department crying hysterically. She had, she told me, something on her bottom and it was growing larger by the day."

I slipped my hand inside his jeans. "Bottom?" I laughed.

"Ass," he corrected, looking over at me. "That feels good, and she said bottom, not me."

I worked my fingers around the tight denim, shoving it down his thighs. "Got it, on both counts."

"Anyway, I was expecting to see a small lump or spot that needed to be biopsied, so I asked her to lower her pants so I could take a look. As I bent down to peer at the spot, I poked it and something erupted, and I swore it was looking at me." He said this arching as he lifted his hips to allow me to undress him.

"What was it?" I cringed.

He looked over at me again, his eyes hooded and filled with desire. "A very large worm that had burrowed into her skin. And I vomited right there in the exam room."

"You did not?"

"I did. My attending ripped me a new one for it, too. It was the first and last time I ever threw up, in front of a patient, anyway."

My breathing was ragged. "There were other times then?"

He chuckled. "Yeah, more than a few. My first year of residency was rough."

I kissed him on the lips. Soft. Sweet. Intimate. "You'll have to tell me about them, later."

He kissed me back. Hungry. Desperate. Needy. "Yeah, later."

That's when I dragged my mouth down his throat. Lower. And lower. Kissing a path down to his chest, the smooth skin above his navel, and then down to his cock, I took him in my hands. Full. Thick. Beautiful. The crown of his cock was swollen and dripping . . . *with desire for me.*

I licked that drop, and then I stared up at him. For some reason, I couldn't look away as his eyes flashed in the sunlight. His beauty was so strong, his body so incredibly perfect, and his being made just for me.

He was watching me with a predatory look in his eyes. And then as if anxious, he cupped the back of my head and tugged me closer—closer to his cock.

Gripping the base of his cock with my hands, I tucked his broad head into mouth and sucked gently as I pulled him in. The sharp inhalation that was audible in the quiet told me he liked what I was doing.

Those butterflies I got every time we were together flitted and spun and tumbled around in the lowest part of my core.

I fucked him with my mouth and tongue, my teeth, and then I let my jaw go slack to take him even deeper.

Overwrought with lust, he arched under my touch and twisted his fingers in my hair. My pulse stuttered and my body ached with wanting to please him, maybe even more than I wanted pleasing.

He let out a long, tortured groan, and then whispered my name, "Juliette."

His hands slid from my head to around my shoulders and pulled me upward. He fumbled between us to shove his jeans down even further than they were. He twisted out of them and kicked them aside. I had already ripped my shirt over my head and thrust my shorts off.

And then we were both lying face-to-face totally naked.

I cupped his cheeks against mine and fluttered my lashes against his skin, over and over, and he laughed softly, but the laugher faded quickly.

Moving swiftly, he was hovering over me and then inside me in one solid thrust.

My mouth dropped open in a soundless gasp when his hands rushed up the back of my thighs and he hooked my knees over his forearms.

In this position, he took me hard and fast, the pace turning almost frantic. Our bodies pitched and strained, grasped and clutched. I raked my nails down his back, and he bit me hard enough to bruise.

And then he turned me so he could take me from behind. He pounded into me. Like this, we were nothing but flesh on flesh. The headboard creaked from how hard I was gripping it and he yanked my hair until my head tipped back.

My orgasm hit me like a shock wave that ripped through my core and erupted as a passionate cry from my throat.

Jake growled and turned me back around. His face contorted,

and hot, rough hands grasped my knees, forcing them apart. Then his mouth was on me, his lips devouring me as much as his body was.

More pleasure rushed through me. Desperately, my fingers dove in his hair. I held and gripped him, never wanting this to end.

Never wanting us to end.

I cried out his name as my orgasm surged throughout my entire body.

Jake's face contorted, and hot, aggressive hands grasped my knees, forcing them apart wide enough to allow him to go deeper inside me. Maybe even deeper than anyone had ever been.

Sensations burst behind my eyes.

"Fuck, Juliette." Jake's movements were harsh and rushed, his body jerking, his breaths short and ragged.

I stared up at his face, watching his eyes close as he came. It was erotic and wild. It sparked like a wildfire out of control, and it was the most beautiful thing I had ever seen.

Moments later, he opened his eyes, and warm blue irises looked down at me, and that was when I knew for sure . . . I loved him.

Really loved him.

I loved him with everything I had.

He kissed me softly and then crushed his chest to mine. When he rolled to lie beside me, he buried his nose in my hair and whispered something I couldn't hear.

We stayed that way for the longest time, neither of us able to move, our bodies locked tightly.

"I love you, Jake."

There it was.

His eyes flew open. I thought he was going to jump out of the bed, run out the door, flee as far and as fast as he could away from me. He didn't. I think what he did might have been worse. He just stared at me in bewildered silence.

Right then I knew they were words I shouldn't have spoken.

Words that slipped out.

Words he didn't want to hear.

Yet, I'd said them and there was no taking them back. I had to own them. Then again, I felt as though they were written in the stars.

I held out my hand to his, but I didn't move to take his. I simply held it out, waiting. Waiting for him to accept my love or reject it. The seconds that ticked by were torturous, but I kept my hand right there, held up, and offered.

Accept or reject.

I had no idea what he was going to do or what I was going to do if he rejected me. Once again I'd acted before thinking. Jumped without looking. Dove without a net.

Taking a breath, he slowly reached for me and slid his palm on top of my upturned one. "I quit my job today," he whispered.

Everything went black, and I started to free-fall. His grandmother was dying, there was nothing anyone could do to prevent it, and as soon as she was gone, so was he. We weren't written in the stars after all, but the fact that he was leaving was.

Those feelings of panic I never could control started to take over.

I needed air.

I needed to be alone.

I needed to get out of his room.

I tried to pull my hand away, but he wouldn't let me go. He squeezed it tighter as if he wasn't going to allow me to flee. My heart thundered erratically in my chest when I raised my gaze back to his. "You feel the same way. I know you do."

His eyes looked icy blue. "What does it matter how I feel? You know I have to go." The words raked from his throat as sharp as a razor.

"It matters, Jake. It matters. I could go with you."

He shook his head. "I need to do this on my own. So please,

just stop."

And I did.

Yanking hard, I jerked free of his hold and threw my legs over the side of the bed. I needed to get some air. I needed to breathe. To take a few moments to put things in perspective.

Determined to keep me in his bed, he pulled me back to him. I threw myself backward to break free of him once again, but he got hold of my wrists and pinned me down. "I'm not letting you leave like this, Juliette."

"I just need a few minutes alone."

He shook his head but said nothing. He was shutting down. I could see it in his eyes.

I tried not to sob, but the sound I made instead was even louder. It was a tortured cry of rejection that I couldn't contain. He closed his eyes as if unable to witness my reaction.

"Let me go," I said quietly. I wasn't looking for drama or to cause a scene, but I felt like I couldn't breathe.

Opening his eyes, he pinned both my wrists with one hand and lifted my chin. "I love you! Is that what you want to hear? I fucking love you," he said louder.

Tears sprung hot from my eyes. From the day I met him we were hard and soft, up and down. Both good and bad. Gentle and rough.

He truly was the Ying to my Yang.

The realization stunned me, and I stopped trying to run.

Once I'd settled, Jake dropped down beside me and pulled me to his chest. "The thing is it doesn't change anything." This he said softer, quieter.

I closed my eyes, wishing I could take those words back. They caused too much pain. Too much heartache.

"It doesn't change anything," he said again, stroking his hand down my back.

"I know," I whispered. "I just wanted you to be my North Star."

He sighed, and it was full of pain and torment.

I said nothing more.

Minutes of silence passed. I had no idea how many, but the sun had set, and the room went from bright to dim in a heartbeat. It was a perfect reflection of the state of our relationship. Exhaustion hit me hard, and I hoped sleep would take me under sooner rather than later.

He was right. Saying those three little words didn't change anything. In the end . . . it would only make parting ways that much more difficult.

Breaking up was going to be so very hard to do.

Hit The Nail On The Head

JULES

THE BIG DAY had finally arrived.

You would have thought I was the one getting married by the amount of butterflies in my belly.

With my nose pushed to the glass, I watched from the French doors in the parlor as the florist transformed the garden into an elegant and elaborate tea party meant for the queen.

There were white lace linens and fine china in all kinds of pretty patterns on the various sizes and shaped tables with the most beautiful flower centerpieces done in every shade of pink.

The floor of the main tent had already been filled with at least one thousand white roses, creating a dance floor that seemed to come straight out of a fairy tale.

I took a moment longer to admire the view. The crisp white covers on the chairs. All the shades of pink, from the palest to the deepest, blooming against the shimmer of tulle and lace.

It made me giddy just thinking about it.

Montgomery and Archer were also hard at work under the air-conditioned tent adding finishing touches to the seven-layer cake that was as spectacular as a white diamond. There were no birds or hearts with initials. Instead, textured petals adorned each tier. Some blush, some cream, some white, and a pale green shimmered all around. More petals were scattered over the cake board and on top stood a hand-painted porcelain statue.

Mimi knew it was right as soon as she saw it in one of my catalogs. She said it represented Rory and Remy in the most perfect way. The way they used to sneak off for hours at a time to be together. The statue was of a bride and groom sneaking a kiss, with the bride's legs positioned in a dangling fashion so the porcelain could be set at the edge of the cake.

Additional tents, tables, and sofa settings were also being arranged out in the garden in such a way to make it easy to move about.

Turning around, I strode into the kitchen and opened the refrigerator in the butler's pantry to inspect the flowers for the bridal party. Pink and white ribbons streamed from the lilies in the bridesmaid bouquets. They were large, simple, classic statements turned modern. The boutonnieres were done similarly except there were no ribbons just touches of pale green.

When my eyes landed on the bridal bouquet, it brought tears to my eyes. With a trail of silver-edged orchids accented by clear beads, it was one of a kind.

I closed the door and leaned against it. I was not going to cry. I was not going to cry. I patted the tears from under my eyes and left the kitchen.

Feeling nervous, I fidgeted with my diamond earring as I strode through the house to the foyer. Assuring I could move about without restraint, I'd worn a blush colored jumpsuit and matching ballerina flats.

Too bad I hadn't thought about how difficult it was going to be to use the restroom beforehand. It had taken me five extra minutes to put myself back together.

I sighed.

I should have just worn the strapless knee-length dress.

Opening the door, I smiled at the big pots of hydrangeas. The intense antique pink created such a strong statement, I thought, dramatic, romantic, and eye-catching.

The sound of engines had me jerking my head up, and I watched with nervous jitters as the first caravan pulled through the gates. Three black town cars and two Suburbans carrying Remy and his entourage. The Governor and his wife and his security detail, the groomsmen, and the pastor and Jaxson, along with the groom were all arriving. Finn and Uncle Edward were with them, helping to coordinate the groom's side of the family.

It was almost go time.

Seconds later, they parked next to the vintage Jaguar and I couldn't believe the ceremony was expected to begin within an hour.

Nearly five weeks of planning, countless hours spent on this one wedding in hopes of making everyone's dreams come true, and it was about to commence.

Still teary-eyed, I patted under my eyes and tried not to think about the fact that I had no more clients after this one. That Easton Design & Weddings had been sold to a franchise, and they took occupancy on Monday.

Instead, I focused on the now. On the fact that the five hundred or so guests arriving very soon were royalty in their own right. Politicians, movie stars, high-society families. And they were going to be treated to a performance by singer Charlie Puth, who would be singing, "When I See You Again." It was to be dedicated to Rory's father. And Lana Del Ray was also coming. *Lana Del Ray!* She would be singing, "Love" and "Lust for Life," which were both sure to set the dance floor on fire.

And to top the evening off, at midnight there would also be a dazzling display of fireworks in the gardens to top those anywhere in the world.

Wedding guests were not allowed to bring cameras to the ceremony. This was mandated by the Governor's security detail, but Jaxson, who was the official wedding photographer, would be releasing photos to the news media on a timely basis.

I waved at Uncle Edward and Finn as they got out of the car. Just then Jaxson snapped his camera. "Looking good," he said, walking up the steps.

I smiled at him. "Yes, it does."

"I mean you. You look good. Not a sign of nerves anywhere."

I watched as Finn and Uncle Edward brought the groomsmen and family over to the pool house. "I'm a nervous wreck on the inside. Are you ready for the bride?"

He nodded.

"Okay, let me go check on her and then I'll come get you."

"I'll be around back."

Exhaling for courage, I turned around and headed up the grand staircase. I automatically veered right toward Jake's room, but then realized it wasn't him I needed to see. I turned direction and veered left toward Rory's room.

Things between Jake and I had been undefined. It's the only way I knew how to describe it. After the night we proclaimed our love for each other, we never spoke of it again.

Over the days that followed, I stayed with him at night. Mimi's condition had continued to decline, and he spent most of his time during the day with her. When I could, I joined them.

The sex between us bordered on desperate. It was a mix between lovemaking and fucking, but that had happened before I'd said those three little words.

Last night was the first night we hadn't slept in the same bed in weeks. After the rehearsal dinner, he went to Remy's bachelor party, and I spent some much-needed time pampering myself. I glanced down at my nails and smiled. The pretty pink gloss looked perfect.

My ears perked up as soon as I hit the landing. I could hear the hysteria from here. I picked up my pace and knocked loudly on the bride's door. When Rory's maid of honor opened it, she had fire in her eyes.

"What's going on?" I asked.

My eyes bounced around the room, from one lace bridesmaid to the next fringe-covered one to the one in chiffon, and then to the tall, lone figure standing incredibly handsome by the window with his hands in his tuxedo pockets and his bottom lip in a pout.

Why was he in here?

"Remy's oldest brother hired more than a dozen strippers for the bachelor party last night. Look!" She shoved her phone displaying an Instagram photo, that must have somehow had been leaked, in my face.

At first, I gave it a quick glance. I'd been through this a dozen times. It was my job to remain Switzerland and neutralize any impending disasters before they happened.

But then I took the phone from her and studied the photo a bit more. The guys in the wedding party were in the private room of some club seated at a table. Each with a barely dressed woman on their lap, including Jake.

I wanted to enlarge it. To see if he was turned on. Look at his facial expression. I did not. I was here for Rory. Not myself. Yet, I couldn't stop my mind from wandering back to last night. To the text he'd sent me around eleven.

Him: Are you in bed?

Me: I am.

Him: Are you thinking about me?

Me: I am now.

Him: Touch yourself for me.

Me: Where are you?

Him: It doesn't matter. Touch yourself and tell me if you're wet.

Me: Have you been drinking?

Him: I've had my share. Are you doing it?

Me: Come over and do it yourself.

Him: Can't.

Me: I'll leave the door unlocked, come over anytime.

He never did say yes, and he never came over. He called me this morning and told me all the guys passed out in the suite at the Ritz, and I left it at that.

I glanced toward him. His gaze looked so very male, and as our eyes locked, he didn't show an ounce of regret. It made my stomach constrict painfully. "It wasn't at all how it looks," he sighed as if he'd already been through this.

Obviously, this was why he was in here.

"Where's Rory?" I asked, only just now realizing she was not in the room.

Twelve girls shouted out different things, but the only voice I heard was his. "She locked herself in the bathroom, and I can't get her to come out."

The wedding planner in me kicked into action. "Everyone out," I shouted.

After protesting, they all finally filed out, all except Jake. As soon as the door closed, he was on me. His hands on my hips drew me close. "Nothing happened. They were strippers doing their thing."

"I know," I said, my voice low, steady.

"No, you don't. I can see it written all over your face."

I lifted my shoulders in a careless shrug and turned away, refusing to meet his dark stare any longer. "Rory," I pounded on the door. "Come out here, we need to talk about that picture."

"I am not coming out. You can tell everyone to go home."

I sighed in frustration. "Did you even look at the picture?" I asked.

"Do you want to talk about this or not?" Jake said.

Unimpressed by the fact that his tone was bordering on angry, I knocked on the door again. "No, I don't."

"Why not?"

"Because I don't want to," I whispered. "Rory, please come out and look at this picture."

"You're pissed because I never made it over and I get it, but I passed out with the rest of the guys and then when I woke up, I had to get Remy home."

"Or was it because you were hot to get in that floozy's pants, or panties, I should say."

His laughter had me seeing red.

Incredulous, I whisper-shouted, "It's not funny. You texted me all hot and bothered and then never replied."

He took the phone from my hand and blew the picture up with

his fingers. "Look, I wasn't even paying attention to her. I was texting you when she was on my lap, and then Remy took my phone because the guys had taken his, and went out to the car to call Rory. I never found it until this morning."

My heart leaped into my throat when I looked a little harder. He was right. "Oh," was all I could say.

Jake threw his head back and laughed. His shoulders were still shaking when the door flew open.

Rory came out in a white silk robe that had the word 'Bride' monogramed on the right breast pocket. She narrowed her big blue eyes at her brother. "This isn't funny, you manwhore."

He didn't stop laughing. "Rory, just look at the picture."

I handed the phone to her.

"Remy isn't even one of the guys with a girl on his lap. Look." She shoved it back my way.

"I know," I told her. "That was what I was trying to tell you."

"He really does love me," she grinned.

Jake was shaking his head. "Can you finish getting dressed, Mimi wants to see you before we all go downstairs."

Practically bubbling over, she ran back into the bathroom. "I have to get ready!"

Jake pulled me to him and I could smell his fresh scent and as soon as I got close, he smacked me on the ass.

I yelped in surprise. "What was that for?"

"You know exactly what it was for," he murmured, and then he slid his tongue in my mouth and I forgot all about the floozy with the big boobs who was sitting on his lap, mostly.

When Rory finally emerged from the bathroom, I broke free of Jake's lustful hold and stared at her in awe.

"You two are too cute together," she said, and I blushed the brightest hue of pink.

Jake ignored the comment all together. "Are you ready to see

Mimi?"

She nodded. "Just need help with the back of my dress."

In her glimmering white dress, sparkling with silver beads, she looked every bit as beautiful as she was. I rushed over to her and fastened the dainty pearl buttons. Then I stepped back into the room and watched as she swept back her elaborate skirt and stepped out into the room. A new light beamed in Rory's bluebell eyes. "You were right," she said to me.

I inclined my head. "About Remy?"

She shook her head. "No, that's old news. About not wearing a veil." She touched a hand to the band sparkling in her upswept brown hair. "This is a statement piece."

I nodded and forced myself to hold back the tears. "It certainly is."

Jake strode toward us and held his arms out to both of us, and once we took them, he led us out the door.

Mimi was sitting in her wheelchair, her portable oxygen tank already connected and ready to go. Matthew was by her side, as were two other nurses.

In her pale green dress and matching turban, she looked every bit as regal as the status she held. She'd been made up and her lips and cheeks shined a rosy pink. None of that hid the fact that she was barely able to sit upright in her chair.

As soon as she saw Rory, she burst into tears and took the mask from her face. "Oh, my darling Rory, you look like a princess out of a fairytale."

Rory rushed over to her and I tried to grab her skirt to help her, but she was too fast. "I love you, Mimi. I love you so much."

Mimi patted her back. "No tears today, my darling Rory. Today is supposed to be the happiest day of your life."

"I know," Rory choked out, "but I can't help it."

"Now, now," she said. "Straighten up."

Rory took a big breath and did what Mimi had told her to do. With trembling hands, Mimi opened the blue silk bag that sat in her lap. "This is for you, Rory. It belonged to my great-grandmother."

Rory stared at the diamond necklace from the photo in the parlor with her mouth wide open. "Mimi! Oh my God, I had no idea you even had this."

When Mimi tried to unfasten it, she couldn't, and Jake hurriedly took it from her. He fastened the fire of diamonds around his sister's neck. "Something new," he whispered. She fingered the necklace and Mimi looked on at the two of them with pride and joy.

Jake then took something from his pocket. It was a thin, sparkly pink bracelet, and when Rory saw it, she burst into tears. "You kept this?"

He nodded. "It's your something old."

I melted right there. He had been listening to me when I went over wedding protocol.

She pulled it over her wrist and then hugged him.

There was a knock on the door. "Are you ready for the photos?" It was Jaxson, and as always, he had perfect timing.

"Yes," I called. "Come in."

I knew Jaxson would capture that iced fire, the lovely lines of Rory's shoulders, the sweep of her vintage dress, but I also knew he would capture the moment that would mean everything. The emotion between the three of them. The love they shared so easily captured on film to last a lifetime.

I watched as Jaxson posed them and snapped away.

"Join us," Mimi said.

"No, no," I argued, with a wave of a hand. "This is for the three of you."

"I insist," she said.

And I knew there was no arguing with Mimi, so I crossed the room and stood between Mimi and Jake.

Snap.

Click.

Snap.

Click.

I felt like I belonged there. Beside Jake. And I knew I shouldn't. I knew things were only temporary between us even though I hated to think about them that way.

"It's time." Roger was at the door looking wistfully at Mimi.

As soon as she heard his voice, everything about her lit up. That's when I knew. I knew in my heart that Roger was the love of her life. The man she couldn't have so many years ago and maybe never had since.

"Yes," she said, and when she spoke her voice was thin and fragile. "I think it is time."

Roger took control of the wheelchair, and together we all went out into the hallway. Mimi and Rory took the elevator, and the rest of us descended the stairs.

The moment came quickly.

The groom took his place, and Mimi was wheeled to her reserved place right up front.

I turned to gather the bouquets and pass them out as Uncle Edward lined the bridesmaids up, who had all settled down and were smiling very flirtatiously for Jaxson.

When I got to Jake and Rory, I felt my knees go week. He looked so incredibly handsome and she looked like a princess straight out of a fairy tale. "Rory, you really do look stunning," I told her.

"Oh, don't." She waved a hand in front of her face. "I didn't think I'd get all choked up at all, but I'm right on the edge of doing it twice."

"One breath in, one breath out," I ordered. "Slow and easy."

"Thank you, Jules." She looked over at her brother and drew in a ragged breath. "She's so perfect for you. You could join me and we could have a double wedding."

"Don't." He gave her hand a squeeze. "I need to be able to walk down this aisle without wanting to knock you off your heels."

She laughed. "I can always count on you to say the right thing, brother."

He brought her hand to his lips and kissed it. "You look beautiful. Dad would be proud."

At that she started to cry for the second time. I looked at Jake, at the man he was, the good man who didn't want to believe he was, and sucked in a breath.

"And two . . . go." Uncle Edward said.

Oh crap!

I quickly wiped the tears from Rory's eyes and stepped out of the way. "Go, go," I urged as the music changed.

"I'm impressed," Uncle Edward told me as Rory and Jake started down the aisle. I looked up at him. "Everything went so smoothly. You really are fantastic at this, Jules. I shouldn't have doubted you."

My eyes filled with tears and I threw my arms around him. "Thank you," I said softly, and I meant it for more than just the compliment. I owed him so much. "Wedding planning comes naturally, it's all the rest I have trouble with."

"You are going to be great at whatever comes next."

Next.

I didn't want to think about that.

"I think we've all earned this." I pulled back to find Finn with a bottle of pink champagne in his hand that he naturally confiscated from the fountain out in the main tent. The label read Cupcake Champagnes. I'd left the liquor ordering to Finn, so I was surprised to see that. I thought they only produced wines.

"Later," I said with a wink, and then I hooked my arms through his and Uncle Edward's. "Right now we have to watch our bride get married."

From the back, I watched as Jake gave his sister away and took his place near Mimi. When he reached for her hand and squeezed it, I let another tear roll down my cheek. She looked so very frail.

I hated that he had to lose her.

I hated the circle of life.

And I hated death most of all.

As the ceremony concluded, and after the bride and groom came down the aisle, I threw confetti at them along with the other guests.

Everyone then began milling around in the garden, and I stood and watched for a bit. It was a garden party to top all garden parties.

Jaxson was standing over near the pool, and I walked over toward him. "Hey," I said.

He looked at me with a sadness in his eyes I hadn't seen in a very long time. "Hey."

"Is everything okay?"

He gave me a slow nod. "Perfect. Just about to take family pictures outside. Are you coming?"

I shook my head. "Go ahead. I've been in enough photos."

"Oh, come on, you have to join them. I haven't gotten to take any shots of just you and the man who has obviously stolen your heart."

"Jaxson, please don't look at it that way."

"Hey," he said, "Do you think if the two of you get married, you could use those monogramed towels we got for our engagement party?"

I knew he was joking.

It was his nature.

Yet, it stung.

I reached for his hand, but he placed it on his camera. "Jaxson, I never meant to hurt you."

He lifted his lens and snapped my picture. "I know, Jules, but that doesn't mean you didn't. The good news is I'll get over it. Now come on."

"I'll catch up," I whispered.

Once he was gone, I reflected on the differences between my relationship with Jaxson and my relationship with Jake. Both were good men. Both handsome. Smart. Sweet and funny. They were similar in so many ways, and yet so different in others. I loved them both, just in different ways.

I didn't want to hurt Jaxson.

But he and I were over long before I met Jake.

There was something missing between us, and it was on his part as well as mine. Even if he didn't see it that way right then, some day he would.

I want the best for him.

I want him to feel what I feel.

To feel more alive than ever.

That's the thing about love, wasn't it—you don't get to pick it, it just happens.

Wistful, I looked toward the west and stared for a long time. I couldn't believe it when the brilliant magenta sun began dipping beyond the horizon.

It was picture perfect.

The day had been one of sparkling clarity, without a cloud in the sky and bathed in nothing but sunshine.

Not too hot and absolutely no rain.

It was beyond perfect.

Too bad it wouldn't last forever.

Whole Nine Yards

JULES

I STARED AT that mouth. Those lips . . .

Oh, my God.

Jake was talking, telling me about a conversation he had had with the Governor about the rural counties of Georgia, but I wasn't listening.

In the vast space of the open ballroom, it was taking all of my strength to fight against the lustful desire that was trying to make its way deep inside me.

Jake glanced over at me, and I knew the moment he became aware of my lustful trance. I felt the blood rush to my face, and I swallowed hard. My parted lips and heavy breathing were a dead giveaway. Not to mention my nipples felt like diamonds, and there was a steady pulsing between my legs that was beginning to ache.

He leaned closer.

He knew what he was doing to me.

My clit felt like it was throbbing.

Space.

I needed space.

Thank God, the ballroom doors were open, and I used that as my cue to put some distance between us. With long strides, I stepped ahead of him and out into the fresh air of the night. He caught up with me, and my gaze rose. Again I found myself staring at those lips.

Those lips that had to send every woman reeling.

I knew they did me.

With a dry throat, I managed, "Looks like everything went off without a hitch."

Jake dropped his own gaze. "All that's left are the fireworks and the send-off, and then it's done. I think you deserve a break."

I gave a huff of laughter. "My break will come at the very end."

He looked at his watch. "We only have thirty minutes until midnight. I think you can relax for a few minutes."

I sipped my pink champagne and then turned to look out toward the party. Moonlight danced on the surface of the tents, and the stars were as bright as I'd ever seen them. "Yes, maybe I can."

I leaned against the open door jamb. I'd changed into that blush silk dress with the thin, sexy straps I should have worn to begin with. The only downside was I had to change my shoes. My toes curled in my heels. My feet were killing me.

Lilies scented the air, and I breathed it in. I loved this part of summer. The dark nights and the warm air whirling around with the scent of the summer in it.

From behind, Jake reached around me and handed me a black velvet rectangular box. "I bought you something."

With shaky fingers, I took it from him and opened it. Inside was the most beautiful diamond necklace. A single solitaire inside an elongated star. A perfect match to my diamond earrings. I looked at him.

"It's your North Star. Whenever you wear it, I want you to think of me."

I knew this was his goodbye to me, but I didn't want to believe it. I just wanted him.

He put it around my neck and then turned me to face him. His eyes turned hungry and electricity sparked between us with just a simple look. This attraction was too much. I didn't know how to deal with it without acting on it.

Dropping my gaze, I looked at my glossy pink toes. He lifted my chin. Excitement stirred in the air. He was so close to me that I could smell his heavenly scent. He smelled of the soap in the shower. He smelled of pure man. Like always I wanted to bury my nose in his neck and sniff him.

Our bodies were almost touching.

I wanted them to be.

Then they were.

Like two magnets, we were drawn together.

He had leaned forward just a bit and then his fingers were on my face, tucking a stray piece of hair behind my ear.

Feeling electrified, my body jerked as his flesh came in direct contact with mine, and my breath caught at the intensity of the physical connection.

"I want you," he whispered at the same time he lightly nipped at my bottom lip. "Right now." I nodded, silently telling him I wanted him too—and right now.

He took my hand and walked fast through the foyer and into the room that had once been his grandmother's office. Behind him he locked the door, and then pressed me against it.

The feeling of his lean, muscular body pressed against mine only served to further ignite my desire. With a desperation I didn't understand, I pushed myself closer. Close enough that my hard nipples pushed against his unyielding chest. I couldn't help myself.

Jake made a sound of approval deep in his throat.

I wanted to close my eyes but couldn't. I had to see him. I looked up into his eyes, those light and dark eyes, and lost myself in him.

He looked at me like nothing else mattered but having me.

I shivered from that look alone.

It wasn't long before his hands were running up my sides and when he lifted me, I felt electrified. I wanted this like I'd never wanted anything. Responding in the only way I could, I wrapped both my arms and legs around him and then buried my face in his neck.

With my lips touching his skin, and his scent invading me, my senses came alive. The edges of his hair tickled wonderfully against my cheek. The feel of his hands, now firmly grasping my hips, seared me as if he were branding me. His heavy breathing was all I could hear.

What came next happened so fast. We were moving. He was setting me down on the desk. His hands were dragging up my body to the hem of my dress. He lifted it to my waist.

My fingers trembled as they unzipped his pants. With a lick of my lips, I allowed my eyes to graze over him—he was devastatingly handsome. He was soft and hard at the same time. Just like the line of his jaw, the shape of his nose—they were hard but those incredible blue eyes outlined in dark, thick lashes softened his features.

My gaze slid down.

Seeing his erection made my heart beat so fast.

Heat flared in my belly.

All of a sudden, everything became about this man.

He was all I could think about. On how he slid his hands to the back of my neck. On how his fingers tangled in my hair to tip my head back. On those lips that would be on me very soon.

Oh, God.

Then he slid those soft lips down my skin and his fingers followed, and I felt each beat of his breath and mine.

Excitement danced in my belly.

My nipples were tight, like hard steel tips. When Jake skimmed his thumb over the silk that covered my breast, I sucked in a breath and nearly gasped. But when he pushed the fabric aside to close his mouth around it, and I felt his tongue, his teeth, and his lips all at the same time, I practically whimpered.

It felt so good—warm and wicked.

He worked his way back up to my throat, sucking the sensitive skin of my neck between his teeth as he did. The small bites didn't hurt, but they did send the most erotic sensations ripping through me.

I bucked beneath him with a crazy, writhing need. I was like a lioness out of her cage, wild and free. With desperation, my hands found the back of his head to thread my fingers in his hair. Tugging it, pulling it, I brought him to my mouth where I wanted those lips.

He groaned, and then he placed his palm and pressed against my clit on the outside of my panties. Again, I writhed beneath him.

I had become a current for his touch, and the way his fingers slid inside my panties to find my slick heat, more than electrified me from the top of my head to my the tips of toes.

Breathless, I moved my hands to his shoulders and slid my tongue down his throat, and just like he had, I pulled his skin between my teeth. I might have been rougher, I might have left a mark—I wasn't sure. I just couldn't control myself.

His responding groan told me he was burning just like me, and his body language told me not to stop, so I didn't. Not until he moved to capture my mouth with his own and take me with a heart-stopping kiss.

If I were romantic, I'd say that although he was bold with his body, to the point of unfaltering, he was almost tender, sweet even, with his mouth. It was that whole hot/cold, hard/soft thing we'd had going on from the start.

The heat of his body radiated and I could hear his ragged breaths. They mimicked mine. He took his cock in his hand and positioned himself at my opening. With the sounds of our mingled breaths the only noise in the room, I placed my palms flat on the cool surface and spread my legs wider.

His exultant groan echoed as soon as he thrust into me. Twin bursts of pleasure sizzled under his touch. I bit my lip to stop from crying out.

With steady movements, he eased in and then out again. In then out. Giving me a bit more each time. Going deeper and deeper. When he was fully inside me, I thrust my head back and closed my eyes.

He was my home, and I was going to lose him.

With his hands tightly gripping my hips, he slammed into me. Hard. And then harder still. Again, I had to bite my lip to stop from crying out.

It felt so good.

His fingers gripped me, pinched me almost, as he slammed into me. I followed his rhythm, and then everything exploded inside me. He pulled back and thrust. His cock slid so deep inside me that my hands gripped the edge of the table so hard that it was cutting into my skin.

And then we were both coming.

Joined together, we were breathing heavy, giving each other pleasure that never seemed to be enough. His head fell to the crook of my neck, and I wrapped my arms around him.

This was who we were, but not who we were meant to be. And I had to accept that.

Outside the office, we heard shouts. "Jake. Jake. Where are you?" It was Rory, and her voice was panicked.

Jake jerked back in a rush and zipped up his pants. He looked at me. "Go," I said, getting to my feet and pushing my dress down.

"I'm right behind you."

"Jake, where are you?"

He rushed from the room and up the stairs toward Mimi's bedroom. I tried to move fast, but I was stopped in my tracks when I heard the sound. The tortured cry of despair that ripped from Jake's throat.

And I knew . . . I knew then, something really bad had happened. *That Mimi had died.*

Once In A Blue Moon

JULES

I FOUND HIS goodbye note on his dresser the morning after the funeral.

The envelope was thick, and my heart pounded as I opened it. Inside were the pearls that I had admired the first time I met Mrs. Beatrice Beau Crawford Alexander and a hand-written note in what I had come to recognize as Jake's handwriting.

I grasped the pearls in my hand and read the note.

Juliette,

Saying goodbye is never easy, which is why I thought it would be best not to put either of us through that.

I want to tell you to wait for me, but I can't because it isn't fair. I don't know how long the wait would be.

I want to stay, but I can't. I have to do this for me. For him. I owe him that much.

I want to say so many things, but the only one that really matters is that when I was with you, you brought my world from black and white to color.

Enclosed is Mimi's pearl necklace. She wanted you to have it, and wanted to make sure I told you to remember how strong you are. You should already know that, but I'm doing as she asked for fear she's watching.

Jake x

Rushing to the window, I looked down. The vintage Jaguar was no longer parked in the drive. It was gone. Probably locked away in one of the garages until he came back.

If he ever came back.

My head was spinning. I stumbled to the bed and held the letter tight in my hand. I took a deep breath. I was not going to allow myself to have a panic attack. I knew this was coming. And Mimi had been right. She knew he would leave the easy way, and he had.

Why hadn't I seen this coming?

I should have.

Tears got stuck in my throat, and I stubbornly swallowed them down.

I looked at the pearls in my hand.

"You are strong," she'd said.

I wasn't.

"Show him the way," she'd said.

I couldn't.

I didn't know it myself.

I clutched the necklace he'd given me with my free hand. He was my North Star. My Polaris. I just couldn't reach him. He was too far away. And it was time to let him go. At least for now.

Rory knocked on the door and stepped inside. The way she was looking at me, I knew she knew he'd gone.

She slouched down beside me, and I rubbed my eyes in an effort to get rid of the fog that was hanging over me.

"He's gone," she whispered.

"I know."

"You have to go get him."

"I can't. He doesn't want that. He wants to be left alone."

She threw her leg up on the bed as she turned toward me. "My brother doesn't know what he wants. I've never seen him as happy as when he is with you, but his guilt is something he's carried for so long that he doesn't know how to let it go. You have to help him."

"I can't." Frustration made my voice edgy.

"You have to. You're the only one who can. He blames himself for something he shouldn't, and one day it's going to break him. You have to help him."

"I don't think I can. I don't know how."

"Jules, Mimi told me you did. Please don't give up on him."

"I have to," I whispered. "That's what he wants."

I clutched the pearls in my hand tighter.

Show him the way.

I couldn't show him the way because I didn't know it myself.

And I doubt I ever would.

chapter 31

Add Insult To Injury

JAKE

I HEARD THE call come in just before nine pm.

"A homeless man on a stabbing rampage in Greenwich Village stabbed two people, assessing injuries and in transit."

Senseless violence I'd never understand.

I'd been at New York Presbyterian Hospital for more than a week and every day I felt further and further removed. The satisfaction I knew my father had gotten out of this job didn't resonate the same within me. I preferred the face-to-face of talking with patients. Discovering what was bothering them and working together to help cure them.

There was none of that here. Just senseless violence wheeled in every day. It was hard to stomach.

I didn't get any satisfaction out of it.

There was no glory.

No sense of pride.

Just a deep sadness that I couldn't seem to shed.

I'd wanted to follow in my father's footsteps for so long, I had no idea anymore if it was ever my dream or just my nightmare.

"What do we have?" I asked the intake nurse.

"Fifty-six-year-old man with a stab wound to the chest very close to his right lung. He's unconscious."

"What about the other victim?"

"Woman about the same age stabbed in both arms. Conscious, but not alert. She may be on something."

Moments later the doors crashed open and the paramedics powered through them. With fast feet, I trotted alongside them as they wheeled the first patient in. It only took me a moment to recognize the man lying on the gurney. "Peter," I said out loud.

"You know him?" one of the medics asked.

I nodded. "Dr. Wright. He used to work here. What's his condition?" I asked, already assessing it for myself.

"He'd lost a lot of blood before we arrived. Pressure dressings were applied. And we started two IV's."

"Has he been given anything for pain?"

"Base ordered morphine."

"Anyone with him?"

"Yes, the other victim."

I looked over to the third year resident that was on my heels. "Rule out other possible injuries and book an OR, stat."

"Yes, Dr. Kissinger, I'm on it."

While this third-year resident followed Advanced Trauma Life Support protocols, I quickly turned around to check on the second victim being wheeled in and froze. The haggard, unkempt looking woman was covered in blood . . . and she was my mother. "Monica," I said hoarsely.

She looked up. Unfocused. "Jake, is that you?" she cried.

I nodded. Stunned.

It had been a long time since I'd seen her.

She reached for me. "Oh, Jake."

Fear seized my balls.

This was a nightmare.

"Jake," she cried louder. "Talk to me, baby."

Ignoring her pleas, I looked over at the paramedic. "What's her condition?"

"Superficial stab wounds. Small pupils. Burn marks around her mouth. Dark circles around her eyes."

I cut him off. "Heroine?" I asked, barely able to get the word out.

"As far as I can tell she's a habitual user. However, there were no traces of drugs on her person at the scene. In fact, her and the male were attacked leaving a church after attending a Narcotics Anonymous meeting." It took me a moment to gain my bearings. I hadn't seen her in so long.

This woman was my mother.

And a drug addict?

Alcoholic I could have guessed, but the other?

I forced away all of my own shit. "Emergency can stitch up her wounds," I told him, keeping my voice neutral, calm, while my insides screamed. He nodded and veered to the right while I went left.

"Jake," she called, but I didn't have time for a reunion right now. I had to scrub up and take care of Dr. Wright.

My patient.

"I'm losing his pulse," the resident shouted.

I sprung into action. "I want four units running of rapid infuser five minutes ago!" I told him and watched as they slammed through the steel doors.

Scrubbed up and gowned, I stormed into the room and took control of the patient. Checking his stats, a cold sweat broke out across my forehead. The signs and symptoms of a hemothorax were all right in front of me. His blood pressure was low, he was experiencing tachycardia, and his skin was both cool and clammy. "Chest X-ray, stat," I ordered.

This man was in critical condition, and we had to work fast.

The team gathered around, clicking into action.

As soon as I saw the X-ray, I knew exactly what we were dealing with. "Send off for a CBC, a chem-20, and grab all the O-neg you can find!" I told the team who surrounded me.

"Yes, doctor."

"Hang in there, Peter," I whispered.

The resident slammed another sedative into the IV. "Massive hemothorax," he told me without question.

I nodded. He saw exactly what I saw. This kid was good.

I cleared my mind and focused on the patient. Not who he was or why he was with my drug-addicted mother, but instead, on the patient in need of care.

By inserting a large-bore needle into the space of the affected side, I was allowing air to escape and hopefully relieving the pressure. Needle decompression was standard procedure in cases like this.

"Suction please," I dictated as I pulled the needle out.

"Pulse is dropping," the resident shouted grabbing for the paddles.

"Come on, Peter," I whispered as I moved aside.

"Clear! Clear! Clear!" the resident called.

"I got a pulse!" the nurse shouted.

"Yes! You are not going to die, Peter. Do you hear me? You are not going to die," I told the patient on the table even though he could not hear me.

With the rapid accumulation of blood in his chest, I knew I had to do more than allow for air passage. I had to drain it. "Prepare to assist with the immediate placement of a 36–40F chest tube and establish two large-bore antecubital IV lines for aggressive fluid resuscitation, blood transfusion, and auto-transfusion. Now!" I shouted out to the team.

Time was short. His breathing was impaired. While I worked, I couldn't help but think of Monica. She'd fucked up my life. I blamed her for my father's death almost as much as I blamed myself. The woman was poison. *What the hell was Peter doing with her?*

"He's stable," the resident called out.

I blew out a breath and performed a secondary survey, reassessing and looking for other life-threatening injuries, of which there were none.

Thank fuck.

While the team took care of readying the patient for the holding room in Trauma One, it was time for me to collect any information about the patient and incident that I could, and I was dreading it.

In addition to circumstances directly related to the injury, I had to find out as much as possible about the patient's medical history, medications, when he last ate, and if he consumed any alcohol or did any recreational drugs.

And the woman I had to solicit this information from was Monica.

Fuck me.

Thinking about what I had to do, but not at all looking forward to having to do it, I stood in the doorway unable to move and watched as the nurses removed all of Peter's clothing.

Since penetrating chest injuries usually involved violence, it was important to collect evidence according to hospital policy. They had to place each piece of clothing in a separate paper bag.

As they cut away the sides of the sports coat he was wearing, an oddly tri-folded off-white piece of paper fell to the ground.

It caught my attention immediately, and I jetted toward it. Picking it up, all I could do was stare as I unfolded it and read the same words I'd read over and over for so many years.

I'm sorry. It wasn't your fault.

Pain.

It struck like a piercing wave of old hurt. My heart started to pound, and my breath came too quickly as I stared stonily at the piece of paper. I had seen this very same thing every year for fourteen years. Last year I hadn't received one though, so I thought they had stopped.

My lips twisted. *Why did Peter have this?*

The man whose life I'd just saved had been sending them.

Why?

The nurse looked at me before continuing what she was doing. I didn't return the piece of paper but instead stared at Peter.

What the fuck?

Why?

He wasn't going to answer me of course, but I knew who would.

Storming through the trauma wing, I marched into the ER and looked on the board. I found her name and was whipping back the curtain and looking at the woman who I knew to be my mother without so much as a thought about what I was doing.

My nape prickled from the resemblance and I slowed my pace, forcing myself to remember she might look like the woman who raised me, but she was nothing like that woman on the inside.

Lying in the hospital bed, looking so frail and thin, Monica was a replica of Mimi only so much younger she shouldn't have been. "Jake?" she said softly.

Desolation settled over me as I held the paper high. "What the fuck kind of sick game have you and Peter been playing?"

Her eyes widened in shock. "I don't know what you're talking about."

I stared at her coldly as I closed the distance between us and tossed the paper onto her lap. "This! Why was it in Peter's pocket?"

Color rose in her cheeks. "Jake, I don't know."

Anger surged through my veins. "You owe me the truth!"

"I don't know why," she cried. "I've never seen it before."

Liar.

I took a deep breath. "Why were the two of you together?"

Monica sat up but said nothing.

"Why?" I shouted.

She shifted on the bed, and the blanket fell from her body. When it did, I saw the track lines on her arms.

This woman was severely broken.

What had she been doing all these years?

Monica let out a forlorn-sounding sigh. "He came to help me."

"Help you how?" I bit out.

She looked away. "I was doing so good, but then I relapsed after Mimi refused to let me come see her before she died. Peter found out and flew to New York to get me back on track."

Bleakly, I thought back to any time Peter might have mentioned my mother and recalled none. "Why would he do that? And how does Peter know anything about your life?"

All the blood drained from her face. "He's been trying to help me get sober and stay that way for the past fifteen years."

My eyes flickered over her. I wanted to call her a liar. And out loud this time. But I couldn't. The truth was they were together when he was attacked, and they were leaving a Narcotic's Anonymous meeting, so some of what she was saying had to be true. "Why did he care if you were high or drunk or sober? What did it matter to him?"

Her brows furrowed in confusion. "Because, Jake, he feels guilty and he says it helps him cope with that guilt."

I stared at her. "What exactly does he have to feel guilty about?"

"He's the reason your father was working that day. The reason your father didn't come to Connecticut to see you and Rory."

If the rug could ever actually be pulled out from under you, it was just done to me. I felt unsteady on my feet, and without thinking, I sat on the edge of the bed. "What are you talking about? I'm the one who texted Dad and told him not to come."

She reached for my hand. "No, baby, your father had called me that morning and told me he'd been called into work and wasn't going to be able to make it. I told you about his call that morning."

I shook my head vehemently.

"Yes, I did. I came downstairs, and you were in the kitchen."

My mind went whirling back to that morning.

I heard the stumbling on the stairs. Monica had come down looking peaked and a mess. She rushed to the sink where she vomited. Looking over at me, she said something I couldn't understand.

I didn't care enough to ask her to repeat it. "I can get us both to school," I barked, and walked away, assuming she was apologizing again for her bad behavior.

I blinked the memory away and felt a chill so deep it shook my body. He hadn't come to Connecticut, that part was true, but not because of me, rather because he had to work.

I wasn't the reason my father had died.

The revelation should have lifted a mountain off my shoulders, but the reality was my father had still died on that tragic day, and the sadness of his death far outweighed the reason he had been in the city.

This city.

And chances were good, he'd have been right where he was no matter what he'd been doing because that was the kind of man he was.

That too hit me like a brick wall.

"You look so much like your father, Jake," my mother said. "He'd be so proud of you."

I looked at her with disgust. "How would you know?"

Her voice was weak, sad. "Because I know. I know."

"You don't. You never cared about him or me."

"That's not true. I wanted to see you, Jake. I did. But I had to get better. And I've been trying ever since you left."

I laughed and took hold of her arm. "Yeah, you've been trying really hard."

Tears spilled from her eyes. "I don't expect you to understand, but every day since Mimi took you and Rory from me, I have wanted to get better and get you both back."

"It's been sixteen years," I gritted out. "It's a little late now, don't you think?"

She shook her head. "I'm so sorry, Jake. I'm so sorry."

I shook out of her hold and stood up. "I used to hate you, Monica, but now I only feel sorry for you."

Her shoulders sagged. "I know, baby, I know. But someday, Jake, I will get better."

"Yeah, look me up when you do," I said, choking on the words.

"I will, Jake, just you wait and see. And when I do, I will fight for your love."

Every bone in my body wanted to reach out and help this woman. Looking at her though, I finally understood what Mimi had been through. The never-ending road. The constant disappointment. The helplessness of wanting to help someone who didn't really want help. Like Mimi, I knew enabling Monica would only make her weaker. Unlike Mimi, I wasn't going to spend my whole life doing it. And I guess, unlike Peter as well.

Dr. Peter Wright blamed himself for my father's death. The man had taken me under his wing, been a mentor, tried to keep me away from a job he knew I was pursuing out of my own guilt, and the reason behind it all had been guilt.

I should have been angry, but I wasn't. I got guilt. I knew what it felt like, tasted like, smelled like.

I'd lived it.

I understood it.

How it ate you up and controlled your life.

I was done with that. I was done with it. And Peter needed to be, too.

The thing was . . . like I said, my father was who he was, and he would have been there that day no matter what. He was a hero, who probably helped save more lives than I would ever know. *He was my hero.*

Shifting my gaze from Monica's to the note, I turned and headed out of the room. I had to make sure Peter knew I didn't blame him.

"Jake," Monica called. I looked over my shoulder. "I will get better."

"I hope so," I told her sincerely. And as I left the ER, I felt like a brick had been lifted off my shoulders. Lighter. Free. A new version of myself.

In the doctor's lounge, I slumped down and took my head in my hands. I'd wanted to be like my father since the day he died. Yet, the truth was, I didn't have to follow in his footsteps to be a good man. I didn't have to be him to make sure I wasn't like her. I just had to be me.

My whole life I'd run from the shadows that hung over me. Blaming myself for my father's death. Worried I was like *her*. Running away from building a life that I only believed would end in destruction, like hers.

Now, having come face-to-face with Monica after all these years, I knew I wasn't anything like her. I wasn't her.

The truth was I was who I was, and it wasn't my father or my mother.

I was just me.

A man who wanted to help people.

A man who knew right from wrong.

A man who, whether I wanted to or not, loved a woman he'd left behind. Loved. Yes, I might not have been looking for it, but it found me.

And maybe it was time to stop running away from my past and run toward the future.

Maybe it was time to do what Mimi had told me I had the strength to do just days before she died . . . *and show Juliette the way.*

chapter
32

Best Thing Since Sliced Bread

JULES

I HAD COME here every year for the past fifteen years.

The 9/11 Memorial Plaza was a tribute to the past and a place of hope for the future. The eight-acre park was a sanctuary where terror once reigned down. Set within the footprints of the original Twin Towers sits one of the largest manmade waterfalls in the United States.

The name of every person who perished in the attack was stencil-cut into parapets around the pools. In the evening, light shines up through the voids of each letter of a name.

It was special.

It was with purpose.

It was heart-wrenching and soul-soothing.

There was a fleeting sadness in my gaze as I looked toward the flags that were lowered at half-staff.

My eyelids hung heavy when at 8:46 the first of the bells rang. I stopped where I was and bowed my head in silence.

I would always remember. Everyone would always remember. The darkness that had come and the fight to find the light guaranteed that.

I shivered under the damp gray sky and drew my coat tighter around myself as I walked. I knew where I was going. I hadn't passed the names of Josh and Rachael Easton on accident. I would run my fingers over their names, over and over, as I had for years, but first I wanted to find another name.

I found his name quickly and stared at it for a long while. Dr. Conrad Kissinger, a hero who died trying to save the lives of those inside. Maybe even those of my parents. I would never know this, of course.

Hot tears pricked my eyelids, and I swallowed them back. Fiercely determined to be strong, I ran my fingers over the letters of his name and said a prayer for him.

I wasn't religious.

I didn't pray often.

But coming here, it seemed like the right thing to do.

When the second bell rang, I knew it was time to move on. I could stand in one spot all day and contemplate the senselessness of the terrorism and the loss of all the lives, but I knew it would never bring my family back to me.

As much as I was a 9/11 kid, I had never allowed it to label me. Until Jake, I had kept my sadness inside, but now I knew it was okay to let it out.

It was okay to be sad.

That didn't make me weak.

It might actually even make me stronger.

A few days ago I had received a call from another 9/11 kid who was putting together a documentary about the children who lost parents on that day. Up until now, I had shied away from any involvement to do with the status that was forced upon me. Yet this time, I said yes. I would participate. I would tell my story. It was time to share my grief with those who felt what I felt.

Time to help heal as best we could—together.

As Jake and I had done for each other.

I'd thought about calling him and asking him to meet me here, but in the end, I decided to honor his wishes and let him do what he had to do. I understood grief manifested itself in different ways, and he was working his out the only way he knew how. I hadn't given up hope for the two of us, but I wasn't sure I was strong enough to fight for him right now. I hoped someday soon I would be though.

I had to find myself first before I could show him the way.

I'd spent the days since Jake had left at my uncle's farm. I'd also gone to see George and Ethel to tell them the truth about me. Believe it or not, Jake had gone to see them before he left and already told them everything. They weren't angry or spiteful. They were only happy to see me.

They were good people.

Step by step, I walked slowly toward the names of my parents, and when I did, I allowed myself to remember that last morning I'd spent with them in our kitchen. The love I'd witnessed between them. The family we'd once been. The person I was then.

Everything that had happened since that day had made me who I was now. I wasn't perfect, but I'd come to realize I wasn't that imperfect either. How could I be when they had helped shape me? Circumstance might have ripped them from my life, but they would always be in my heart.

As I approached the only place I knew my parents to be anymore besides my heart, I spotted a single white rose laid over their names.

I blinked in surprise as a shiver danced down my spine. There were red roses all around. On names to the right, to the left, but this perfect white rose had been carefully set directly between my parents' names. My heart started beating wildly, and I whirled around to find Jake standing so close, and yet so far.

That's when my world stopped moving, and he became the only thing I could see. He was my prince charming. My white knight. My Tony the Tiger. My Ying. My everything.

He had another white rose in his hand, and he looked every bit the same, but at the same time so very different.

I couldn't say exactly why, but I wanted to use the words *carefree, unburdened, lighter.*

It looked good on him.

Jake held out the rose for me, and my mind whirled back to that day so long ago when the boy that he had once been had given me his rose.

It was a selfless act, and so kind.

Who knows, maybe we had formed a bond then and never even knew it.

Could something good really come out of something so very bad?

Maybe we really were meant to be.

Maybe we were written in the stars, after all.

I didn't accept the rose right away, not because I didn't want to, but because I was trembling so much I couldn't move. I was suddenly that lost girl from so long ago. I didn't know what to do, which way to go, where to turn.

Mimi wanted me to show Jake the way, but it ended up that he was the one to show me the way.

He stepped forward to put the rose in my hand and then held onto me. "I love you, Juliette," he said. "And I'm sorry I was such an idiot. I never should have left. I can't stand being apart from you."

"But your job?"

He shook his head. "It's a long story. I'll tell you about it later. But bottom line is that I realized I don't have to follow in my father's footsteps to be like him. I just have to be me."

Tears welled hot in my eyes, and for once I didn't care that they fell. "I missed you."

"I missed you, more than anything."

"How'd you know I'd be here?"

He kissed each of my fingers. "Because I know you. Because I feel what you feel. Because we are the same."

I looked at him in awe. Our connection was unbreakable. That I already knew, but was it otherworldly too? "You mean like some kind of cosmic connection?"

The corners of his lips tilted in the smallest, itty-bitty way. "And . . . I might have called Finn to ask him if you were coming to the city for the memorial and where you were staying. He told me you were on your way, and that he was certain you'd be here first thing this morning, like you are every year."

"I was late this morning."

He nodded and those lips tilted again. "I know. I've been waiting for you. I would have waited all day if I had to. But now that I have you in my arms, I don't want to wait another minute to have you in my life."

I looked at him through teary eyes. "What are you saying?"

He pulled me closer to him. A heartbeat from his lips, and whispered, "I want to be your North Star. Will you let me?"

I closed my eyes.

He was the Ying to my crazy Yang.

He was my perfect.

He was my soulmate.

Of course, I'd let him.

Breath fast and ragged, I opened my eyes. Jake was down on one knee and holding out a box. "Juliette, I want to come back to Atlanta, and I want you to be my wife."

With trembling fingers, I took the box and opened it. Inside was the perfect match to the necklace he had given me, but it was a ring.

A huge sparkling diamond.

"Will you marry me?"

I looked down into his bright blue eyes, which were clearer than a summer's day. "Oh, Jake," I cried, and went to my knees so I could throw my arms around him. "Yes, I'll marry you. I love you so much."

The bell rang again, and for that silent moment, we stared at each other. And then his mouth was a fever on mine. It was burning grief and spiking love. There was need and desire poured into it—his running as deep and desperate as mine.

Even on my knees, I could feel my leg kick up and toe point. The love I felt for him was like a wild surge. It crashed into me and left me unsteady. Giddy. On cloud nine. I had no idea how I was going to stand up because I felt like I was floating.

I broke away fighting for air, and Jake took my hand to bring me to my feet. His was a rock. A boulder. The steady I needed in my unsteady.

"Come on," he said.

Blurry eyed and love swept, I looked up at him. I knew he wanted me to take him to my parents, but I couldn't move.

Lacing his fingers through mine, he showed me the way to the names cast in bronze, and together we laid the second white rose on top of the first. Like an x between my parents' names, it linked them to Jake and to me.

I sucked in a breath, allowing my grief to pour out and my love to wash all over it.

People around us had stopped to look on with mild curiosity, but when Jake took the velvet box from my hand and with steady hands slipped the ring on my finger, they clapped with joy.

I looked at the ring. I looked at the names. I looked at Jake.

He and I were children of 9/11.

We might have been damaged, but I knew in my heart we were

not broken.

And together we would make each other whole.

epilogue

Piece of Cake

JULES
Eight Weeks Later

UNCLE EDWARD NEVER missed.

He was that good. Thank goodness he'd come out of retirement for one last wedding—mine.

The dress *was* me to a tee.

With its acres of frothy tulle and hint of sexy in the sparkle of the low-cut silk bodice, it was both romantic and modern.

Looking at my reflection in the window, I beamed at the garden of fabric roses that practically bloomed on the warm white of the elaborate pick-up skirt and along the sweeping train fit for royalty.

I felt like a princess.

The long veil no longer shrouded my face, but now framed the upsweep of my hair. I was covered in silk and satin and pearls and lace. All I needed were a pair of glass slippers, and I would be Cinderella.

I touched my earrings, the fire diamond necklace Rory had worn, my wedding ring, and the pearls Mimi had given me. My something old, something new, something borrowed, and something blue, which was buried under all the fabric of my skirt for Jake's viewing pleasure.

In the reflection, I saw the wonder that surrounded me, and I reached out and touched my fingertips to the cool glass.

I no longer felt so far away from it, but rather I felt a part of it.

Everything was soft, soft, soft, and so romantic. Twinkling lights and white candles were everywhere. White roses and eggplant calla lilies had been scattered across the entire barn. And the crystal chandeliers that Jake had insisted on and installed himself really made the place sparkle.

"There you are." Jake's voice alone sent shivers racing up my spine, but in the glass, I could see the way his gaze swept over me, and the hunger in it brought goose bumps to my skin.

I smiled at him. "Yes, I saw you talking to Dr. Wright and thought I'd give you a minute. Everything okay?"

He nodded. "More than okay."

"Did he say anything about how your mother is doing?"

"She's in a rehab center."

"That's good."

He nodded again, moving the tulle over my shoulder and kissing behind my ear. "Have I told you how beautiful you look yet?"

I turned and wrapped my arms around his neck. "As a matter of fact, yes, but I don't mind hearing it again."

He kissed the corner of my lip. "You." He kissed the other corner. "Look." And then his lips brushed against mine, soft and sweet. "Beautiful."

I closed my eyes. The warm air, the easy play of his hands, his velvet lips, they made stars explode behind my lids. He made me weak, and it was the kind of weak I didn't mind being. He completed me.

"Mimi told me to show you the way," he said around his kisses, "But I think you showed me."

I pulled back. "She told me to show you the way, and I think you showed me."

We both laughed and said at the same time, "I think she showed us."

He lowered his lips back to mine and this time his hands moved to my rear. "There's an awful lot of material around your hot little body right now. It makes it hard to touch you the way I want to."

"I know," I beamed, "That's why I didn't wear any underwear."

His eyes went wide. "Fuck me. You're killing me, Juliette. Come on," he said, taking my hand. "It's time to cut the cake so we can hop in the limo and get started on our honeymoon."

Music pumped out hot, drawing a crowd to the dance floor. This wasn't the large-scale wedding I had planned for Rory, but it was what Jake and I wanted.

Small.

Intimate.

And ours.

Stars winked on through the windows as we walked across the wooden planks and the moonlight creaked in from the slated roof of the barn. This was the new and improved Sunshine Farms, which was not only where we had chosen to get married, but also my new business and our new home.

Remy and Rory would be moving into Rosewood right after graduation, and Jake and I and Mimi's seven dogs had already moved to the country.

As it turned out, George wanted a change and Jake and I wanted what George no longer did. So while George and Ethel moved to California to help run the Champagne label of Cupcake Wines, which Jake had funded, Jake and I purchased Sunshine Farms.

I would soon be opening my new wedding planning business here. And as for Dr. Kiss, he had already opened a family practice in town, where he worked during the day, but came home to be with me every night.

Jake stopped, or rather was stopped by an older woman in a peach chiffon dress. "Gladys," he said cheerfully, "I want you to meet my wife, Juliette."

Juliette.

I liked when he told people to call me that.

"Nice to meet you," she said.

"Nice to meet you, Gladys," I smiled. "I heard you're coming to work for Jake in his office."

She smiled brightly at me. "That's right. Someone has to keep him in line."

Jake shook his head. "She's a kitten," he whispered in my ear.

"I heard that, Dr. Kiss."

He rolled his eyes. "Not you, too."

Laughing, we said our goodbyes and Jake continued to beeline toward the cake.

It stood proudly on the pedestal table in the far corner, and Jake practically ran the rest of the way to get there.

Picking up my skirt, my sparkly Converse were on full display. I'd ditched the heels right after Jake and I had said I do over on the riverbank with the magenta sun setting over the water.

The music stopped as we took front and center. I felt like all the air was floating around us. Montgomery smiled at me as he handed me the sterling silver knife. "Here you go, my darling."

I got up on my toes and kissed his cheek. "You outdid yourself this time."

"You say that every time."

"This time though, you really really really, outdid yourself."

"You did, darling," Archer said, taking his hand.

And I think he blushed.

They were too cute together.

This cake was truly a masterpiece. A mix of silk, real, and hand-made sugar-paste flowers covered four round layers. It looked like a dream. I really hated to cut into it.

"I'm so glad he didn't go with the birds," Jake murmured in my ear.

I elbowed him in the stomach.

"Ouch."

Turning my head, I got up on my toes again to kiss his cheek. "Sorry, but not sorry," I snickered. "I really liked those birds. And just so you know, I packed that dress to wear on our honeymoon," I added smugly, but then quickly glanced back at the sky. This was the calm before the storm, and the weather would be turning very soon. I just prayed it didn't turn before our flight. "If we have a honeymoon, that is."

He slid his hot mouth to my ear. "Oh, we're having a honeymoon, and I don't care what you wear while we're on it as long as I can slide my dick into your wet pussy while you're wearing it."

Pink now painted my own cheeks and I suddenly felt incredibly hot. I went back on flat feet and looked behind me at his gorgeous face. My knees started to wobble, but it wasn't nerves this time, it was the flutter of excitement in my belly. This was a new chapter in my life, and I couldn't wait to start it.

"Are you two lovebirds ready?" my uncle asked.

Jake snickered, and I rolled my eyes. I was never going to live the lovebird's thing down. Not ever. Now even my uncle was in on the joke.

Jake tossed his hot baby blues at me, and he looked like the happiest man alive as he covered my hands, and together we sliced through the cake.

Jaxson was beside us with his camera, and he was snapping away, capturing these moments that would last a lifetime.

When he lowered his lens, he looked sad once again.

I frowned at him, but he smiled back, wiping away whatever sorrow he'd let bleed through, and then he raised his lens and started snapping again.

He'd won the photography contest and would be jetting off to some tropical location tomorrow, permitting the forecasted storm didn't ground all flights, including Jake's and mine.

"Smile," Jaxson mouthed.

And I did.

I knew then that although he might not be happy right now, he would be soon. And Sundance deserved happiness.

Archer plated the first piece, and placed it right on Montgomery's favorite silver-lined dish, and then he handed it to me along with two forks. As soon as he did, Jake moved beside me and took the forks to set them down. I gave him a curious look, but not for long.

Not even a second later, the piece of cake was off the cute little plate and in his hand, and then he was smashing it in my mouth. Chocolate morsels fell from my lips and onto my dress when I opened my mouth wide in shock and surprise.

"Paybacks are a bitch," was all he said as he picked me up and twirled me and twirled me and twirled me. Crashing his mouth to mine, he licked at my lips and shared the chocolate cake with me, along with one heart-stopping kiss.

"That was classic," Finn bellowed, almost doubling over he was laughing so hard. And he wasn't the only one. Uncle Edward, Archer, Rory, Remy, Jaxson, and I swear even Mr. Darcy was laughing hysterically.

In the echo of laughter that surrounded us, Jake set me down and wrapped his arms around me. Then he took my mouth again, cake and all.

Soft.

Sweet.

Romantic.

Laughing, because really, how did I not see that coming, I held him strong and close, and tasted chocolate and him.

My two most favorite things.

When I was breathless, I laid my head on his shoulder and knew this was my home. He was my home.

I'd not only learned so much from him and so much about myself, but I'd learned that love wasn't just one thing . . . it could be many things.

It could or could not conquer all.

It could be patient or impatient.

It could be kind or ugly.

It could be happy and it could be sad.

It could make you feel like you were climbing the highest mountain or free falling from the tallest cliff.

It could be so many things I never knew until him.

And each and every one of them were beautiful in their own way because they were a result of being in love.

The problem all along was I'd been looking for perfect. And who knew, maybe Jake and I were perfect together, and maybe we weren't.

It didn't really matter.

The thing about love was it didn't have to be perfect.

It just had to be right.

THE BEAUTIFUL END!

LOOK FOR MORE STANDALONES
IN THIS SERIES . . . COMING SOON!

Come A Little Closer
(Jaxson moves on, and Sadie isn't anything he was expecting)
*If you had a chance to turn someone's
life around . . . would you take it?*

&

Something Just Like This
(Finn faces his demons with a girl from his past)
Do you control your past . . . or does it control you?

ABOUT THE AUTHOR

Reader * Chocolate Lover * Writer * Coffee Lover
Romantic * Beach Lover * Yoga Beginner

KIM KARR IS a New York Times & USA Today bestselling author of eighteen novels. Best known for writing sexy contemporary love stories, she enjoys bringing flawed characters to life and creating romances that are page worthy.

Her stories are raw, real, and explosive.

Her characters will make you laugh, make you cry, make you feel.

And her happily-ever-afters are always swoon worthy.

From the brooding rock star to the arrogant millionaire to the Football Player. From the witty damsel-in-distress to the sassy high-powered businesswoman to the boutique owner. No two storylines are ever alike.

If Kim's not writing, you can find her wandering through antique stores with her husband, trying out new fitness classes with her sons, venturing out to new coffee shops with her daughter, or with her nose stuck in a book.

www.authorkimkarr.com
Facebook, Twitter, Instagram, Amazon

also by
NEW YORK TIMES BESTSELLING AUTHOR
KIM KARR

CPSIA information can be obtained
at www.ICGtesting.com
Printed in the USA
LVOW13s0306230218
567666LV00024B/1179/P